NINE

D.M. KING

SNOW LEOPARD PUBLISHING

NINE
Copyright © 2016 D.M. King

This book is a work of fiction. Names, characters, businesses, organizations, places, events and incidents either are the product of the author's imagination or are used fictitiously. Any resemblance to actual persons, living or dead, events, or locales is entirely coincidental.

For information contact :
Snow Leopard Publishing
http://www.snowleopardpublishing.com
email: info@snowleopardpublishing.com

ISBN: 978-1-94436111-2 (paperback)
       978-1-94436112-9(hardcover)
       978-1-94436113-6(ebook)

LCCN: 2016939410

Cover Design by J Asheley Brown Designs

First Edition: May 2016

10 9 8 7 6 5 4 3 2 1

1

Dying for your country sounds so noble, until you uncover the real reason they want you dead.

I do my best to disregard Dr. Busby's words as the traffic swells down Route 402. Ever since he got his PhD over the Internet, he's certain he can solve all of humanity's problems. If he only knew how many kids have a habit of calling him Pretty Heavy Dude behind his back, perhaps he'd lose some of his lofty goals and bizarre ideas, especially all his government conspiracies and infatuation with little green men. If Martians existed, wouldn't they already be here taking over this lame world? Or marrying our grandmothers? Insanity must be a requirement for teaching these days.

"About another hour to the facility," says one of the caseworkers, better known as our security guards—his face nearly as white as his clothes. "Traffic's like a funeral procession, but don't worry. You'll all find out your day of departure soon enough." He chuckles as if he's told the best joke in the world, but the riders and I shoot him a dirty look. He yaks it up with the other two chaperones, their breath steaming up the windows. I write *you suck* on the glass, but he's too preoccupied with the sudden slow-down to notice. The five other vans ahead and behind us remain at three-car intervals at least.

"Guy's an a-hole," A thin *Richie Rich*-like kid with dark glasses whispers in my ear from behind. I nod, but I'm in my own little universe—only one of three girls on this transport this fine morning, all because we got the call. *Now that you have reached your 16th birthday, please report to your nearest tracking station if you wish to know your expiration date.* Yada-yada. No matter how I see it, government policy is lousing up my normal Saturday routine.

I guess Busby and I do have one thing in common. We respect but don't trust the government. Ever since they insisted on implanting expiration chips into infants just before I was born, they lost my vote. Maybe in the long run old man Busby has it right. But I'm not too worried about my life expectancy. I've already lived longer than some people predicted I would.

"Hey, Blondie?" Someone akin to David Beckham scoots into the seat next to me. "What's up?"

What's up? That's the best line he could muster? "Nothing much. You know, just following government procedure." I share a phony smile, and he retreats to the back to pester someone else. I'm kinda glad. It woulda been a shame to dash his hopes. I'm more of a geeky guy type of girl. Strong mind. Strong body. You die either way, right? I'll take brains over brawn any day. So you can lift over 300 pounds but can't balance a checkbook? No thanks. It might save me from having to shop at the Big and Tall shop one day.

I'm daydreaming a lot these days, but what else can I do riding in a stuffy van with a bunch of strangers? We would have already been at the tracking facility if it weren't for the drivers who think a Saturday morning trip to the grocery store is a contact sport. A three-car accident slows us down to a crawl before we speed up again. I keep a steady beat with my bubble gum, mimicking the sound of the tires thumping over the uneven road. My mind drifts off again.

Bang. Bang. Bang.

Gunshots ring out. I wince and glance at the rest of the riders, but they're as shocked as I am at the flying bullets and glass. Their mouths hang open as if they're attempting to speak but fear won't let them. My heart races—a sudden coldness freezes me at my core. Our driver slams on the brakes, swerves onto the berm of the road, and I bite the inside of my mouth.

Ouch!

Blood and strawberry gum's not a great mix. Soon a cluster of unknown assailants surrounds us. One boards the bus.

"Run," The black-masked gunman screams. He and four others waylay our county transport vehicle with one goal in mind. Too bad they keep it a secret.

I'd seen plenty of movies where people get shot, but nothing compares to seeing it in real life. As many times as I hit re-set in my brain, the scene never changes. A splash zone of blood from the driver covers the windshield and starts a steady red ooze down the exit steps. Social workers in white, now reddening jackets, lie slumped in their seats— their eyes still ajar in astonishment. Meticulous bullet holes mark their foreheads. Squelching my vomit is a chore as I clutch the seat in front of me, unsure of my next move. I'm such an easy target, since my feet won't budge. Either someone's put crazy glue on my sneakers, or my brain is busy disengaging from my body. Right now, I'm betting on my brain. Thankfully, my choice is spelled out for me, as the gunmen shout their orders.

"Move. All of you. Leave before they send reinforcements," he barks.

Stunned we're not the next victims, all twelve of us navigate around the dead bodies and spread out through the Georgia pines running in wild snake-like patterns. According to all the survival shows, it's the best way to keep from being shot. But having never been a target before, I decide maybe it was high time I figured out if it worked. So far, so good.

Thankfully the underbrush is thin, but I trip nonetheless. Several days of rain make each step a challenge, but the woods are our best cover. I skid through the mud as it builds up on my shoes turning my sprint into a steady jog. My calves tighten along with my chest, but I keep moving.

Four of us remain within shouting distance—still no clue why this happened. Tree limbs take turns slapping me in the face as we flee like prisoners. My throat burns from the frosty air, and try as I might, there's no stopping my chattering teeth. Pure adrenaline supersedes my thinking.

I have no time to be afraid because the only thing on my mind is escaping, but from what, or whom?

We put some distance between the highway and us, but needing answers gnaws at me. The other three eventually catch up, and I'm hoping they'd thought the same thing. We huddle together to converse. Our noses are red and running, like we've been out all morning hunting or out all night drinking, which doesn't sound like such a bad idea right now. Glistening tears sting the corners of our eyes. The four of us stretch our lungs for one more ounce of oxygen, but there's only so much air. Kind of ironic, considering just last year Atlanta was voted cleanest big city in America. We launch back into a trot.

"Wait!" I screech out in between breaths. "Why are we running?" I stop again. The others follow suit.

"Because they told us to, that's why," A blonde-haired short girl with a modified Mohawk replies, her voice shaky but confident. Blood dribbles down the side of her mouth and chin. "We musta been in some kind of trouble? I dunno." A nervous laugh spills out, breaking the tension. Mom used to tell me that fear can exist inside a vacuum, but it can't stand being in the same room with humor. Adopting cynicism as my life mantra has worked pretty well so far, though *this* experience might put a dent in it.

"Yeah," A bald African American kid adds *his* two-cents worth. "Where I used to live, when people were shooting at you, you didn't stand around to find out why. It wasn't logical." His voice was a cross between a rapper and a smooth-talking psychologist. Shock changes people. Makes them say and do strange things. Their random words don't help me, so I jump in to add clarity.

Proving my shock theory true, I draw blanks at first. It's not every day you witness a massacre. I gawk at them as if that'll help me form my sentences, but I babble instead. Their eyes beg me for answers, but I can't hide my ignorance. Without even knowing each other, we embrace for a five-second hug. A momentary calm washes over me.

"We were going to the expiration station in the city to discover our dates, right?" Everyone nods. "So what's wrong with that? It's what we're supposed to do around our 16th birthday. So why spring us loose ten miles from the place? I mean—"

"Don't know 'bout the rest of you, man," A boy declared," but I'm kinda glad. Knowing when I was gonna kick the bucket wasn't my idea anyhow. It was my dad's. The name's Rico. Rico Lopez."

"I'm Faith. Faith Monroe. Nice to meet you. Wish it was under better circumstances."

We don't bother shaking hands, since our hug initiated our new bond. Our silence speaks volumes. There's no need for words right now. Finding safety is our priority

We meander through the rest of the forest until we reach a clearing. A strong smell of wood smoke permeates the air. Conyers, Georgia is still a bit chilly for early April. Now I'm glad I ran back to my room to snag my coat before I left. Parental advice *does* work occasionally.

Star Woodley, the blonde with the stout body and muscles like a county wrestling champ, introduces herself and leads the way this time. I guess she forgot *her* jacket. A thin red vest lay over a black and white Japanese symbol t-shirt, and it at least braces the wind some. She's the only one who looks like she's in her element and unaffected by the cold or the primitive environment. Unlike the rest of us, she seems to know the area well, almost as if she's been here before. It piques my curiosity. Seemingly choosing just the right path to take and relying on an uncanny instinct, Star scours the ground for other footprints and blazes a trail, snapping off tiny limbs as markers in case we get lost. At first, I think maybe she's one of those back-to-nature girls. You know, the kind who sit in the woods for hours admiring the flora and fauna and draw or write poetry. Anyhow, she doesn't *look* like that kind of girl, but who knows? I'm appreciating her skills no matter what type she is.

Ozzy Baker tosses *his* name out into the chill and follows close behind leaving the Latino-looking kid and me to bring up the rear. Several Army vehicles are parked on the dirt path leading toward the main road, so we stop just shy of being seen. Ozzy, with his height and his shiny bald head, nearly gets us recaptured or at least questioned, but we tackle him behind a row of thorn bushes just in time.

"Ouch!" he complains. "What'd you do that for? Maybe they can help," Ozzy says.

Rico, with his mildly broken English, chimes in immediately with an angry smirk on his face. "They'll *help* us, all right. Help us all go to jail for killing the driver and social workers."

"Wait a minute! We didn't shoot those people! Those ninja soldiers did!" Star objects. "Besides, we all have cell phones. We should just call. My dad's in government. He'll get us out of this mess. I promise."

"*Stop*," I beg. "You're right. We probably *should* call, but why us? There were probably, what, ten or more transports running today. Did anyone *else* see the big black number nine spray painted on the back of the van?"

"Yeah," Rico agrees. "I caught it, in between peeing my pants and running for my life. I thought it was just marking the number of us riding in the vehicle."

"Well, obviously then you can't count. There were *twelve* of us," I correct.

"Who cares? Let's just call our parents and hop a ride on the next transport. There's absolutely no evidence to link us to the shootings. We did what we were told. We're not suspects." Ozzy gets up and pushes himself away from the rest of the group, striding out into the open field to get a phone signal. He's disappointed. But it isn't until he tries to flag down a soldier that we all want to strangle him.

"Halt! Over there in the woods. It's the rest of them." Three soldiers take off in a slow jog at first and approach, waving their M-16's back and forth. I wasn't a cross country phenom, but for some reason I was blessed with the ability to run like a politician's mouth, tirelessly and non-stop. So my first instinct is to scramble away, leaving my new acquaintances behind, but one carefully placed bullet at the base of a tree barely missing Rico's leg, stops us in our tracks.

"You. Out where we can see you. Now," he bellows.

We climb up from our prone positions and step through the shrubs. We're the Munchkins on the *Wizard of Oz*, eyes and mouths wide open in fear, all shouting our innocence in a muddled effort. Then the soldier who seems to be in charge tells us to shut up, forms us into a line, and marches us toward the Humvees. We're quite the mod squad with six-foot plus Ozzy in the middle, flanked by me on his right, with Rico and Star to his left. Frankly, the idea that the *four* of us could survive on our own for very long was remote anyhow, so you could see the sighs of relief when we turn the corner to see who's behind the Army truck.

"Dad?" I shout. "What the hell?" We nearly collapse in shock. Rico shouts Hail Mary's to the sky. He looks ridiculous, but I give him credit. If his God got us out of this jam, I might have to reconsider my *own* unbelief soon. Who names their kid Faith when they've never stepped foot in a church except during the holidays? I guess *my* parents do. That's who.

My father meets me halfway between my jaw-drop and before I can even ask my justifiable question.

"Look! We don't have much time, so I'll give you the shortened version, okay? I'm so sorry it had to go down this way, but we needed to stay hidden. The FBI's been tailing us for days and tracking us since we left. We *had* to stop that transport. All of you are *minus* the expiration device. It doesn't matter how or why right now, but if you would have shown up at that facility, eventually you would have been killed."

"Killed?" Star questions, her voice weak for the first time since our meeting. "And those were *fake* bullets y'all were shooting at us? Why? Couldn't they just fix us with a chip now, and we'll all be official? Why didn't my parents tell—" Before she can complete her sentence, both her mother and father poke *their* heads out from the Hummer. Her father, the mayor, gives a convoluted explanation.

"When you were born, we just couldn't do it. So we bribed the hospital officials to *pretend* you received the device and create your official documents. We hadn't given much back to society until recently, kept most of my family's money to ourselves. We were greedy. Swindled the IRS. Those expiration dates? They're based on parents' *contribution* to society, their money, community service, and their talents. We knew you wouldn't have many years. So that's why we did it. We're not sorry. We did what we had to do."

If *their* presence there that day wasn't enough to make us relive old episodes of the *Twilight Zone,* in a matter of minutes the rest of our families arrive. Ozzy's step-dad and mom and Rico's mother are there. His father had been busy tied up at work. And when I say tied-up, I really mean it. Apparently, the little *rescue* operation today had leaked out, and some government officials showed up at the factory to extract some information. His dad got off a quick text message to his wife to head for the safety point, but *he* wasn't so lucky. I'm the first to ask the next most relevant question.

"Okay. So, what now? We get hauled off to some safe house or military research facility like Area 51.5? What's the big deal? I mean, if we don't have the chip, can't they just give us a death date anyhow, or hook us to an electric chair? Same result, right?"

As soon as I finish, Dad tears up—and he was never one to cry much, other than when my mom died. There must be more to this entire situation than they are admitting. Dad cradles me in his strong forearms and kisses me on the cheek. A remnant of his tears sting the small wound on my face I'd received trying to hide. Note to self. Upon going

undercover in the future, pick a set of woods *without* prick-
er bushes. We share a few more minutes of sentimentality
among families, but it doesn't last.

"Drones. Three of them at nine o'clock—surveillance,
we think!" Our new soldier *friend* wastes no time forcing us
into the army cargo truck and ordering us to keep low.

I have so many questions, such as why wait so long to
tell us that we were illegal? And why let us go in the first
place? But there's no time to gain answers, as our parents
are ushered back to *their* Hummers, and our caravan is on
the move. In minutes, we hear the sound of mini-helicop-
ters or giant bees dive-bombing our truck, an array of pings
bounce off metal. Bullets. *Surveillance drones, my ass.* Someone. Some *thing* is shooting at us, like we're a bunch of terrorists. And the only thing we have in common is we'd all
somehow managed to escape government protocol when
we were born. Lucky us.

The front right corner of the truck's ceiling is reinforced
with a triangular piece of metal barely large enough for the
four of us to huddle under. Bullets pierce through the heavy
green canvas and ricochet off the truck bed as we grab a
few blankets and cover our heads. Not that any moldy army
blanket is capable of stopping bullets, but it's all we have.
Previous riders musta forgot to leave us their helmets and
body armor. Remind me to write Congress as soon as the
chaos ends. Provided I have any fingers left to type.

In the darkness, Ozzy's teeth chatter like a roller coaster chain taking its riders to the top. *Clickety, clickety, click.*
Muted prayers and more Hail Marys from Rico add to the
mix. I can't hold back my own screams of terror either. I'm

too young to die cooped up in a military vehicle traveling way too fast over a bumpy country road. I definitely had *other* plans for the rest of my day. None of which included an air to ground battle with weaponized robots. I guess studying for my chemistry test is gonna have to wait. But what an excuse I'll have come Monday.

A quiet Saturday drive through the suburbs suddenly turns into a war movie, minus Sylvester Stallone and his friends to save the day. The only person who fails to fit the mode of hysteria is Star. She appears to be in a weird meditative state. But either it isn't exactly our time to go, or somehow fate intervenes because after about fifteen minutes of playing duck and cover, three explosions from behind launch us onto a major highway. The onslaught is over. No more drones. No more gunfire.

As we uncover, thin rays of light poke through the myriad of holes in the canvas, and we put a little more distance between us. Bouncing around in the back of a military truck isn't my idea of a thrill ride, so it's great to be on a smooth road. To no avail, we attempt to communicate with the soldiers up front because we have the desperate need to use a bathroom. We yell for twenty minutes, but it isn't until Ozzy seizes a tire iron and shoves it through a small hole on into the passenger side of the front cabin that we get our wish.

"Hey," We hear from the soldier sitting on that side. "Rest stop ahead."

I guess 'rest stop ahead' means something different to *some* people because it takes at least another *thirty* minutes before our pleas for a bathroom are acknowledged. Our

discontent with our riding accommodations brings no response from either soldier, but at least we won't add urine
to the blend.

A typical rest area with three snack bars and a mini-bak-
ery bring us relief as we all rush to eliminate over an hour
of anxiety. Our militia men keep watch at the doors, so we
don't get any foolish ideas like running away or calling the
cops. *Their* bladders may be equipped to withstand a roadside slaughter and high-speed chase, but mine's not. A faint
siren speeds up my routine that I barely wash my hands and
skip the automatic blow dryers. Ozzy's hoodie makes for a
nice towel as we meet once again and ask to buy food.

"Hurry up! Your limousine awaits." The bigger soldier
seems way too thrilled with himself.

If that's his subtle attempt at humor, it isn't funny. None
of us laugh. We are still shaken by what we've seen, why
we're running, and where we're headed next. About the only
part of me that feels somewhat normal is my sarcasm, but
even *it's* threatening to cower in the corner and not come
out 'til Christmas.

Sirens increase a little more, but they're still far enough
away to buy us some time. Who knows when we'll stop
again? When we'll get a meal? I think back even two hours
ago and time feels like a blur. It's not as if I could have out-
run or overpowered these soldiers. Having all the answers
was never an option. Blind trust makes the most sense, even
though my brain tries to convince me otherwise. Besides—
Dad has rarely been wrong. Here's hoping he keeps his stel-
lar record alive. I may have to add this adventure to the
time he assured me he'd turned off the main power before I

replaced my burned-out power outlet. I think my hair's still a bit curly from that blunder.

We notice some stirring in the kitchen as we place our orders, but the sirens have ceased. A collective sigh accompanies the *cha-ching* of the register as we pay and return back to our *kidnappers*. They seem nervous as we approach as if they sense something we don't. Rico shows no fear by making fun of them.

"So, isn't the army, like—*allowed* to buy a cup of coffee and a donut? You two look hungry. And whaddya do for a bathroom in the front of the truck; pee in a bottle up there?"

Both soldiers consider his questions no more than a couple of seconds before they point us back toward the doors. The smaller one *almost* grins at Rico's last comment then goes into his usual trance staring at the flat screen TV in the corner. It's the transport van, the blood and bodies. Traffic held up for miles. Our faces on the monitor are lined up in a row like a *Guess Who* game, only we *know* who. And now? So does everybody else.

2

Rico's the last to leave the roadside rest stop because he stays as long as he possibly can to hear the details. For some reason, *his* picture's not included in the fugitive line up. *How did he get so lucky?* We aren't exactly riding in first class, and being able to walk upright and grab a snack and drink from the concession provides much needed relief, but we have to move quickly.

With the longest arms, Ozzy offers to carry our chip bags and bagels, with each of us responsible for our own drinks and candy. I know, not exactly soup and salad, but it's the best we can do on short notice. Renegades can't afford to be choosy. The bigger soldier always hangs back to keep a steady eye on us, but really? Where would we go? Home? More than likely the *first* place they'd show up. I have no interest in perpetuating movie director typecasts. You know, blonde bimbo always heads back *toward* danger not away from it.

Much to our disappointment, three teenagers leaving the place at the same time as us, two girls and a guy our age or younger, recognize us from the recent news report. And before we can dash away inconspicuously, they ask to take a *selfie*. All four of our heads shake *no* in unison, but that doesn't stop these persistent brats from causing quite a commotion. In a jiffy, we'll be stars all over Snap chat and Instagram. We might even make *America's Most Wanted.* I shake myself out of my fifteen seconds of fame.

Minutes later, we hear one of the cashiers yell out the door, "Fugitive alert! It's them!" We don't get ten yards into the parking lot before a couple of local police cruisers block our way to the truck with not even a siren to warn us. Just the random flashing red and blue lights. Our two soldiers peel back in front of us to stand guard like our protective wall. Part of me just wants to give up right then and there. I'm tired of playing runaway of the week. No matter how much protection, we'll eventually be caught anyhow. There's some crazy quote about a needle wrapped in a rag will be found in the end. I think *we're* the needles—just not too sharp.

Things look bleak until four police officers, guns pulled, ask the soldiers a few questions and then simply get back into their cars and drive away. No attempt at a daring rescue. Not one, "Hey, kids? Are you all right?" Nothing. Nada. It's as if our hedge of protection used mental telepathy or Vulcan mind control to get us out of our predicament. But how? Since when does military training include smoke and mirrors a la David Blaine?

Both soldiers are too good at pretending to be mute *and* dumb. Our barrage of questions continues to fall on deaf ears as we get back on the road. We feel rather dumbfounded, but we also aren't doing much complaining. Not when we have already had two close calls. Speaking of calls, our cell phones are almost dead, and Ozzy's got smashed when we tackled him earlier. We help him pick the glass out of his pants pocket; otherwise we have to endure his constant yelps from it poking him in the thigh. It was ancient anyhow. About time someone put that dinosaur out of its misery.

As far as we can tell, we're headed northwest. An occasional squawk comes over the radio and a cell phone rings on and off for miles, but the rumble of the engine keeps us from listening to any details. Surprisingly, the dissonant drone of the engine and sound of tires on the road act like the perfect sleep machine. Coupled with the fact that we've devoured two bagels apiece, a bag of chips, and three Snickers bars, and we're more than ready for a nap. It isn't too long before we're overwhelmed by the events of the day, and we pass out cold, bellies full.

When we awake, it's almost dark. We have no idea how long we've been traveling or where we are. Stress builds up the more and more I think about how we ended up here. *If they knew about our expiration date issues, why wait to tell us? Besides, you mean to tell me we were the only ones who beat the system? And most of all, why kill us when we get there?* Getting *anything* out of the soldiers has proven impossible, so we decide to quiz each other instead.

"So, Ozzy?" I begin. "You're built like an NBA star, but you sound like an Ivy Leaguer," I say.

"Ozymandias Quentin Baker, at your service. While I had quite the monumental opening to my life, being born in the bathroom at a Mary J. Blige reunion concert and given up for adoption, my step-parents found out quickly that I was *special.*"

Rico, Star, and I grow fascinated by Ozzy's eloquence. His exterior screams jock, but in a few more sentences we know he is so much more.

"What?" Rico interjects. "You could dunk a basketball by age three?" We all need a laugh. Hearing Star's intermittent snorts make her seem more like the rest of us instead of some kung-fu warrior princess.

"Actually," Ozzy continues. "I was *thirteen,* but that's not what I was referring to really. I was speaking full sentences at two and a half. Started reading at four. And I don't mean Dick and Jane books, either. I was proficient in addition and subtraction before I reached kindergarten. So my folks had me tested. *Four* times. My IQ is about 210 right now. They just kept at it until it got higher and higher. Pretty sure it doesn't work that way though."

"Whoa. So why do *you* think you escaped the expiration device?" Star asks.

"Born in a bathroom? Adopted? I guess they left out that detail. Not sure. What about you?"

"Me?" Star grows uncomfortable. "Well, as some of you may already know, my dad's the mayor of Rutledge."

"Really?" I interrupt her. "I'm from Madison."

"White Plains, here," Ozzy says. "Heyyyy! We're within a forty-mile radius of each other. What're the odds of that? Rico? Where do you live?"

"Panthersville, but I was staying with my uncle in Oxford. That's probably why I was the last one on the transport."

Star continues with her introduction.

"I was a preemie. Chip on my shoulder. Felt like I had to prove myself. I'm a third-degree black belt and a dancer; a lover of anime. I dunno, maybe I was so small my parents didn't think I'd make it, so I didn't get the chip. You heard my father's explanation. Rico?"

"My mother and I were kidnapped a month before I was born. I'm the great nephew to Mexico's President Eduardo Lopez. We were held for ransom in the USA, but my mother? She tells me that when I was born, I had a rare heart condition. Maybe *that* is why I wasn't date-stamped like a carton of milk or a candy bar."

Rico has a way of bringing a smile to everyone's face. I'm sure he could have read us the directions to making instant pudding, and we would have been entertained. His face is so animated, like a living, breathing Avatar. His dark-black eyebrows wiggle up and down with each word, and he has just enough hint of an accent to prove he's an immigrant. I go last in our pass-the-time game of Who Are You?

"I'm Faith Monroe, and I was named after Faith Hill, the country singer. I've been raised by my dad the past few years. Mom died when I was thirteen, kinda weird circumstances."

"Weird?" My new companions' voices sound out in chorus.

"Yeah, she'd been having countless fainting spells for about a year, but none of the doctors could find anything wrong. I, on the other hand, was born with low platelets. I bruised easily. Walked around looking like a boxer who'd just gone ten rounds and lost. Kids talked. Teachers called home. My dad worked long hours because Mom spent many days and nights in bed with horrible headaches and couldn't work. Mom never had the energy to go into school to clear things up."

"What about your dad?" asks Ozzy. "Why didn't he go in? Or call? I mean, especially if abuse was suspected?"

"Things had already spiraled out of control, so I guess he figured just moving would make things better. I got my platelets under control, but my mom kept getting worse. One day I went in to check on her, and she was dead. Rumors spread again. Everyone blamed me for her death. Said she was beating me. I dunno; it was all such a mess. I try not to think about it anymore."

Star seems to recognize my rough feelings and changes the topic quickly. "Hey, that's a pretty cool tattoo on your back, a praying mantis. It goes well with the green eyes and the blonde corn rows."

"Thanks. I got it when I turned sixteen in January. Dad hesitated, but since I'd had such a crummy life so far, he let me. Doctors gave me the clean bill, so I traced it and had it done. *Non-needle* technology at its finest."

"Why a mantis?" Star asks. "It's one of my fighting styles."

"Well—you know—everyone's always so curious about

'em, so many myths and stories of females biting off the male's head after sex and taking down scorpions. People *wanna* get close to them, but they keep their distance because they're scared. That's me to a T."

"Hey—you're not gonna like bite all our heads off the next time we fall asleep or anything are ya?" Ozzy takes his turn at lightening the moment. I chuckle, but deep inside I still feel the sting of having even some of my so-called *friends* turn away from me after my mother passed. Her autopsy showed a cerebral aneurism beneath her brain stem. It was rare, something never seen by researchers or scientists anywhere. Leave it to Mom to be an exception.

"No, Ozzy. I think I'll wait until I get to know you better. Besides—I'm full. No room for anybody's head right now." *My* subtle attempt at easing some of our stress works. Everyone grins.

After a few more minutes of sharing, either the fumes from the army truck or our exciting day besets us. We're all fast asleep again. Spread out into the four corners until Rico wakes us up with a better idea, his garbled words clear enough for us to distinguish but barely.

"Stick to—gether. Warmer. I'm freez—inggggg!"

We sleepwalk to the front right crook where he lay and practically use each other as pillows. Not even Star's gurgling stomach is enough to keep us awake. But the strangest thing I notice before blacking out again is how our two drivers look. They finally have their helmets off where I can make out a few more of their features. As the lights from the cars on the highway fly past, I recognize an odd texture to their skin. In the light of day, they don't look much older than their late twenties or early thirties. But at night? Each face shines like they'd had some bad plastic surgery.

I'm certain that both soldiers know I'm watching them. And as the digital clock on the dashboard, 11:09, begins to criss-cross in my vision, my body feels the pressure of at least one elephant pressing me down to the oily floor. My heart slows, and a gentle peace washes over me. I manage to force open one eye just before letting go, and both soldiers smile like a couple of grandfathers tucking in their grandkids.

3

A series of shotgun blasts act as our alarm clock the next morning as panic grips our chests once again. Rico's the first to peek out the front window through an empty cab, and he describes the scene. The rest of us brace ourselves for a battle that fortunately never comes.

"So? Whaddya see out there?" Star whispers through a deep yawn. Her Georgia accent is slightly more pronounced.

"Not sure, but it appears to be some kind of a shooting competition. Our army guys versus a bunch of rednecks. Hay-stuffed targets are shaped like people. Big red X's on their faces. Three heads from the targets already dangle from the neck like boogers."

Still somewhat uneasy about revealing ourselves, we un-latch the back lift gate, finally getting some much needed air. Ozzy takes the lead, but only because we force him into it. Our two soldiers spot us first, but they sound *different*. Changed. They were speaking like they're from the south.

"Well, good morning. Did ya sleep well?" The main driver speaks. A stupid grin spreads across his face, maybe he knows something we don't.

"Where are we?" Star asks glancing into the bright sun. Shielding her eyes, she approaches unafraid. "I want to talk to my dad." She reaches for her cell phone, but it's gone. The rest of us check for our devices too. *Each* of our phones must have been removed while we were asleep. But how? Normally the tiniest noise would rouse me awake. When I was a toddler, Mom and Dad used to have contests to see who could be the quietest, so I wouldn't wake up. Without the chargers, our cells would be useless anyhow, so there's no point in fussing about it.

Two of the younger rednecks alternate turns firing at the targets once again missing badly, but the elders and soldiers step in to give further instruction. One would have thought they'd taken the time to introduce themselves and find out who we were, but they seem mesmerized by our two escorts. Who, in the light of day, look just like your brother or your uncle. No signs of the wax-like glow to their faces or their penetrating eyes. We stroll a few steps toward them, and we're intercepted by two women and a girl about our age or maybe younger bounding out of a cedar shed, their arms full of boxes.

"Luther Bennett?" she shouts. "Why didn't you holler and tell me we had company? I swear you're addicted to shooting the stuffing outta those scarecrows."

"They ain't scarecrows, momma," The younger boy says. "They're CIA agents!"

"FBI!" The older boy corrects.

"Oh, never mind. Lunch'll be ready in ten minutes, so get your shootin' outta your system. You've got lots of chores to do today. And it looks like we'll have to add a few places 'round the table."

Feeling totally like we'd just arrived at a bad movie set, we stand in shock and frustration that nobody seems to care too much about us. In fact, Ozzy and I communicate with our eyes and eventually get the attention of Rico and Star to attempt an escape. But that's when our gracious hostesses come back out of their house empty-handed this time except for a pitcher of orange juice and four paper cups.

"Hi, I'm Kandy Bennett, and this is Loribelle, my sister and my daughter, Misty." She quickly pours us all a cup of juice.

"We used to have another brother, but he died," Misty says, her eyes tearing up.

"Misty, dear? Why don't you go back in and check on the potatoes. And we'll get to know our guests. Run along now."

"But momma? Why can't I stay and get to know them too?" She kicks the dirt around by her mother's feet and continues to whine. Kandy's slightly embarrassed, so she gives Misty a gentle swat on the backside.

The oldest member of the hunting party steers his way over to us leaving the rest of his gang back with the soldiers. His military cut, square jaw, and lack of facial hair aren't typical of my idea of a backwoodsman until he opens his mouth. But there's no doubt who's in charge of this band of merry misfits.

"Misty Ann?" he emphasizes. "You heard your momma. What's our rules?"

"I know, Pa. I know. We do things when we're asked when they're asked and no complainin'."

"Don't you worry yourself, girl. There'll be plenty of time to get to know them at lunch." He proceeds with his introduction. "Luther Bennett. You've already met my wife, Misty, Loribelle. Over there's my brother Otis, my sons Micah and Junior. He's got a name, Winslow, but he prefers Junior. Kids don't make fun of him that way. So, I'm sure you have tons of questions, and we wanna answer as many as we can. Maybe you'd like to get cleaned up first, and after some eats, we'll fill y'all in on why you're here. How's that sound?"

As soon as I step into the rustic cabin, my expectations and biases melt. While a couple of deer heads line two of the walls in the living room, no opossums hang from the ceiling half-skinned. No stuffed bear rugs lie on the floor in front of the stone fireplace. As neat and as tidy as a mountain hotel, the Bennett's place is a sanctuary. Fresh bakery smells constantly tease our noses. Overstuffed cozy furniture calls to us as we remember our terrible ride.

After a round of much-needed quick showers, lunch, as they described it, consists of a full-course meal. Pot roast, potatoes, cornbread muffins, green beans, and a strawberry Jell-O dessert. Just when we think we can't possibly eat any more, Kandy shows up with something else. The food that didn't seem like it could feed the seven of them actually ends up feeding 13 of us with leftovers to spare. Like a well-coordinated group of waitresses and busboys, the table's cleared, and we're settling down in the family room to talk. I'm thankful for the amazing food and the gracious hospitality, but in the pit of my stomach something still seems a bit off, just too perfect. Were we just four fully fed parakeets in a cage waiting on a bunch of starving cats? Or did our new caregivers understand our plight and really want to help?

"Mr. Bennett?" I begin the inquisition.

"Luther, please. We ain't formal folks," he corrects me.

"Thanks so much for the meal, sir. But we're at a loss here. I mean, it's not every day you get whisked away by the army, shot at and almost killed, and end up in a backwoods retreat, you know?"

"And what about our families?" Rico questions.

"Yeah? My mom and dad are probably worried. We haven't talked for hours," says Star.

"And I missed church today. My mom's going to freak out," Ozzy adds.

"Ya'll have to understand something right off," Luther explains. "We're just doin' what we think's right. Ain't no government gonna tell us what to do. And we'd like to tell ya'll about your families, but we ain't heard nothin' for a few hours now. Ain't that right Commander Gleason?"

At least we finally have a name to go with *one* of the transporting soldiers now. I keep hoping they'll step into the conversation and shed a little more light, but suddenly they're as dull as a couple of tarnished forks again, upright and standing at ready by the front door. They took the time to eat with us but were the first to rise and return to active duty. A milk moustache still lines the driver's mouth until Ozzy offers him a napkin. Not even one of them takes the time to actually ask us *our* names.

"All right, you can't say anything about our families, but where are we? Why is everyone acting like it's the end of the world?" Star's bold words finally capture their full attention.

"We're about five miles south of Waverly, Tennessee. And as you could probably guess, we ain't like most people these days. Momma and Papa raised us right and showed us how to farm, cook, and store food and ammunition. They wanted us to be prepared."

"For what?" All four of us ask. I have suspicions but need confirmation.

"Well—let's just say—we knew sooner or later something like this would happen, with the government puttin' objects into our babies and stuff. Marking down the time we're supposed to die. But it's a good thing we got high-quality people like Captain Gleason and Moore over there. They came a long way to help."

Luther chases the rest of his family outside or to their rooms like the place is on fire, but we stay as cozy as ever, almost floating in a sea of kindnesses. Captain Gleason and Moore now hover over the back of the sofa, the lights dimming on their own. The peculiar look I'd noticed before I blanked out has returned, only this time I'm fully awake but frozen. Both soldiers' eyes burn piercing cold cobalt, and even though we can't explain it, we end up in a pitch black room with a giant white screen in front of us. A warm breeze blows at our backs. The taste of strawberry and our recent meal enhances to the nth degree now. My breath grows shallow, but never once do I feel frightened like we're going to be harmed in any way. A complete calm.

Soon images appear on the screen. There's a planet similar to Earth but smaller. The image zooms into a gigantic room, a series of leather chairs with exotic people in them. They have darker than normal skin and eyes beyond blue, almost robotic in nature. Men, women, and a handful of teens are seated and conferencing over something. Their mouths open, and words spill out, but there is a slight delay in our own ear's retrieval. Almost like an interpreter is feeding us their comments in a form of English we could understand. It takes a few minutes, but we adapt and their mouths are totally in synch.

A deeply-tanned woman at the head of the table speaks first. Her coal-black hair flows past her shoulders partially covering a stark piece of golden jewelry. A necklace. Gangster-like bling that draws one's attention right to her perfect chest. Her skin-tight white dress reveals the body of a personal trainer. Authority fills the room when she speaks.

"We have no more time, my friends. We need to test the solution now, or all the citizens of Nine will perish. We have no choice."

"Why can't we test it here? On a few select people? Those who are already near death?"

"Oh, Rama? I wish it was that simple," her voice resonates in my head. "This technology can only be implanted right out of the womb. Past five days, and the body will reject it. Besides, we're still in need of a *new* home. Overcrowding has made our planet uninhabitable. But we have *found* a planet much like ours. Almost triple our size. Earth. They also have population concerns, but we can use that to our advantage. And—we have something they may want."

"Our *auric*?" One of the male teens takes his turn to speak. He looks familiar to me. Like I've seen a more grown-up version of him somewhere before. The intensity in his eyes is a dead giveaway. It's Commander Gleason, one of our army rescuers.

"Yes. Their resources have diminished. Their government is weak and just waiting for our help." Their leader makes her reasoning clearer.

Gleason continues his respectful but formidable comments. "They may be weak, but they're not stupid. I have studied their kind. They are not afraid of conflict *or* war. There's no way they'll allow us to test the expiration codes. I say we find a new—"

"Nonsense," she interrupts. "There *is* no other way. They'll accept the codes because we'll feed their minds."

"You mean *manipulate* their minds, imposing our will and removing their freedom to choose. Our ancestors would be ashamed of us for using our talents to harm." Anger grows in his voice as he stares up and down the table at the esteemed council pleading with them to listen.

"I hear your compassion, Marek. It is admirable. But we have run out of options. You must admit that even our ancestors, as you say, would have done everything they could to survive."

A heavier teen sitting just to Gleason's left stands up in support of his neighbor's position. Once again I recognize him as a younger version of our soldier Moore. There's enough of a resemblance for them to be related.

"Not if it meant the extinction of a species," he yells. "What if another planet did that to us? Would we simply stand by and do nothing?"

Their regal leader grows impatient. She pushes herself away from the table and moves back toward a window. Our bodies move in conjunction with her steps until we're perched over her shoulder and staring through her eyes. The city is a bustle of people, high-speed trains, a Dubai-esque modern Manhattan. Thousands upon thousands of ants traversing the sidewalks to the point that we can barely see pavement. Our eyes focus in like binoculars on all body types and age levels. Street urchins and businessmen coexisting like a finely tuned engine, each gear and part in perfect sequence, without a skip in the population's heartbeat. It was a well-adjusted and incredibly sewn societal fabric.

The four of us stand like museum statues unable to move on our own or to speak, but the blood that flows through the city now flows through us. Its intricate system of sustaining life and maintaining the patterns envelope our minds. We understand the heart of their leader. Her desperation surrounds us. Suddenly *we* are her, and *she* is us.

In a matter of seconds, our positions change once again back to where we first started as her Excellency pivots back toward her council to address them again. Her countenance alters, and she appears even more confident.

"Bale? You spoke of extinction, but that's not what we're proposing. One by one we will *replace* those who expire on Earth. Our researchers have already connected our life forces to the perfect matches. It will be a seamless transition.

Our higher order of living right alongside them. Until—"

"Until there are no more of *them*, and *we* run the planet," A balding older man with a fresh red scar on his face interrupts her. He bears a close likeness to the lady in charge minus the fierce wound. "We've no more time to waste. Our scouts have already met with a few people on Earth, and they are waiting for us to deliver the technology and the auric. We can send small groups through unreliable intermittent worm holes already, but tomorrow the first of four convergences will be here, so we must act. Let us vote!"

A few more motionless minutes pass before each council members' vote registers on a digital display in front of them. From our vantage point we see, only three people vote no while the rest are yes. I can't be certain, but at least 17 people decide it would be okay to place expiration or date of death chips inside of us. Their planet could no longer sustain all its inhabitants. Such technology would insure their planet a brand new home without killing their own. I guess the truly insane part is that for the past dozen or so years on Earth, it's worked like a charm. Some people dying only a handful of years after their sixteenth birthdays. Others were given thirty to forty maximum years, for those who actually *wanted* to know their expiration number.

So after our trip through our alien night at the movies and our enlightenment period, we finally discover the *origin* of the idea to mark us for expulsion. As inexplicable as it all sounds, being immersed in it handles whatever doubt we can muster. We keep waiting to wake up in our cozy warm beds in a sweat ready to explain our strange dream to our family and friends, but sadly that moment never comes.

Some nightmares are real, and we're in one.

A parallel planet called Nine had a much better plan than any terrorist group could comprehend knowing our weaknesses better than we did. They are using our greed and our will to survive against us, and in the process, making it too damn easy to move right in like unwelcomed relatives. Only these aliens aren't just *vacationing*. One by one they're unpacking their suitcases, hijacking our bodies, and pretending like they own the joint. But it's a good thing some dissenters on their planet weren't too keen on the plan. Otherwise, the four of us may have already been body-snatched. A perilous escape from a government transport is making a lot more sense now, considering the *hidden* details we didn't find out through our out-of-body journey to Oz.

Waverly, Tennessee? There's no place like home. It's too bad we can't stay. I click my heels a few times just in case, but to no advantage. I may never see my farmhouse again or my distant relatives. Here's hoping *this* witch leaves her flying monkeys at home and a freaking high-rise falls on her. She definitely does *not* look like the melting type.

4

I'm not sure how Luther, his family, and the aliens are connected exactly, or how my father knew to send us here. But much of that ignorance gets erased the moment the special Skype transmission arrives. We fade back to our cozy living room from our trip down Alien Lane just in time to be interrupted by a high-pitched whistle. Misty was in her room watching reruns of *Gilligan's Island* but now dashes out like a scared animal and blowing her whistle until she's blue. Apparently it's her job to alert the family when her computer screen displays an official incoming message. I just wonder how they keep all the stray wolves from showing up on their doorstep. All the technology in the world at their disposal, and she uses a whistle? Strange.

Luther ushers us all into her room including our two

aliens. Light blue walls with aquarium murals and the view of a gorgeous beach sunset continue to change our view of what a yokel home should look like. Not that any of us had ever truly been inside one before. Misty has her usual pile of clothes neatly assembled in one corner near the window, but the rest of the bedroom remains pristine. No leftover food or dishes. Hardwood floors dusted and clean, a meticulous bed with a half dozen or so stuffed animals and pillows occupying their own creative space. I'm no slob, but this girl must have been doubling as a professional home stager. Each piece of furniture is perfectly matched and coordinated; a computer desk and entertainment center is adorned with the latest gadgetry. Family pictures and artwork fill one wall, including a few shots of a younger Misty holding a large fish and one standing next to a big deer hanging out the back end of a Ford truck.

I tilt my head back and exhale a huge breath when the first person's face on the screen is my dad. It had been way too long since we'd communicated. His military training gave me confidence that he'd be able to handle himself in most situations, but now that a secret alien race has been added to the equation, I've been concerned. *Check that.* More like freaked out.

Ozzy's step-parents, Rico's mom, and Star's family all appear too as the camera shot widens. While all the women on the other side of the webcam hold back uncomfortable smiles and tears, the men huddle together as if they are about to give us the details to the next football play. My father speaks first.

"If everything occurred as planned, all of you now realize this is *real*. And—we're not dealing with something *ordinary*. Faith, honey? You haven't been hurt, have you? Those drones were relentless."

"Hi, Dad. We're fine." I motion to the other three. "Right? I mean, not hurt, but still a ton of questions. Right, gang?"

"Yup," we answer.

"All right. We'll do our best to explain, but it's critical that you listen to Luther. And Gleason and Moore won't steer you wrong. They really *are* the good guys. Believe me---we need all the allies we can get right now."

"We will," Star says. "No panic here. You taught me well, Dad."

Both her parents move closer to the screen not realizing it makes them look awkward. Two giant heads doing their best to be strong for their daughter. My father pulls them back to a clearer distance adding to his previous thoughts.

"Faith? You were too young to remember this, but Luther and I served together in Afghanistan. We took turns saving each other's asses. When I'd heard he was running off to the mountains to become a hermit, I made a point of demanding that he keep in touch. His parents always had an open mind about what our government was doing, yet at the same time prepared for the future. They didn't care whether we got invaded by some terrorist group or aliens from outer space. They'd stockpile enough food, supplies, and ammunition to survive years without any intervention."

"No offense, sir." Ozzy stops him. "We already figured most of that out already. We want to know what we're supposed to do *now*, and why does the government want us dead? Sorry to be so blunt, sir."

"That's quite all right. I understand. I'm sure your hosts haven't had much of a chance to fill you in on the rest of the details. You four would have been killed because the final alignment of our planets is almost here, and Chancellor Azuna and the rest of her higher council members can't transcend or whatever the hell they call it, without you."

"Without *us*?" We question, staring at each other with raised eyebrows. I'm more than ready to crawl into a giant hole and hibernate until the coast is clear. All of this crap's way too difficult to process. Human-like beings need us? What for, we're the Neanderthals. *They're* the Steven Hawkings.

I struggle with my own turmoil and watch as the rest of my new friends pace back and forth in an obvious panic. Star is normally the rock of the group, but she blinks her eyes as if she's trying to change the channel and attempts to calm herself with her tai-chi. Ozzy and Rico are split between thinking this entire adventure is dreadful and quite possibly the most fascinating thing that's ever happened to them. They're shouting out random things.

"Can you believe it? Freakin aliens," Rico yells.

"I just knew they were real. How the hell did we get messed up with this?"

"This is some serious shit. We're never gonna get outta this alive. I just know it," Rico continues his rant.

Luther picks up on our emotional breakdowns and settles us back down for the rest of the meeting. His flair for calming a raging sea of hormones and nerves is impressive. After this alien takeover, he may want to consider teaching middle school.

Allowing us to vent for a few more minutes, he joins in on the conversation placing his arms around our shoulders from behind. I can sense some tension in him too; his bottom lip quivers before he proceeds to blow our minds with his next sentence.

"Perfect matches. Blood, DNA, body make-up—everything." In a drastic change of character, Luther's a scientist and not just a country bumpkin. "The hierarchy of their planet links directly to you four. If you don't *die*, they'll never be able to live here and take over."

"You gotta be shitting me!" Rico tumbles off the chair. "We're not even related!"

"True," Dad continues. "For different reasons, none of you got the chip, so that's the essence of your *connection*."

Ozzy rises next. It's *his* turn for trying to make sense of our new information. "Astronomical! What were the odds that we'd all be living in the same state let alone within a forty-mile radius of each other? Statistically, the chances were nearly impossible."

"Huh, you would think," Luther helps. "But that isn't important anymore. We gotta get you trained and ready for the next phase of the Niners' plan. If we don't, we'll be outta time."

"Trained?" Star asks, her voice a little hoarse from her two minutes of chanting. "I'm already a black belt. I can handle myself."

Before anyone on the other side of the computer can respond, the transmission starts to pixilate, audio still coming in clear but the picture distorts. One final series of sentences leave my father's mouth before we lose the connection.

"They've found us! Kill the trace! Kill the trace! I love you!"

A half dozen or more well-wishes break through the static from the rest of our families until the screen goes blue. Then Luther rips the wireless modem from the stand, throws it on the floor, and obliterates it with his heel. Shards of plastic fly in all directions whizzing by Rico's nose and landing on Misty's bed. Either Luther works out a great deal in-between smashing computer equipment, or he's got some superhuman strength. A puff of smoke dissipates.

"Daddy," she cries. "That's the third one this month!"

I watch as Luther and Misty share a hug and a big laugh together. I ache for the moment I'll be back with my dad reunited and just carrying on with normal life. Getting my dad's voice out of my mind isn't easy. He and I had gotten much closer since Mom's death. I dread thinking I might lose him too, but I'm not the superhero type. While I enjoyed an action movie occasionally, my tastes tend to lean more toward comedy. I'd had enough sadness in my life already.

How am I supposed to train myself for something I'd never dreamed I'd be doing? Battling an alien race of people, who for the most part looked just like us and loved their fathers and mothers. Sacrificing—whatever, just to stay alive and working hard to solve their problems. I keep thinking that what if the roles were reversed and I was the emissary of Nine? Wouldn't I have made the same decisions? How could the four of us even *begin* to change what's already occurred? Nothing was making much sense. So for the first time since they whisked us away from our ambushed transport, our two soldiers act more like our *friends* instead of a couple of memorial statues.

Our group moves away from Misty's bedroom outdoors to the peaceful river flowing just behind the Bennett's cabin. It's hard to believe that the mid-afternoon could look even more picturesque than the morning scenery, but it does. Many of the trees are in their initial stages of new life after a colder than normal winter, the sky with a band of wispy clouds amongst the cerulean blue. Clear water bubbles on down past the dozen or so boulders jutting out from the river bed. The constant smell of baked bread permeates the air mixed with the earthy odor of mud. While the members of the family go about their daily chores like putting clothes on the line and chopping wood, the four of us and our *saviors* sit down on the shore. Though their voices indicate urgency, they allow each of us to digest this new information at our own pace.

"Azuna is smart, beautiful, but extremely ruthless. *Her* mother was a victim of the very last disease our planet permanently cured," Bale, the smaller soldier, gives us a history lesson. "Orion Fever is similar to what you here on Earth refer to as blood cancer. She'd succumbed to the disease and passed a year before our researchers figured it out. Azuna's father, the man with the scar, wears it in remembrance of his wife."

"I don' get it," I say, my brain nearly too full to respond but somehow I find the courage to delve further into our dilemma. "What about compassion? You'd *think* since she'd lost her mother, she wouldn't be hell-bent on destroying our planet."

"Yeah," Rico interjects, "doesn't she have a soul?"

Marek turns to Rico acknowledging his question faster than he expected. "No. As a matter of fact, no one on Nine has a soul. Our Maker never gave us one. So when you say that we Niners need to borrow your *bodies* in order to live? That would be an incorrect assumption."

"Our souls?" Ozzy and Star join in.

"Do we even have proof that we have 'em?" Star asks. "I mean, I'm not saying we don't, but there is just no evidence, is there?"

"Plenty of evidence, as you say. If you want to count the fact that *we're* here. Both of us. Bale and I—we borrowed a couple of souls." The four of us back away in complete understanding. We're not sure we can trust anyone at this point.

"No worries. They were already—expired. We didn't have to kill—"

Marek eases our fears a little, but it's still way too difficult to digest. Without our souls, Azuna and her alien entourage can't exist on earth. But they're way more advanced. How in the hell are four 16-year-old Georgia teens going to stop them? Maybe we *should* let them take over? Our government's been messing things up for decades now.

We begin a purposeful stroll down the riverbed away from the cottage. Our two soldiers follow, taking us into a new realm of understanding. The details of our training procedure don't sound too terrible until Bale reveals the major *catch* in the process. Rico's brimming with a positive attitude until he hears the latest.

"Hey, I'm not worried 'bout doing a little running and lifting weights and stuff. I always wanted to learn how to use a light saber anyhow. Just don't make me do any of that yoga crap. This svelte body doesn't move that way." Once again Rico reminds us not to take ourselves too seriously, even when facing possible world domination.

"I'm afraid it's not your bodies we're concerned about, my young friends. Azuna has done her research well," Marek explains.

"Very true," Bale continues. "She knows all about the strength and will of the human species with their innate ability to fight a war, although the odds are against them. So it's not your physical skills she hopes to overcome."

Before he can finish his thoughts, we are struck down to the ground by an intense pressure in our skulls. Like something is forcing its way into our minds and giving us instant migraines. A coercion starts in the head and moves through every inch of our bodies. No way to resist. Nausea mixes with a slow tingling of every nerve ending in my limbs. In seconds, I'm hearing a clear female voice in my ears, but it's not emanating from *outside* of my body. Both Marek and Bale's eyes sparkle day-glow blue as they do their best to prove their point. Smiles on their faces, they seem to be enjoying our affliction.

Several minutes pass with continuous messages being given to us by way of hypnosis or mental telepathy, something I've never believed in, but now am succumbing. Their eyes go normal, and we all slump to the ground in a heap. We're still processing the thoughts pushed into our brains with no strength to retaliate.

Star is the first to shake off her temporary paralysis. Her instinct to use her martial arts skills very strong, she takes a half step toward Marek swinging her right leg around in a roundhouse kick, catching him squarely in the back with no effect. And that is the only blow she can muster. He's way too fast and strong; dodging each maneuver almost like he knows exactly what's coming next.

"Please," he cries. "We are wasting time. Your earthly talents may help you in a dark alley or in a ring, but that's not how you'll beat Azuna."

Beads of sweat pour off of Star's nose and chin now and glisten through her short hair. She's breathing steady still, but we can all tell she's exhausted from her epic two-minute clash. There's no doubt she could handle herself with most people, but Marek and Bale aren't *most* people. They're freaking aliens! Lesson number one: If Azuna wants to take our souls, no amount of kung-fu gyrations are going to stop her. We positively need a plan-B.

5

As we soon discover, our alien soldiers already *have* a plan-B. But none of us truly comprehend exactly what we're agreeing to until Marek and Bale give us the run-down.

"While the human body may be strong and able to withstand a degree of punishment, the mind—the soul can be weak. You wouldn't take a pea shooter into a nuclear war, would you? No. That's exactly why—"

Ozzy cuts Bale off to place his own genius slant on things. "We're no match for a higher-level of species. You just proved it. How does one train their soul anyhow? Frankly, I'd put my *mind* up against anyone's, but my soul? Not to use a cliché since we're right next to a river, but we're dead in the water."

He's still rubbing his head from the mind control tactic and reaching high into a tree to retrieve a red Frisbee. His skin looks pale for an African American now, and his eyes are bloodshot and swollen. I guess being brainy doesn't make you invincible or unemotional. He's just not living up to my preconceived notions at all. Maybe stereotypes have finally faded, and I can keep looking stupid. It seems to come way too easy for me.

Marek leads us back toward the cabin shaking his head the whole way. I figure he's about to give up on all of us until he wheels back around, passion on his face. This is the first time we have witnessed his annoyance.

Out of thin air, a black shiny metallic spear appears in his right hand, and he jams it into the ground. Before we even have the chance to react, a swirling wind kicks up fallen leaves and twigs in a horizontal tornado pattern around the now glowing lance. Mud and dirt zoom past our faces as we attempt to shield our eyes from the debris. Suddenly a kaleidoscope of colors form right before our eyes, and we're all stationary once again. Our eyes are the only part of our bodies sharing the same fear, though deep inside I'm about to heave. I'm wondering what vomit looks like suspended in mid-air, but just as if Marek can sense my terror, my pulse settles. He's a quiet lullaby calming the blaring infant. Just like that, my dread subsides.

I stare back and forth at the others and recognize they feel the serenity in the chaos too. We gaze into what I can only describe as a gel-like window or vortex, a whirlpool of intense lightning and thunder. Bale strides into the swirling light show and carves out a full doorway with his two hands. His actions leave behind a clear entrance minus the storm.

"You'll have one more day to decide. Step into your training or walk away. Just remember. Once the Alignment occurs, there'll be no stopping Azuna and the elders from stealing your souls." Bale forms both hands into fists, and the portal disappears leaving a giant hole in its wake. Our bodies are ours again, just as we're released from our mannequin hell.

"Wait!" Our shouts ring through the trees. A flock of birds scatter in all directions when we gather back in a group and head to the cabin.

"Yeah," Ozzy blares. "You two seem all high and mighty. Why can't *you* stop her? It's not like we can raise up a mini-thunderstorm and create a vortex ourselves."

"Yeah, or invade people's thoughts or pause time. We're no frigging comic book heroes or anything! We're just—just—I dunno, normal, for chrissakes. We didn't sign up for this, ya know? Geez. And I thought getting *kidnapped* was scary," Rico freaks for a second time then re-engages. He's a cartoon character waiting for his next frame to be drawn. We're all waiting.

Marek and Bale don't say anything on the way back. Their force diminishes, and I swear both are smiling their pretentious smiles again, maybe even laughing at us inside. It's a crazy idea, but I think they already know our decisions, as if they can see the future or something. I know for a fact that I'm not in the least comfortable with any of this training ritual or stopping this Azuna lady from taking my soul. I can't speak for Rico, Ozzy, or Star, but I'm seriously considering leaving in the middle of the night. If this Azuna wants my soul, she'll have to *find* me first, and I don't plan on making it easy for her. That's for sure.

Luther's the first to greet us when we return to the cabin. He sits in his wicker rocking chair on the porch drawing. It's a young boy, maybe around five or six years-old at the most. Bale and Marek glide into the home and leave the four of us on the porch. In minutes, Misty flies through the screen door with a basket of fresh blueberry muffins. We thank her and converge to the extra chairs. Luther's fixated on his drawing, but it's actually Misty who reveals the subject's name.

"That's Leeland. My baby brother," she whispers matter-of- factly, tears starting their descent down her cheeks. "He died last year. But we didn't know, did we, Daddy?"

Luther pulls his daughter onto his lap like Santa as she rests her head on his shoulder. He passes the portrait to Ozzy first, and the rest of us share it. Luther's an amazing artist. An actual photo wouldn't have captured all the details in this drawing.

"What happened, Luther?" I drum up enough courage to ask. "You're a wonderful artist."

"Well—you see; I was away for a couple of weeks tending to some business a couple of towns over. Kandy wasn't due for over a month, so I thought it would be okay to go. I took the boys. But then—"

"Kandy went into labor early, didn't she?" Star tries to follow his story.

"Yeah, she did. But that wasn't the tough part. Our normal midwife was ill, so neighbors didn't know what to do. There were complications this time. They took her to the regional hospital in the big city where they gave him the chip with his expiration code."

"Wait!" I interject. "I thought everyone was supposed to be guaranteed 15 years? He looks no more than five or six. How could he—"

"Doc Johnson was a good friend of ours just west of Waverly who claimed he had a way of *removing* the code without any side effects. Turned out he was wrong."

Misty can't bear to listen to the story once again, so she excuses herself and sprints back into the cabin. Luther continues.

"Operation went fine and all. Looked like it was gonna work until the seizures. I guess these latest chips don't kill you right away like the first ones back in 2009. When they're removed, there's a time release on 'em. It was detached, but the timer had already been set. The toxins already released into his blood. Five and a half years, though. We're thankful we had 'em."

A dark silence permeates the cool mid-afternoon air. Luther's words rattle around in my brain and trigger my own dreadful memories. We hadn't known his family and him for very long, but I can sense that we all feel the void like we're not just acquaintances anymore; we're family now. Ozzy's holding back his emotions sniffling like a young child, Star's reaching for something to wipe her tears, and Rico's already moving to embrace Luther. The drawing's more than a piece of artwork; it's a son. One who died way too soon.

Suddenly my heart's starting to re-think my escape plan. I've never had any brothers or sisters, but it's been over two years, and I'm still grieving over my mom. Losing a boy like that, especially after you've spent time with him is horrible. Somebody has to fight back and show the administration there's a better way. America probably has no idea where this expiration device came from or about the Niners' plans. The economy's flourished with the new gold discovery, but that's just another ploy to catch us when we ain't looking. All that auric came from their planet. Probably a bribe. While all the politicians are peering through their rose-colored glasses and counting their golden eggs, the Niners are jumping in and out of portals swiping people's humanity.

But how? I'm sorry, but there's only so much training a person can withstand. *What makes Bale and Marek think we could have any chance against Azuna?* There's gotta be something more he's just not telling us. Like our great, great ancestors were all aliens themselves, and we have secret powers we never use.

Feeling so much less than *powerful* at the moment, I hand the drawing back to Luther and take my turn at offering my condolences. I know he spent several years in the military with my father, but there's a strength he radiates beyond his rock-like exterior. There are more than two people keeping secrets around here. And before I meet with Rico, Ozzy, and Star to discuss our options, I'm determined to find out exactly what they are.

Kandy appears at the screen door as chipper as ever until she sees the cry-fest on the porch, but she's not asking to join our pity party. On the contrary, she's too busy spreading her *own* version of hope to the rest of us.

"Leeland may have been the most difficult child I've

ever birthed, but after he was born? Well—let's just say he more than made up for it. He drew all of us together. He made us closer and helped us to believe there'd be a better future, one without those hideous expiration codes. We'll get there yet." She glances at the four of us. "You'll see. He didn't die in vain. No one does. We all have a purpose."

Rico's the first to rise up from his chair as he storms past a surprised Kandy going into the house. Ozzy follows closely behind. Star and I wait a moment with Luther, deciding it's the perfect time to get the rest of the story. Based upon the determination in Ozzy and Rico's faces, I knew they were ready to face whatever our alien friends had in mind. When testosterone calls, men often leap before they look, which is why they get hit by so many semis. If we're putting our souls on the line to save the world, I want to be sure we don't miss anything. Somebody has to be the brains. It might as well be us women.

Luther steps off the porch into the brightening sky and works his way toward the barn. Star and I trail along behind him. It's not easy to keep pace as Luther's strides are swift and long. Our mysterious hermit in the woods feels the pressure on the back of his head and neck from our burning curiosity. We reach the main doors only to be intercepted by Luther's brother, Otis, and his two sons, Micah and Junior.

"Stop," Micah yells. "You can't enter unless you know the password." He smiles, proud of himself for keeping the rules.

"That's right," says Junior. "We can't have strangers lurking 'round. Might git hurt. You're too pretty to get hurt, ma'am."

Having never been called pretty before, I blush, but my interest grows stronger.

Otis joins into the conversation placing himself in between the boys and us. He's not as large as Luther, but you can definitely tell they're brothers. Same square jaw line, military cut, clear blue eyes. For a second I swear his eyes glow just like Marek and Bale's, but I dismiss it as the sun playing tricks on my tired eyes.

"It's okay, boys. Luther thinks it's time they find out. We're gonna exempt them from the code this time. Come on in, ladies. Try not to go into shock."

Fully expecting the aroma of hay and horses, Star and I are stunned by what we see as we enter. Luther's barn is more decked out in computer gear and technology than NASA. We see locked cases of every weapon known to man. Projectors and screens, 50-inch television monitors, and an open section with a rubber mat, almost like a wrestling room.

"It's a fricking command center," Star whispers. "What the hell's going on here?"

Luther pops his head out from behind a row of file cabinets with a couple of push pins and his latest portrait. One entire wall of the place is filled with Luther's drawings, mostly of Leeland and the rest of his family. He sticks this picture up with the rest of the photos and strolls over to a silver desk with a comfy black leather chair. There's no place for us to sit down until Junior flicks a switch and six rounded bar stools rise up through trap doors right in front of his desk.

"Welcome to my inspiration," Luther says.

"Your what?" Star and I question together.

"My reason for rebellion against the government. Now—I know what it may look like."

"That you're crazy?" I say. "Some lunatic with a revenge motive is seeking to take down the government?"

"Exactly."

"Nope," Star responds. "Go right ahead, fine by us. Then we won't have to—"

Luther stands holding a cell phone like device in his hand. It's a remote control. He taps it twice, and a hologram of our current leader Chancellor Stevens appears in mid-air. She's signing an agreement surrounded by the press snapping pictures of the historic moment.

"I know you two weren't even born yet, but here's what started all this expiration code nonsense. Have you any idea why they're called Niners? Marek and Bale? Azuna?"

"No clue," I say. Star shakes her head in agreement.

"It's the Ninth planet to be discovered, if you're counting Pluto, which we are. Xisto is its real name, but translated it means *nine*, a truly parallel planet to Earth with one exception."

"No souls," Star says.

"Yes. And technology way beyond anything we have here, of course. During the alignment and sometimes without it, Niners are able to travel through these, oh how can I explain it?"

"Vortices?" Ozzy's voice echoes through the barn from behind us. He and Rico join our merry roundtable along with Marek and Bale. They're even more impressed by the surroundings than we are.

"Come. Join us. We have much to discuss before your training begins."

"Our training?" Rico asks. "We haven't even made our decision yet, have we?" He stares at us puzzled.

"No, we haven't. But I'm glad you're finally putting all the pieces together for us, so we can make an informed choice. Right, guys?" I respond.

Ozzy is busy taking his own tour of the facility in awe of all the latest gadgetry. He examines a red button-like contraption with a solid white knob in the center. Before Marek or Bale can react, he turns the knob clockwise and a light ray flies out from the device blowing a three-foot hole in the front doors.

"Oops! Sorry. I didn't mean to—"

Micah snags the apparatus from him, makes a quick adjustment, and re-fires. In seconds, the damage is reversed. Just like that. No sign of any explosion. He places the contraption back into its case and seals the container.

"Now, where were we? Our training. You see, so far none of you have convinced us that we're the right people for the job," I say, not bothering to even comment on the blast. If magicians can make the Eiffel Tower disappear, a ten-foot hole in a door fixing itself is a breeze.

"Stop!" Luther slams his hand down on the table, his darker side finally shows up. "Pardon my outburst, but you don't understand that you are the only ones who can turn the tide in this war. *We* didn't choose you. That was predetermined by your DNA. You would think that Azuna and her leaders could find four other people with a perfect match, but that's not the case. Faith? Azuna herself needs your soul. Ozzy, Rico, and Star are all perfectly matched to the four greatest leaders on their planet. They can't be allowed to cross over. We'll have no chance then."

Surreal, every ounce of it. Overwhelmed doesn't even come close to describing how I felt learning that our whole planet's survival rested on our shoulders. Whatever happened to anticipating your driver's license? Dating? Finding a college? Stopping an alien breed from taking over never made any of *my* lists.

My ocean of fears includes having kids, getting shipwrecked on an island of cannibals, and gaining more than five pounds. Those are rational, clear, and common concerns. Well, except for the cannibal one. Preventing an alien takeover? Really? Rico's God is brutal. And He didn't even give me any special powers or wings, just a damn disease. Hey, maybe *that's* the solution? Let her have my soul, and she dies of a blood disorder. Oh, if it were only that simple. Hail, Mary? Any chance you can bring me some sleep? *I Didn't think so.*

6

I toss and turn for at least an hour before the sandman knocks. I let him in, but not without a few questions first. *Why sleep now? Don't you know an invasion is coming? How am I gonna make sure I keep my soul?* He stays quiet, but what can I expect from a childhood urban legend, especially when he's so fickle? *Stay awake. Stay awake. Stay awake.* You repeat over and over during your favorite teacher's lecture, but no matter how hard you try, your eyelids rebel. *Faith? Faith? Are we keeping you awake?* It's not like you can't overcome the embarrassment; it's just the last thing you wanted to do to the hottest male teacher whoever walked Heritage High halls.

An alien entity needs your soul to survive on earth. I'd love to say, "No thanks. I'll just sleep through that if I can." Yeah, right. I may never sleep again, ever.

Luther's remarkable cabin in the woods is a cozy place to lay one's head but not when the fate of humanity scrapes at your soul. Rest sounded good to Star and the others too, but we have plans first thing in the morning to make our final decision over breakfast. If I don't sleep, I may miss that engagement.

I drew the long straw and got my own room while the rest shared the guest bedroom. My room's right next to Luther and Kandy's. Their whispers stop around midnight, but I'm unable to decipher anything tangible.

The wind has picked up outside spinning Misty's favorite weathervane, a golden rooster, around and around. I gaze out the window and listen to its sporadic squeaks hoping the noise will finally settle my nerves and take me to dreamland. And that's exactly what happens.

"Faith? Faith, honey? Could you run downstairs and get me more water?" Mom's voice is barely audible from my room next door.

"Sure, Mom. Be back in a minute," I assure her. I tiptoe downstairs and grab two water bottles from the fridge and head back up to her room. Her door's ajar, and when I enter she's not in her bed like normal. She's lying on the floor nearly *under* her bed. Moving, but she's obviously in no position to get back up on her own. As she turns her head toward me to speak, I blink my eyes a few times trying to clear my view. My mother's body is hers, but she's got Marek's head. Their faces change back and forth like they're in a battle to see which one wins. Marek speaks, but it's Mom's voice I'm hearing. I keep waiting to awaken from my nightmarish encounter, but I sense that Marek, I mean *Mom*, has something important to share.

I set the water on the nightstand next to her bed and lift her to her feet. In seconds, she's stronger than I've seen her in months now. Unscrewing the lid from the bottle and drinking, something I've had to do *for* her the last few weeks.

"Please don't be scared," Marek's lips in sync with her words. "Your friends? They understand what's at stake, but they want to give up. Run. You must lead them, Faith. We are out of options."

"I know. But Mom? I'm just a kid. I should be thinking about proms and part times jobs. Planning my future. Not how to resist an alien conquest."

"That's silly, dear. Shit happens, right?" Her award-winning smile makes me melt. "*Dad* didn't put a tumor underneath my brain stem. I was *born* with it, I guess. Look. None of that matters now. Besides, I'll always be right here. Through the training and when you defeat Azuna." She pauses to take another sip from the bottle. Suddenly my mouth feels as dry as dirt. "Look at Luther. His dead son got him through *his* training."

"What? Luther went through the training too? Why?"

"His whole family did. Only Leeland got the chip, and that was by necessity. Kandy would have died if she hadn't gotten to the hospital."

"But why would *they* need the training?"

I feel myself struggling to wake from my dream. I'm clawing at the blankets and screaming in my head to wake up, wake up! Mom's body disappears and is replaced by

Marek completely now.

"We needed allies here on Earth, people we trust to do the right thing. And as you already know, basic human instincts or talents aren't enough. Kandy and Luther volunteered to enter the training as a *back-up*. In case we couldn't convince you four to comply. But that still doesn't solve our conundrum, Faith. Azuna and her cabinet need *your* souls not Luther's family."

"But how? My mother? I'm so confused!" My legs shake out of control as I attempt to walk or maybe run myself out of my sleeping spell.

"Your mother's soul. I—*absorbed* it—when she died. She wasn't my identical counterpart, just a temporary substitute. That's how I knew you were the one. Azuna is a perfect match. It led me to Luther who led me to your dad and you. So you see, it was all meant to be. I know Azuna's nature. What drives her? It's not power or riches. It's her people. She won't let them perish. It's why her father placed her in charge. With her here and calling all the shots, full assimilation could occur in a matter of years. Everyone's expiration date altered to suit their needs."

"But if she had my soul, wouldn't she change? See that all of this is wrong? Maybe change her mind?"

"Well, you see, it doesn't quite work that way. Think of a soul as a battery. In a Niner, it's present just to keep our bodies functioning. Unlike earthlings, it has no effect whatsoever on our reasoning or morality. It just keeps us *ticking*."

"Oh, really? Just a battery, huh? Then why were there tears in your eyes at the sight of Leeland's portrait? You're changing. Aren't you?" I press him a little more because there's *some* reason he's decided to help us. He and Bale just aren't like the other Niners.

"Emotions? Tears? Merely an *involuntary* response. I assure you, we feel nothing."

"Yeah, right. Speaking of feeling things, I can tell there's at least *one* more thing you haven't told us about how this entire training procedure actually works. I've watched you and Bale dodge it long enough, thinking you could just mention it in passing."

Wham! Wham! Wham!

I'm startled awake by the wind whipping up something outside my window desperate for Marek's answer, but in moments the conversation fades. A large piece of aluminum continues its assault on the house. My stomach growls, and suddenly I'm focused more on feeding my face than worrying about any training strategy. All the while I'm thinking there's more to these Niners than I first believed, as if they can erase memories and stuff, especially dreams.

Bits and pieces of my nightmare linger as I leave my warm bed and walk to the breakfast table. Misty peeks up at me with a mouthful of corn flakes, a half-eaten apple next to her bowl, and an enormous glass of chocolate milk. Kandy cracks two eggs into a pan and pops down a couple of slices of wheat bread into a toaster. I'm praying the food's for me until Rico bounds in from the second bathroom, his hair a shaggy wet mess from a shower.

"Morning. I have dibs on the eggs. First up, first served 'round here. Kandy's rules. Star's up going through her tai-chi, and Ozzy's been reading something since six. Says he'll be down soon. How'd you sleep? I mean, with all the stress—"

Not wanting to sound weak, I lie. "Fine. Real cozy night. You?"

Kandy offers both of us a cup of coffee, but we both opt for hot tea instead. I've never been much of a coffee drinker. Mom and I had a family tradition of enjoying a cup of tea together every morning. Somehow even though I knew she wasn't feeling well, she always made me believe she was improving. Just the thought gave me hope.

"I slept all right. Tough time getting there, but once I dozed off, I was good. Don't wanna seem rude, but you look like crap." He insults me, but I'm so starved I don't even care. He makes a show of dabbing butter and hot apple jelly on his toast. I swear, he'd make a perfect comedian one day.

"Thanks for the compliment, Shaggy. You might wanna use a comb soon, or you're gonna look like a black used Q-tip," I joke.

"Seriously, man. You look like you went a few rounds with an MMA fighter last night. Sure you're okay? Bruises cover your forehead, your neck."

I panic. My platelets must be out of whack again. *I can't imagine why.* Fortunately I always travel with my current prescription and oral meds. The low dose of Prednisone usually does the trick. I must have been thrashing around last night, but currently I'm quite foggy as to why.

"Thanks, Rico. It's my platelets again. I'll take my pill after I eat."

Right on cue, Kandy delivers my version of breakfast, and I waste no time devouring it. I'm curious about Misty's handheld device she's been playing with since I arrived.

Normally not shy or speechless, it's dominated her attention.

"Whatcha playin? A video game?" I ask.

Rico glances over her shoulder, his eyes suddenly wider than normal.

"Check it out!" he says. "All the characters look like us. Luther, Otis, Junior. How did you do that?"

"It's a simulation. Program a situation, the people, and all the troubles, and then you figure out a way to get through it. I've just been stuck in one spot for hours, and I can't seem to get past this level."

Ozzy and Star move into the scene overhearing some of Misty's explanation. Ozzy offers his services.

"Here. Let me take a look. Maybe I can solve it."

Misty's reluctant at first. Glancing back and forth to her mom and back to us. Not exactly the expected impulse from a pre-teen who's been stumped. In between her next round of eggs over easy, Kandy gives Misty a nod, and she lets Ozzy take a stab at it.

"Whoa! Is that me? Looks just like me. Am I really that tall? Where are we? You need to clarify this level. Okay?"

"Well, you've all decided to run through the forest, and you come upon this cave. But it's not just any old cave, really. There are many twists and turns in it."

"Kinda like a maze?" Star says.

"Yeah, but a *lot* harder. And you only have one life left, so I have to be careful. Or you'll die, and I'll get bumped back to the start."

"Where's Faith? She's not in the cave," Ozzy says.

"That's because *she* decided to stay—with us, to beat the

aliens. And now I just wanna get all of you back together again. So we can be a team."

Luther steps through the back kitchen door allowing the aroma of wood smoke to filter in and mix with Ozzy's order for fried ham with his food. He's holding an email message probably taken from his tricked-out barn. The four of us are still in awe of Misty's game, but Luther snaps us out of our daydream.

"All's well with your father, Faith. Each of your families is fine. We finally received word. They're on the run, but they'll reach the safe house in a few hours. The government's been relentless. They must know something's up. So what's it gonna be? Training's gotta start today if we hope to beat the alignment."

Star's voice quivers as she's the first to speak. "Well, I've never been afraid of much, but this alien junk scares the shit outta me. I gotta be honest. Almost beat it outta here last night. The odds are against us. I'd rather take my chances and hide. There are plenty of places to go."

"Oh, really? And we all did so well a couple of days ago in the woods. I'm kinda liking my new accommodations. I mean, it's not the Hilton, but it's pretty close, ya know? I'm in, if you're in," Rico sounds cautiously optimistic. His drawl makes it easy to forget he's from Mexico.

I hear my new friends speak, continue to watch Misty battle with her game, and scenes from my nightmare come back. My mom, Marek, and my final question. I could walk away from all of this. Consider it all a nightmare. Go home. Leave the rest to decide. But then Mom's words creep their way up my spine like a pair of freezing fingers. I have no idea if it's just another one of Marek's mind control tricks, but suddenly I don't even care. I want to *do* something with my life besides mourn my mother's death and explain my bruised body over and over again.

Luther and his family have all endured the training. Why can't we? How difficult can it be? Junior? He can barely hold up a rifle. Misty's a pretty little porcelain doll. Micah barely says anything, but he seems smart, like the quiet ones in school. They don't speak much, but they all get straight A's. If *they* can do it, so can we. I shake my head out of my halftime internal motivation speech and demand to see Marek and Bale. A surge of energy I've never experienced because of my disease, races through my veins now. I can't wait to start.

Luther leaves out the door he entered, and in minutes we're all one happy family gathered around the dining room table. Ozzy, Rico, and Star feed their mouths with the last bit of breakfast, and I launch into my quest to persuade us all to do what's right.

"Before we agree to anything, I'm sure my friends and I deserve to know the rest of the details of our training. Marek? In my dream? You were about to tell me, and then you played your hocus pocus, and I woke up, not remembering I even asked. Well, now I do. So spill it."

"In your dream, huh? Rico asks. "So *that's* why you look like you've gone a few rounds with Anderson Silva. I knew it was something."

"Marek, we want the details now, or the four of us walk." I don't back down.

"Fine. But I think the rest of the family should fill you

in, since they've experienced it already, don't you think so, Luther? Kandy?"

7

"We have to do what?" Our voices carve out a niche in the sweet country charm of the cabin placing an ominous stain on the atmosphere. If there had been paint on the walls, it wouldn't be peeling; it'd be melting.

"You all have to die," Luther explains.

Star's the first to back away from the table and begin her pacing. Her hands move back and forth over her cropped hair and then out to the sides in reaction to the news. I feel terrible about demanding to know now because I can tell the rest of the gang's not as enthusiastic as I am in the least. In fact, 'Let's get the hell outta here' seems to be etched on all of their faces, and I know I'm going to have an even harder time inducing them to die for their country. Thankfully, there's an army of people more on my side than theirs.

"Please, everyone? Take it easy. I mean, look. Luther, Kandy. Do *they* look dead to you? Misty, Micah, Otis, the others? There must be a logical explanation. Maybe they don't mean *die* die."

"No. It's pretty much the dying we're all used to," Otis says. A tiny smile sneaks across his lips. "But, hey, look at the bright side; when you're finished, you can do this!" He catapults himself up to the ceiling nearly fifteen feet in the air, touches the wooden beam, and lands like a superhero. Junior grabs the fireplace poker and bends it like it's a pretzel then fixes it just as easily. Micah pushes his thoughts inside my head, but it's not what I expect.

I was scared too, but you don't feel a thing, really.

I know I don't look it, but I'm more confident than I've ever been.

If a Niner comes after my soul, I'll be ready.

I take a quick peek at the other three, and I can tell they've all gotten the same message as I did, but they're not as gung-ho as I am still. Rico's shaking head back and forth like he's just witnessed a miraculous soccer goal. You know, the ones where the player does a back flip and slams the ball past a diving goalie? All Ozzy can seem to do is laugh in a loud disjointed pattern.

"What's the purpose? I mean, for dying? Isn't there a way to train us while we're alive?" I ask, showing my friends a little love.

"Our scientists have been experimenting with creating an *artificial* soul," Bale explains. "I was the lead researcher on the team. What we discovered was when *humans* die, they separate from their fragile bodies. Without the soul, the body is like a light bulb without any electricity. Niners can easily overwhelm a human's *body*, but it's often the will of the soul that resists complete assimilation. There's just something about a human's emotions that act like a wall. So when the body dies, although many souls are ripe for the taking, some fight back. It appears your creator did that on purpose as a failsafe device, so you're not so easily possessed by anything. We now know why, so our training pinpoints strengthening *that* part of the soul. Of course, you'll require some physical skills as well, but that's in stage two."

Bale's words leave his mouth so matter-of-factly like he's done it a thousand times. He's confident and sure of himself; I wish I could absorb it. I hear every word, but they don't seem to penetrate, just bring more questions. How many of these training sessions have they actually done here, on Earth? Other than Luther's family, I mean. What makes them so sure it'll even work with us four? This kind of thing only happens in science fiction books.

Ozzy's high IQ helps him to follow Bale's logic better than the rest of us. There's still dread on his face, but he doesn't think like we do. "This is kinda like a sports team protecting home court advantage. No aliens are coming into *our* house and taking what's ours. So you're going to teach our souls to resist. But we gotta die, huh?"

"Great analogy, Ozzy," Bale commends him. Star stops her pacing and moves to the family room floor where she sits, crosses her legs, and begins to meditate. "Dying ensures proper training because there's no breakable body to worry about. So far, it looks as if a human soul *cannot* be duplicated. Believe me. We've tried. We don't *need* emotions, a conscience, or morals on Nine. They make us weaker. When our bodies stop functioning, we're placed into a decomposition chamber."

"I think it makes humans *stronger*," Rico says. "I never would have made it without my will to survive. In two days, I would have been dead. My kidnappers tortured me as it is. They would have had no problem killing me. But I wouldn't let them break me."

"And that's why we gotta do this, guys," I say, moving toward Star who seems a little more at peace now. I offer her my hand to help her rise, and although my body is shaking, she embraces me. A clear sense of resolve fills her face. Her grey-blue eyes focus on Marek and Bale as she guides me back to them in the kitchen. An eerie silence accompanies us, but it's obvious that all of us are approaching the same page now. I'm just not sure how we got there. How difficult would it be for Marek or Bale to manipulate our thoughts and force us to comply?

"You hurt any of my friends, and I'll *find* a way to kill you," Star speaks with gritty determination. "Whadda we have to lose? I mean, it's not like we can spend the rest of our lives on the run, right? And no matter what, there's no fairy tale ending in this scenario where we're all happily ever after back with our families, going on summer vacations, and choosing a new pet. I've lived and breathed politics in my house. They're not gonna change things, so why don't we help them see the light? I'm ready, if you are."

Star's speech warms my heart, even though my brain's still calling me a coward, making excuses, and forcing me to doubt. I doubt my own will to survive.

After Mom died, I wanted to join her. I didn't just lose the person who birthed me; I lost my best friend, the one person who taught me to accept every bruise, every scar from my disease and wear it like a medal of honor. I'd grow up and be able to help others go through the same things. She made me recognize the beauty in my affliction known as TTP. (Thrombotic thrombocytopenic purpura) Too bad remembering the past can't change the future. I guess we'll need to do *that* ourselves.

Even a raw piece of marble has to be bruised and broken, before the masterpiece is formed. Can we ever escape adversity? Sooner or later the challenge comes. The fork in the road where you decide to curl up in a ball and give up or tell the monster in your bloodstream he's not gonna win. I still recall the day my doctor informed me that he'd finally found a way to at least halt the process or slow it down dramatically. I'd never heard of gold salts before, but apparently mixed with a half dozen plasma exchanges and a new version of Prosorba, the blood demon retreats. It's probably not gonna be as easy with Azuna, but I'd rather be a lion for a day than a sheep for a lifetime.

It's crazy. Now that I've *found* a way to die, I don't want to. And who knows what strange things the training might do to us? But I'm *already* a freak. So I guess I'll become even more of one. It's not like I'm ever going back to *normal* anyhow. I mean, not now. Depending upon what happens, that is. Who cares what others think? Just wait until we foil these Niners' master plan and turn the government right-side up. I better order a box of Sharpie markers for all the autographs I'll be signing.

Marek and Luther huddle in the kitchen hallway for a few minutes before they return. Luther speaks first.

"You're not in this alone. We'll be right here, understand? Let's say, we meet outside the barn in an hour. Wear comfortable shoes, clothes, and I promise your journey won't hurt."

Kandy continues to encourage us. "In fact, when you're finished, you'll be even better people than you are right now. Take Misty, for example. I couldn't get that girl to keep anything organized in her room: books, toys, clothes everywhere. Now look at her. She's nearly a saint."

"Thanks, Momma," Misty says. "And when you come out, the whole world seems brighter. Like food tastes better, and when you're sad, you *really* feel it, but you don't stay that way for long. And I don't even mind my brothers hogging the television."

The four of us thank Kandy for the wonderful breakfast and her moving words. Misty gives us all hugs, and pretty soon the whole family is joining in on it. I step out into the fresh air aware of my decision and wanting so badly to talk to my dad before we enter our training realm, just in case things don't exactly go as planned. We lock arms and head for the stream knowing that in less than an hour, we'll be chest deep into alien quicksand. Once we're in, there's no escaping until it's over.

Ozzy, Rico, and Star pick up a handful of flat rocks and start skimming them across to the other bank. They're as restless as I am, but it's not until Star finally breaks down and sobs uncontrollably that we start to feel even closer. Emotionally disturbed but more like family, as if we're long lost relatives meeting for the first time in years.

It wasn't *our* fault we never got the expiration codes or happened to be the perfect matches for these alien leaders. Leaving has always been an option, but as we share our fears and tears, we accept our fate. Fighting about it now is a waste of energy. We'll need every ounce of strength when we return. It's better to regret what you do than what you don't, right?

"Did Marek ever mention the actual *date* of the alignment?" I wonder.

"Don't think so," Ozzy says. "But if it's in conjunction with Syzygy, the Convergence, on April 14th, we're about three days away. How on Earth are we going to be train—"

"Uh—Otis can jump through the roof?" Rico reminds us. "Who knows how long this training takes, but if *that's* the result, I think we'll be finished in time. I'm kinda looking forward to having my Spidey senses tingle. You?"

Star lifts her eyebrows and grins almost like she's flirting now, her eyes red and swollen. "Oh, I don't know. I'd like to think there's nothing wrong with *my* Spidey senses, at least when it comes to *boys*. I can tell when they want something they're not entitled to yet. I may be blonde, but I'm not dumb." Out of nowhere, Star proves she really *does* have a sense of humor. Her calm behavior refreshes, helping us forget the fact that a few minutes ago we were all a crying mess.

A half dozen or so black birds congregate in the pine tree in front of the cabin and squawk. A couple dive bomb us as we return to the porch, reminding us of our new purpose. Whether we wanted to be or not, we're targets now.

We can all fly through the sky like we know where we're headed, or we can land on the fence in a row and let the big bad aliens pick us off one by one.

Nevertheless, I lag behind the others baffled by one question I've either been too frightened to ask out loud or maybe don't really want an answer to anyhow. But it slips into my stream of consciousness again like a speed boat as I say 'excuse me' and pass by Marek and Bale. *What if we're just being controlled right now? We didn't make this choice on our own?* No audible answer spills out of either of their mouths as I proceed through the screen door, but an answer comes soon enough in the form of my mom's voice once again.

"Niners like Marek and Bale won't steer a human into training. The procedure is doomed to fail that way. Commitment comes from the heart not the mind. You're either all in or not. There *is* no half-way."

Both men follow me a few steps toward my bedroom, and I peek over my shoulder as a gesture of thanks. They acknowledge my look by pushing one last idea into my brain. *Those who win, believe they can before the war even starts. Do you?* Not sure if my response can be forced back their way or not, I answer. *Guess we'll see, huh?*

8

It's incredible how the Tennessee Mountains make almost every early spring day look the same, no matter what time it is. Noon rolls around quickly, and the sun does its best to burn off the morning fog over the stream. The gentle wind is just enough of a reminder that winter doesn't give up easily, but there's crispness in the air today I've not recognized until now. I recall Misty's words about how everything in life enhances after the training. So I use that thought to continue building my resolve. Maybe I'm suddenly looking forward to what's in store for all of us. Perhaps it can even make sardines taste better 'cuz there's nothing on the planet that can make them *smell* better.

We gather near the barn entrance just like we were told, weaving our way through the four dogs and field of chickens and kicking up dust from the well-worn path. The first thing that comes to mind is why have a command center in the middle of the country, and who's really running it? Luther is anti-government, so where did he get the money and resources to pull this off? I contemplate a few minutes before Marek and Bale throw open the doors and welcome us inside.

The place looks about the same except for the physical training section which has Marek's staff sticking up out of the middle of the rubber mats. He's already started the vortex, but the window hasn't turned to gel yet. We brace ourselves for our journey in, but before we go both aliens give us a few last-minute instructions.

"We have pre-determined a training order for each of you," Bale says.

"Based upon your personalities, your thoughts, your fears," Marek adds.

I'm curious to know how they gathered such information. "Wait! How would you know any of that in just this short time?"

"Your rooms were equipped with monitoring devices as you slept. We've done background checks, health exams, DNA studies, and inoculations," Marek explains.

"Inoculations?" Rico and Ozzy pipe up. They're busy circling the vortex trying to figure out how it works. Neither appears to be as nervous as Star and me. Never seeing her do this before, she's in her meditative state sitting Indian style on the floor, but she's having trouble concentrating and is chewing down each fingernail as she attempts to calm herself.

"Yes. Keep in mind that Azuna and her staff can use all kinds of weapons against you including sickness to wear you down," Bale says. "Your human bodies are quite vulnerable to disease. Niners have eliminated disease, which is one reason why our planet is overpopulated, you see."

"Any more secrets?" I ask, placing my hand on Star's head hoping to gain a little of her peace myself. I throw out a couple of, if there's a God, now would be a good time to prove it sentences in my mind, but I'm not sure it does me much good. My knees continue to rebel wanting to give out on me with each movement. I give in and sit next to Star. Marek goes on with his directions.

"There's no set time limit for your training sessions. In fact, you'll not even worry about time once you're in because it doesn't exist in the module. You'll stay in training until—"

"Until what?" we say in unison.

"Until the module deems you're ready for the physical world again," he says.

"You mean we could be in there for weeks?" Rico shouts.

"Technically, yes," Bale says. "But we have very little time. The alignment is less than three days away. Azuna can enter and live for 48 hours without a soul, so she'll be zeroed in on you as soon as she transfers worlds. We've *advanced* the procedure some."

"Geez. That's nice to know. As soon as we get back to the land of the living, we'll be running for our lives," Star complains.

"Not exactly." Luther walks into the training area eating a sandwich. He never made it to our *last supper* at lunch before we met in front of the barn. "Running isn't part of the plan. You'll be moved to a more secure site closer to where Azuna will enter. If we don't catch her unaware, our chances of success minimize exponentially."

"Phew. Shouldn't we have known this *before* we put our butts on the line? What's it gonna be like anyhow? Let's get ready to rumble! Big time wrestling! TV? Reporters? Pay-per-view?" Rico's joking but not really.

The rest of us chase back a smile because we realize even though he pokes fun at our eventual war, humor won't change anything now. His depiction of an Alien Royal Rumble is a clever thought, but I'm kinda hoping for something a little less strenuous. Like my soul beats the crap out of Azuna's synthetic attacks, or I dodge a few silver bullets on my way to watching her melt like the Wicked Witch of the West after the sun rises on her 3rd day here. At that, I realize I've wasted way too much time watching television.

"Anything else we need to know?" I ask. "Any subterranean monsters in our training, or ogres with hatchets or swords? Elves? Personally, I don't know about the rest of you, but I'm horrible at video games."

"Actually, I'm not too bad," says Star.

"Yeah, me too," Rico admits.

"Waste of time," Ozzy adds, "but I've created a few of my own, and I can out-think myself out of *most* situations."

"Stop," Marek whispers. "All of you. Remember what I've told you. Your human bodies, habits, and tendencies will do you no good once you're in. Do you understand? You'll be absent from your bodies relying solely on your souls. You'll *seem* alive, but you won't be. Azuna probably already knows all of your weaknesses. And fortunately, so do we."

His next move surprises the hell out of us. He waves his hand to form the gel doorway and with one full motion sweeps everyone into the vortex.

****

No amusement park ride comes close to explaining what our trip into training hell feels like. Drowning in the ocean would come close because I try to breathe but my lungs refuse to cooperate. I see my three friends all ahead of me sliding down the same gel-like substance being sucked toward a yellow light at the end of our tunnel. If this is what doing LSD felt like in the 60's, those people were insane. We're streaking through the jelly at mind-boggling speeds, our legs and arms pinned back by the sheer weight of the substance. I'm enthralled by the fact that in spite of the un-comfortableness in my chest, my vision is clear, hearing ex-ceptional, and an eagerness to reach the ending grows.

We sail past the yellow light disappointing me as I was sure it was our landing point. Now we're moving even fast-er as the jelly turns to turquoise, and even though I try to change my position by moving my arms and legs, my at-tempts are futile. It's not too long before I notice my friends' bodies have changed. A hazy purple glow surrounds us like we're all a piece of blown glass cooling after our trip through the million degree furnace.

Gradually we slow to half-warp speed, and it's a good thing because something solid seems to be approaching at an alarming rate. A wall? A door? Maybe a building, I'm not sure. But in seconds we experience the stop button.

Wham!

It's a cold tile floor in a glazed intricate pattern extending out for what seems like miles in all directions. The three of us stand shaking off our rough landing, and I say three because Ozzy is missing now. Our bodies still glow, and we discover that tiny rays of light flow out of our mouths as we speak.

"Whoa!" is about all any of us can verbalize for the moment.

"I thought Marek and Bale said it wouldn't hurt?" Star says.

"Well, it didn't," Rico speaks, trying to catch the light as it leaves his mouth. "It was kind of an abrupt ending though, huh?" He's fascinated by the look of our bodies, but that reminds me that I should more than likely be calling it a soul instead. Not sure which train station we left our *real* bodies, but our souls aren't anything like I expected. I guess I had no preconceived notion, but a violet permanent day-glow never came to mind.

We all freaked even more when we tried to touch each other. Our hands touched solid, but there was jelly underneath. Like we *became* the material we sped through or something. Yet it still felt like we had mass. So intent on figuring out our surroundings and the awe of our current condition, we totally forget about Ozzy.

"Hey? What happened to Ozzy?" I ask.

"Not sure," Rico says. "He was right in front of me through the bright yellow light, but I blanked when the floor came up. He's gotta be somewhere, right? I mean—"

Evidently our souls still have the ability to reason and think, as a deep sense of understanding reflects back to me.

Something about a specific order of our training and how it was determined by our personalities and their research.

We establish our bearings as much as possible, and I'm wishing I spent a little more time playing video games now because that's what this feels like. I take charge and begin moving to my right a few steps. A line of silver three-dimensional dots spring up from the floor, and I am drawn to them. Rico and Star follow closely, each footstep a gooey slosh that still echoes through the expansive space. It's not exactly pitch black due to our incandescence and the lit grid of the floor pattern. We reach the dots and aren't sure what comes next.

"Maybe it's a door or portal?" Star determines. "Quite possibly where Ozzy ended up when we landed."

"Sounds reasonable, but what's the trigger? If Ozzy was here, he'd figure it out. He's pretty humble, but the guy's a whiz," I say.

"We gotta try something, right? Can't wander around aimlessly," Rico encourages. "Maybe there's a button or a code? Here. Let's try waving our—"

Rico's hand rises above the magical spots, and he's right. Amazingly a new portal opens and pulls us all inside. We slide to a halt in a white room with padded walls and two doors in front of us. Ozzy sits strapped to a chair in the middle of the room, his head dangling, and drool forming a small puddle on the floor. His eyes are closed as we approach. We reach to relieve him of his shackles, and his eyes open like a maniacal ventriloquist doll. An uncharacteristic fiery rage from Ozzy slams us up against the far wall and back down to the floor. We're stunned but feel no pain whatsoever. Keeping our distance now, we try to speak.

"Oz? It's us. Remember? Faith? Rico? And Star? We're all on a training mission?"

My words elicit the same response as before, and we're picking ourselves back up off the floor once again. Ozzy's laid-back personality is gone—replaced by his evil twin. Only it's not like he's comprehending a word that we say. He's mumbling bits and pieces and making odd gurgling noises, so we stare at each other praying for one of us to decide our next course of action.

"I don't think he means us any harm." I stick up for him.

"Coulda fooled me, sister," says Rico. "Those weren't hugs he was giving us."

"I know, but Faith could be on to something. Our *weaknesses*? Not sure why, but that's just jutting out like a red F on an essay. What would be one of Ozzy's biggest fears?" Star asks.

"I dunno. Maybe that he'd lose his smarts? Become stupid?" I say.

We study the room a little more coming to the conclusion that it resembles an insane asylum. Padded walls, no windows, strapped to a chair, so he doesn't hurt himself. Two doors instead of just one is a quandary, though. Carefully moving along the perimeter, we make our way to both doors and try each one in vain. Both are locked. I'm not sure about the others, but all along I'm wondering the same thing. *How can a soul get stronger by doing this?* Turning Ozzy into a slobbering idiot by taking away the *one* thing that brings him joy, makes him confident, and feel like he belongs? I have no clue why I'm traveling down this line of logic, but it's almost as if I'm the one that's supposed to *fix* this somehow. With very little else to focus on but the doors, I expect our first test is to decide which door gets us to the next stage. But we aren't sure what to do for Ozzy in his current state.

"This is bringing back way too many memories for me," Rico says. "There weren't any padded walls or anything, but my mother and I felt pretty hopeless. Our kidnappers sent one last video tape of us being alive to my father, with our death a certainty the next day if he didn't pay up."

"So obviously you're here. He paid the money, huh?" Star guesses, tracing the outside of one door with her fingers looking for some type of switch.

"Nope, the FBI broke in early that morning and took everyone down. Dad was waiting for us in an abandoned building five blocks away. I don't think any FBI team knows about us though. I mean, our training and everything."

The last part of Rico's sentence sparks a nerve through my brain; something Luther said an hour before we got pushed into the vortex. He said he and his family would be there for us. Maybe it meant moral support or perhaps *they're* our FBI?

I step back closer to Ozzy now, his eyes back open and not so troubled. We don't waste time approaching again, but we form a half-circle in front of him, looking for anything, a magic control knob or remote tucked inside his clothing. We need to communicate with him. But how? Star's wheels are turning as she moves through a variety of ballet positions and dance steps. She indicates that it helps her to think. Her purple haze trails behind her creating an artistic spectacle. In moments, she stops. Sparkles shoot out of her mouth before she says one word.

"Gavin Reynolds!" she yells.

"Who?" Rico asks.

"A little boy I babysat who lived a few doors down from us. Anyhow, he was deaf, so I taught myself sign language. Maybe Ozzy—"

"He's a vegetable, Star," I remind her. "I don't think he's deaf."

"Hey! You got a better idea, Little Miss Sunshine? Standing here gawking at him hasn't gotten us much, has it?"

"Fine. But what should we say?" I mutter.

"How 'bout, *how the hell do we get outta this place?*" Rico nearly chokes on his words. He's enjoyed his joke way too much.

Star begins with a few simple hand motions like hello and how are you doing, which seems rather silly since he's strapped to a chair in a nut house trying to train his soul to resist an alien takeover. Ozzy closes his eyes a few times, but then we see a slight change. He closes his mouth shutting down the leaky faucet of spit, and we're all amazed to see what he does next.

9

He smiles. Not one of his patented Ozzy the genius-like grins, but noticeable enough to give us some hope. *Maybe we won't need the FBI after all.* Star continues her gyrations, and his mouth starts to move like he's trying to form words but can't remember how. He's trapped in his Alzheimer box with no way to extend any of his intelligence or ideas. He's a mere shell of a human or rather a soul who is dead to our dilemma, *his* dilemma. Smiling uncontrollably like he knows what Star's saying but unable to talk back. Of course, a pair of freed arms and hands would help matters, but we've already seen the ending of that episode. No pain but quite the jolt from flying into the wall.

I reason that now we've established some type of communication, maybe he won't toss us around like a rag doll.

So I move closer and manage to get my hand on one of the belts undoing one notch. Ozzy's eyes flash back to his initial fury, and I'm spun upside down this time and bounce off the ceiling before I smack the floor. Both knees banging together as I hit, my head and feet playing tag with each other. The only saving grace is that I lift myself right up like Wile E. Coyote after a bad day, no worse for wear, just increasingly annoyed. *We're already dead, right?*

"I loosened it!" I cry. "Tell him to loosen the rest."

Star signals, indicating for him to break free from the rest of his bindings. He watches a little while, then starts to shake his head back and forth like an eternal "no."

"Maybe he can't move his body," Rico says, aware of how dumb he just sounded.

"The restraints?" I say. "Don't think he'd need them if—"

"I get it. No need to explain. Just a little stressed here. Man, when Marek and Bale said our bodies would do us no good against Azuna, he wasn't joking, was he?" Rico speaks, slamming his hand into the wall followed by a quick kick.

"That's it!" I shout, directing him away from his tantrum to re-focus.

"Huh?" he says.

"Our bodies!" I shriek. We're acting like we still have 'em, but we don't."

"So?" Star says, trying to follow my logic but still confused.

"Ozzy's relying, heck, we're *all* relying on our bodies now. This is supposed to be a proving ground for our *souls*. How do we get him to stop fighting with his *body*, so his soul can take over?"

"Yeah, good question," says Star. "Ozzy's the only one with enough smarts to figure it out, and he's as dumb as a hoe handle." It's her turn to make jokes as Rico high-fives her, splashing violet mist through the air.

"His body is dumb, his physical mind, but not his soul. Obviously a soul can exist apart from the body. We just need to get him to split. Appeal to his soul instead."

"Nice theory, Sigmund Freud. But exactly how do you suppose we do that? Rico questions.

My thoughts race. I scan the room over and over again in search of anything that might help. No matter how many times I look, I'm left feeling empty. Ozzy's right back to drooling, which makes the air reek. Apparently souls have olfactory senses because one is putting off quite the stench. Another source of aggravation is the constant flow of sparkles from my mouth, from everyone's mouths. I remind myself this is real. I'm not having a *My Little Pony* cartoon nightmare.

Rico's placed himself in the corner on his knees praying. He says it's what he did when he thought for sure his life was over, and the next day he was rescued. I figure that maybe the message would get to God faster since we're already a soul. I'm open to any suggestions. Star works through her tai-chi as graceful as a ballerina. The intensity in her eyes is unmistakable. I'm feeling left out now. There might as well be a *second* chair in here for me because I've no special place I can go to find peace. I'm as helpless and as hopeless as Ozzy.

Watching my two friends face this first test with such courage gives me shivers, if a soul can *get* shivers. Instantly this brings a new thought to the forefront. Star's used sign language, I've loosened one strap, and Rico's searched the doors for a way out. All *individual* attempts to find a solution.

"Hey, gang?" I motion them over to my current position about six-feet from Ozzy's chair. They leave their "me time" and join me.

"What if we've been doing this all wrong?"

"Whaddya mean?" Star asks.

"My mom used to tell me when I went to a new school to make a few close friends. That there's strength in numbers. If we're going to get through any of this training, we need to help each other. We can't go it alone."

"We haven't, have we?" Rico says. "I mean, we all stayed together when we were traveling down the laundry shoot and landed here."

"True. But before this place? It took us a while to even realize Ozzy was missing."

"So how does that help? Get him to leave his body and become like us again?" Star says.

"Well—" I ponder for a few seconds. "What do we know about him? His past? His childhood? Maybe we can help him remember?"

"I dunno. He said he was born at a Mary J. Blige concert—in the bathroom. Then he was given up for adoption because his mother couldn't take care of him," Rico summarizes.

"Separated from his birth parent, where he grew for nine months and developed his soul?" I say, feeling like a shrink trying to analyze the source of Ozzy's internal conflict or something.

Star starts her incessant pacing again waving her hands in the air, like a mad scientist on the brink of her latest invention. She repeats the same word over and over.

"Separated, separated, separated…"

Rico's having the toughest time dealing with our sudden epiphany. He's slid half-way down the far wall, head in his hands, laughing at first. His cackling gives way to crying as he's almost on the floor clutching his chest. It's kind of funny because he's making sobbing noises, but they're no tears. There's no need for concern since we're already deceased, but Star and I rush to his side anyhow.

"Pull it together, Rico," Star whispers. "We're really close. I'm gonna try something, just for the hell of it."

"What's that?" he says.

"C'mon. One of us needs to wake him back up," Star explains.

"You don't mean?" Rico cringes.

"I do. But since we're in this together, let's *all* approach him at the same time. Ready?"

Not sure of what's about to happen next, we hold hands and take long but gentle steps toward our friend. He's even worse than he was when we first saw him. The entire front of his shirt and pants a wet mess. No enchanting purple glow, his head slumped in an awkward position over his left shoulder. There is very little movement in any of his extremities.

"Ok. On the count of three, we all slap him," Star says.

"Slap him?" I question. "He's gonna love us for that one. We may all go *through* the wall this time."

"Yeah. Maybe *that's* how we get outta here!" Rico's finding his usual personality again.

Star starts the countdown, but before she even gets to number three, Ozzy opens his eyes. He's reacted as if he's aware of what's coming, but he doesn't brace himself.

Smack!

Fully expecting a violent reaction, we duck putting our arms over our heads, ready for the recoil. But no recoil occurs. We lift our eyes back to him and see a familiar haze beginning around his ears and the top of his head. In utter excitement, Star rears back and hits him smack dab in the face once again with a different result. She's spun several times like a tornado and thrown head-first into door number two. It doesn't open, but half her body is through the door and the other half still in the room.

Rico and I swoop in to pull her back into our reality. We turn back to Ozzy who's thrashing around like a maniac now trying to escape his chair. I'm not sure I *want* this Ozzy loose, so I ask Star to use sign language again. Convince him to stop warring against his restraint. To consider when he was born, taken away from his mother, and began his new life. A better life. More stable, more loving.

Star completes her message, and pure energy leaps from his body sending all three of us down on our butts. We shake off the force of the blow and coldness envelops us. Fog replaces the sparkles that flowed from our voices, and ice crystals form on our lips, our eyebrows, our entire souls. Our glow is still present but suspended in animation. Ozzy's body has gone limp. No evidence of life remains. Each movement is a chore, but we gather as one and find one extra soul has joined us. It's Ozzy. He's been freed from his tortured shell. His gigantic arms pull us all into a ball. Nobody speaks, but we can hear each other's voices.

It worked. We did it. He's one of us again. What's next? We're still trapped. I wanna go home. I can't take this anymore. We're never gonna make it.

Who said *what* means little now. We're a team. Hard lesson learned. We get outta our training session? Our bodies really *are* useless. No match for our usurpers. Our souls will be the only thing that lasts, the true remnant of our power. We don't simply *have* a soul; we *are* a soul. And if it's not stronger by the time we're finished, that's *our* fault.

Ozzy finally lifts his head from the ground spreading countless thanks to us. Thanksgiving sweeps over us all. Again Misty's words encourage me. *Food tastes better. Everything is enhanced. The world is brighter.* She was just trying to be helpful, but I doubted her the entire time and made fun of her naiveté. Not now.

We break our hugfest and realize we're still stuck in a padded room with no way out.

"Great!" Rico breaks the silence. "Now what? It's not like a magical key's gonna suddenly appear from the sky."

Ozzy chuckles. It's incredible to hear him again. The *real* Ozymandias. Not the dead body in the chair.

"Don't be so sure, my friend," Ozzy says. He skips over to his body and is about to stick his hand in his soaked shirt pocket.

"Wait!" Star shouts. "Uh—you sure he's not all electrified still? He packs a strong wallop. That's for sure."

"Yeah, just watch." Ozzy reaches into the slimy pocket,

but before he can remove the key, his dead body re-awakens. A sharp flash like a million cameras goes off, and we shield our eyes expecting to find Ozzy on the floor up against the wall once again.

We peek over our fingers. Ozzy is on his knees in front of the chair. His body gone, and a gold key lying in the center. His soul snatches it and flies over to door number two. Before he even raises the key up to the knob, Star is screaming.

"Stop!"

"Why?" The rest of us chime.

"I've seen what's on the other side. My head, remember? Already been through that one, and I don't think it's the way out. At least, not based upon what I saw."

"Why? What did you see?" I ask.

"Earth; back in the forest at Luther's cabin."

"What about it? Maybe this is it?" Rico wishes. "We passed? Our training, I mean. It's our way out and back to solid ground."

Star's not buying anything Rico is selling. It's clear that she knows something we don't. Something she saw on the other side. I'm leaning toward choosing the *other* door. This can't be it, the extent of our training. I pound door number two with my fist, and it goes right through now. I waste no time asking the rest of the gang what to do, so I stick my head through the padded door.

It doesn't take very long for me to figure out why Star was opting for door number one. Luther's cabin? The covert barn? His entire property is demolished like a couple of F-15's leveled the place. No sign of anyone—just the remnants of Luther's perfect hiding place. Parts of the house and barn still glowing red, a heavy black smoke blocks my view of the trail to the stream. I'm scanning side to side hoping I see someone alive and well, but there's no movement, just destruction and overwhelming sadness.

From behind, I feel a giant tug on the lower half of my body as my three friends pull me back into the training grounds.

"She's right. That's not the right door. Try the key in the other one," I whisper, hoping neither Ozzy nor Rico pushes me on why. I'm not so lucky.

"What's inside? What did you see?" they insist.

I take a quick glimpse at Star whose face has turned ghost-like, and she looks at me as if to say, "It's your call."

"Well—I might as well spill it. The compound, the cabin, and Luther's barn are all gone. They're trashed, like a military wave came through and blew it all to pieces."

"Any sign of Marek or Bale? Luther?"

"No, a few things still on fire and just a big black hole of smoke."

I guess souls can faint because the floor rises up to greet us, and I've never felt more powerless and alone.

10

A ripple of pure panic washes over us as we mull over the gravity of our situation. If what I saw represents the *current* condition of Luther's secret hiding place, we may *never* leave this training module. We'll be stuck here forever bouncing from one extreme soul test to another. On the other hand, what we saw may be another *trial* we're supposed to pass while we're in here.

"Okayyyyyy." Star breaks the silence. She's taken the key from Ozzy's hand and is fumbling with it trying to decide which lock it fits best. Before we can even argue about it, like magic, it flies from her hand to door number one and slips into the lock like a dollar in a vending machine. *Click!* The door pops open, and we're sucked inside like before.

Our roller coaster ride is shorter this time and slightly

more violent as we all tumble head over heels unsuccessfully avoiding each other. It's not easy when you have a six-foot seven inch Ozzy, flailing away trying to find some sense of balance. Rico's retreated to his Hail Mary mode, praying out loud allowing the force to slam him back and forth against the sides of the tunnel with little to no resistance. Apparently God's not opposed to a little hostility now and then.

Somehow I catch up to Star, and we lock arms. This time we make sure neither of us gets separated. Regrettably, this swirl of energy kicks all of our butts again, and when we land my partner gets ripped from me. She's gone, just like Ozzy the first time.

"Star," I yell. A blinding beam of light from above us nearly pierces our souls and wipes out our vision in the process. As the fog clears, we see that the purple haze around us diminishes for a few moments then surges back even brighter than before. *Why do I feel like we're flashlights that just got recharged?* Still almost face-first on the floor, we rise to our knees. The intensity of the light decreases, and we notice a new venue, an auditorium or concert hall with a boxing ring in the middle. The echoing hall is empty until we stand up and begin to explore further. Thousands of other souls appear jammed into the seats screaming and cheering like a mob of fans. They don't seem to notice us at all. Ozzy waves his arms in front of a patron and is totally ignored.

"Oh, boy," Rico mutters. "What now? We get thrown in the ring like gladiators and have to beat each other into submission? Lions and tigers and bears, oh, my!"

He's kidding, but that's exactly what it looks like right now, minus the outfits and the spiked ball and chains. One thing is for certain; our loyal fans won't be much help at all. They're mesmerized by the action in the ring, which must be a secret because although we try a half-dozen angles, we see no one. No combatants. No referees, nothing.

"Any idea?" I shoot a question Ozzy's way, counting on his IQ to kick in and get us to the next level. It's nice to have him back with us. I hated seeing him like he was, a feeble-minded shell. Ever since we've entered this training, I've found some compassion. It's not that it wasn't there before. I just have a good way of hiding it behind my wise-cracks.

My friends are suddenly so much more than three random passengers on their way to find out when they'd die. Being an only child, they're more like family. Brothers and sisters I never had but often wished I did. I can't be sure, but perhaps they're feeling the same way about me. Even when they barely knew me, they never brought up my obvious bruises that still show up occasionally even though I'm in remission. They treated me like they'd known me for much longer. Almost like we'd grown up together and had already established a bond. Music is useless if there's no audience. It's nice to finally have one, an audience that is.

I can sense Ozzy's grasping for a solution, without having much luck. It's not until Rico, being his usual playful self, climbs up into the ring and does his Muhammed Ali impersonation that the dominoes begin to fall.

A small contingent of men emerges and surround someone in the opposite corner of the ring. A bell sounds, and they separate back outside the ropes revealing Rico's opponent. Star, wearing a tank-top, tight black leotards, and a red mouthpiece. It's clear she doesn't recognize Rico *or* us, and she's acting like a raging badger about to destroy her prey, and we know Rico's in a heap of trouble.

"Get out of there! You'll be killed!" I scream.

"I'm already dead!" He laughs, trying to find a spot in the ring to exit. Each time he steps through the middle ropes to exit, he's bounced back into the ring. No way out.

Star's fury grows as she races around the ring trying to engage her opponent. Finally, Rico is cornered and cannot retreat. The crowd noise level rises to a fever pitch. Star pushes her right leg toward his stomach in a front-thrust kick, but she doesn't connect. Amazingly, Rico's just as fast, as he slips her blow and captures her foot, flipping her back down to the mat. She's dazed for a second then leaps back to her feet to track him down again.

He's as clueless as the rest of us, but she comes at him again with a flurry of karate moves, and he counters everything she tries to do. Rico's fearful eyes begin to change. Soon he's the aggressor, and she's the hunted. Our words and signals for him to stop do no good. The bell sounds for the end of the round, but Rico gets one last blow into Star's nose, and it shatters. *I guess souls can bleed.* Her blood splashes one of her trainers in the face, and that's when we recognize him. It's Otis. Luther's brother.

Ozzy and I dart to her corner hoping Otis will listen and end this nonsense, but much like the people in the crowd, he's oblivious, like he's a hologram. Gangs of people continue to shout their approval, but a few begin a ruckus and are escorted out by the guards. That's when I see that most of the crowd's holding up signs that say *Star, We Love You, Star, Star's Our Champ*. One complete section full of people wailing *Champ-ion, Champ-ion!* Definitely a one-sided affair, only Rico's spoiling her performance rather easily.

The next round is more of the same. Every advantage Star displays has no effect on Rico who's barely breaking a sweat; only confidence waits for him in his corner. *In his corner?*

I grab Ozzy's hand and practically yank his shoulder out of its socket dragging him up to Rico's corner, and that's when *our* view changes. Ironically, we have no immediate concern or worry about Star's condition. We want her to lose just as much as Rico does. Our dilemma about being stuck in the training module has faded as we're focused on Rico's fighting abilities, wondering whether this test is for all of us, not just Star.

Star's face is swollen, her left eye almost shut. A deep bruise forms under her chin where Rico caught her square with his elbow. His skill far surpasses anything Star can elicit, which makes no sense at all. Still, we pull him back to us as the bell rings again and massage his shoulders, squirt water down his throat, and spout some unnerving words.

"You have her right where you want her," Ozzy says. "She's not so tough now, is she? Thought she could beat up on a poor defenseless Mexican kid?"

"Hey!" Rico objects.

"Yeah, it looks like she bit off a little more than she can handle with you, Rico. Knock her out this round, champ! Send this crowd home unhappy. It's your night, Rico!"

The words leave my lips so easily, but then a war erupts inside me as we send him back to the fight. It's *not* me. I fight back. I don't *want* her to lose. I don't *want* him to win. I just want out. No more training. I can't take this. Rico wouldn't harm an ant. Star knows she's strong, has confidence, but she's not a bully and doesn't lord it over anyone. She isn't prideful. So why?

I try to pull Ozzy away from the ring to talk some sense into him but he resists. He's caught up in the frenzy. The crowd's pelting him with racial slurs now, threatening Rico and him if they lose money. Hundreds of guards continue their diligence removing spectator after spectator who've lost self-control, now firing weapons in the air to regain some composure. Some respond and move back to the action in the ring, while others continue their foolish behavior.

Round five begins, but instead of knocking Star out, Rico toys with her often smiling after every one of his calculated blows causes her more and more pain. She's a warrior, as his punches and kicks come at longer and longer intervals, giving her time to regroup. Her eyes fix on Rico like he's somebody else. A stranger, lost in herself and in winning the fight.

She slides past Ozzy and me, and I reach for one of her shoes. The crowd screams their disapproval, but she falls right in front of us. The ref's not much good, more symbolic than functional. The first thing that comes to mind happens as Ozzy's taking a swig of water from Rico's bottle. I snatch it from him and squirt her in the face twice. Star's purple glow short circuits for an instant, so I do it again. She lets go a few choice words as I continually douse her head and face. If it makes her stay down and ends this torture or brings her back to her senses, either will work just fine right now. Ozzy's climbed back into the ring encouraging Rico to finish her off, wiping his sweat-less face as merely a gesture. He's still possessed by whatever evil has invaded his soul.

The referee finally does his job and begins to count Star down. 1—2—3 —4. Before he gets to five, it's clear I have my friend back, at least for a moment.

"Stay down," I yell.

"Faith? Where am I? What's going on?"

"You've been fighting Rico. He's been beating the crap outta you. So please? Just stay down." My emotions take over.

"Rico? Really? I'm—starting to remember."

"Uh, oh. Is that a good thing?" I say in between my sobs.

"Yeah," she says making her way to her knees. 7—8—9.

Star gets back on her feet, and I'm worried I've lost her again. But she eases my fear with two words.

"My father," she says.

"Your father? The mayor? What about him?" I ask.

"He gambled all our money away at casinos, MMA fights, and race track. That's who I was fighting."

I'm still confused, so she sidesteps a roundhouse from Rico and shouts over the ropes to me. "Now! In the ring! My fury? All about my dad!" She sheds more light on her motivation.

Star shakes off the remnants of the trance she was in and sweeps Rico off his feet with a swirl. Before she can finish him with a heel to his face, the bell rings. She stops about three inches from putting his lights out for good. Rico rises up. His cockiness evident but a little less pronounced as he stands high on the ropes in his corner and taunts the crowd. Ozzy struggles to pull him down, and I try experiment number two on him, opening his water bottle and drenching his dark black hair. Sparks fly in all directions, and his head falls limp, and that's when I see why. Just above his left pectoral is a bullet hole. Another shot is fired our way and catches Ozzy in the shoulder. Both fall. Security tackles the gunman, who as they haul him away, resembles Star's father. *I thought we were already dead?* The entire corner of our side of the ring is now a bloody canvas. Rico's not writhing in pain, just lying down in the fetal position over a turned over stool. Ozzy's back is to us both, as his eyes follow the security guards out of the stadium. Star's father is in handcuffs. The audience thrashes, pushes and shoves, and runs in all directions. Thankfully no one is headed for the ring.

I'm not sure, but I think we're all ourselves once again as Ozzy swings back around to assist Rico. The ref's long gone, and the place has emptied leaving the four of us to deal with the aftermath. *Where's the damn key to get us to the next level? What could we possibly learn from watching Rico and Ozzy bleed out? Is this supposed to prepare us for the inevitable?*

An agonizing despair claws at my heart and muddles my brain at the same time. I've felt this before at my mother's death, but I was prepared. I knew in advance that she'd be leaving me for good. Heck. Deep down I'm trying to fathom where all of this grief is coming from since supposedly we're already dead. We won't be losing Rico or Ozzy like I lost my mom. But I can't seem to help it, like I'm *programmed* to steer my way through this dark cloud when

I just want to quit.

So far, each session has been nothing but a heavy dose of reality. Smart people can lose their intelligence, and then what? The athletic and strong can be weak, especially if driven by revenge or unresolved conflict. What do we each have inside us that's greater than anything we've learned or trained for on Earth? A *soul*. That's the best I can do. Nothing, not even a bullet or a mental disorder can damage our souls. Until it's the true source of our thinking and our strength, the world will continue to crush us. Bruise us. Outwit us.

I break from my intense daydream and notice that Star's dragged Rico to the middle of the ring. Somehow she's found a scalpel and a few other surgery tools, and she's removing the bullet from Rico's chest. He lies motionless, eyes closed, almost like he's been drugged. Ozzy's upper arm has been tied off with part of his torn shirt, and he's playing nurse.

"But how?" That's all I can think to say when I join them.

"The ref? He came back and threw a wrapped up towel into the ring. It had all this stuff in it."

"But—" I stutter.

"But I'm not a doctor? I know. Wanna be one though. Dad's got *other* plans. MMA Champion. Already has me signed up for the training in Vegas. I was supposed to leave right after I found out my expiration date."

"Not to be stupid," Ozzy interjects, "but why bother? I mean, saving him? We've said it like a hundred times already. We can't die in here, right?"

Star and I look at each other knowing what Ozzy says is

true, but Rico's lifeless body, uh, I mean *soul*, calls to us. It's gotta be part of the test. In the real world, we'd never stand by and just let him die, would we?

Our wannabe doctor explains how the bullet has potentially nicked a major artery. Those crazy sparkles continually spray from our lips. They're annoying as hell, but I pretend they're just cold weather mist. It helps some, but should we ever make it outta here, I'm gonna recommend removing them from the training program.

We're all in for quite a shock as soon as she clasps the bullet with her giant tweezers. Rico's eyes spring open like he's just seen a monster because he has. Swinging from the auditorium rafters is a gargoyle-like creature ready to pounce on us from the ceiling. Rico sits up, and we grab shoulders and bow our heads to shield ourselves from the impact of the beast, and that's when it happens. *Can creatures enter the vortex?* I guess we're about to find out.

11

I awake to a steady rumble of breathing and a massive black claw attached to a gigantic hand covering my body like a blanket. Wherever I am reeks of a boy's locker room, sweat mixed with horrible breath. I try not to move, or I might awaken my new sleeping buddy. I want to be scared, but I've already seen enough to know whoever designed these instructional modules could have made this devil eat me for dinner already. Though uneasy and claustrophobic, it occurs to me that *I'm* the one separated from the rest this time. This must be *my* turn to teach my soul to what, tame the beast? Take out its thorn? Hypnotize it into my slave?

I'm pinned by the colossal weight and unable to squeeze even one arm or leg free, because apparently King Kong transforms into granite when he sleeps. I have no choice but

to wait it out. I pass *some* time by counting the wrinkle puppy like rolls in its face and try blowing on its nose, which in-
cidentally looks like the Sydney Opera House, only smaller,
but not by much. If the animal wasn't ten times my size and
didn't have two-foot horns and a set of fangs to match, we
might make quite a pair. A quick shower underneath a wa-
terfall and a little aftershave may get rid of the stench too.
A girl can dream, can't she?

I make constant light of my situation because while I'm
buried underneath this unmovable rock, who knows what
time it is in the real world? Or what day it is even? The stupid alien alignment could have come and gone, and we're
still trying to figure out how to overcome yet another hur-
dle. To be honest, I can't *wait* to see how this one turns
out. It's been nothing but pure joy so far. Why does every
test have to be a screw when we only have a hammer? Any
chance we could get a few *other* tools?

A couple of desperate screams fly from my mouth and
light up the darkened cave. Geez. For a soul minus a body, I'm
sure not having much luck breaking away. A tiny glimpse of
relief gets me excited as a sliver of dim light seeps through
the rocks above me where previous knowledge takes over.
*In every gargoyle cartoon, don't the creatures thrive during the
night and turn back to rock during the day?* Since exactly the
opposite is occurring, my hope disintegrates, and I let out
my loudest screech yet.

Unexpectedly, rocky crust and dust blast from its eyes
first as his gaze is transfixed right on me. Some fear forms
near the base of my scalp now and scampers down my back,
but I try to keep it together. His nose and mouth come next,

a frightening yawn that reveals even more sharpened teeth. It is most definitely where the pungent odor is emanating. It smells like it's been dumpster diving for its food for a long while now.

Its entire body animates, but I'm still caught in its clutches. The pressure is even stronger than before, almost as if it's afraid it will lose me, or I'll run away. But to where? Outside the cave where the rest of the clan can fight over me? Now that it's awake, I'm about to formally object to my captivity, but I guess irony is alive and well in the Niners' training manual. It lifts me to eye level, and I do my best fake tears performance, even though I refuse to admit that most of them are real, and he sets me back down on the ground. Free.

While running is an obvious option, I freeze instead. I'm not the *only* one crying. It's lumbered its way to a far wall, its mammoth back toward me, and clearly distraught over something. I force myself toward it, and it looks over its enormous shoulder at me. Weakened knees and tears still streaming down my face, I introduce myself through the snivels.

"I'm Faith," I murmur. "I won't—"

"Hurt me?" It says, as clear and as plain as day. A deep growl in its voice as it speaks.

"You speak English?" I ask a dumb question.

"That's only because you wish it." He turns back to me, and it's only then that I truly see how remarkable he is; strong sinewy arms with emerald green wings big enough to cover a small tour bus, and majestic horns on both sides of its head. He was the perfect guardian to any cathedral or church.

"Why are you here?" I question.

Silence. The beast loses focus like it's remembering something. Something terrible. It cries out, and I'm certain the whole cave will be upon us in seconds. A tumultuous echo bounces off the rocks, and the same hand that cradled me scoops me up just before I am flattened by a boulder.

"Phew! That was close," I say, suddenly grateful for my protector. My protector? I can't believe those words leave my mouth, but it's true.

"Do you have a name?" I ask.

"I do. Roughly translated, I am Blodd, head guardian of the king's castle." We make our way outside the cave traipsing through the rubble, and he continues his introduction. An obvious hesitation in his voice, he explains further. "At least—I used to be."

Blodd places me gently on a large stone. The refreshing air tickles my nose, and I finally get a glimpse of this new environment. Picture the hills of Ireland or maybe Germany with a canvas of endless bright flowers. Reds. Yellows. Blues. Unlike anything I've ever seen on Earth. Most likely replicas of what's on the planet Nine. An occasional cool breeze pushes my hair into my face, my corn rows gone now replaced by a head of wavy curls. Usually what my locks look like after I've undone the tight braids. As I'm taking it all in, Blodd goes down on his knees. He seems to be struggling with something again, and soon I recognize what. His hands and arms are beginning to turn back into stone. He bellows once more, frustration and anger in his eyes. In the back of my mind, I'm leaping for joy at the chance to escape when he finally transforms, but his anguish compels me to climb down from my paradise to dispel his pain.

"What's happening? I thought all gargoyles remained statues until sundown. But you seem to be reacting the opposite, or are you?"

"Upon first creation, I was no different than most. One day a strange rain poured down and changed me. Some type of plague or disease. A spell. As you can see, I've no control over when I transform."

His story cuts right through me. One day I woke up after my 13th birthday, and I was changed too; a wounded mutant with blood vessels bursting left and right. Deep blackish purple and green bruises were all over my body with no previous injuries. There was no way to control what was happening to me. My illness was a wall between the truth and the lies, and eventually my *so-called* friends determined to rescue me from my *abusive* mother.

"Is there anything I can do?" I ask, not sure I desire an answer.

"Afraid not. I'll just—" His transformation completes. I have reason and opportunity to run, but I don't. Where would I go? I have no idea what dangers exist or knowledge of this world. The *old* me may have high-tailed it out, but let's just say that my *conversion* has begun too. My soul is gaining experience; gaining strength. That's the whole reason I'm here, right? Experience has so little to do with what happens *to* you and more about what you do when it happens. Whoa. I'm suddenly sounding like Socrates' sister. Who knew *death* could bring out the wisdom in the unwise?

I decide there must be a purpose for bringing Blodd

and me together, so I wait. And I wait. No sense of time, but at least an hour passes before his thunderous frame re-enters the living world. I can tell he's surprised to still see me. Other than a local exploration of the immediate area while he is solid, I pretty much hang out hoping he'll return.

"Welcome back," I whisper. "Have a nice nap?"

"You're still here. Why?" He questions—a puzzled look starts to form.

"Oh, I dunno. I guess you're kinda growing on me. Besides, I think there's *something* I'm supposed to do for you or *with* you. Just not sure what it is. They don't make these training levels very clear. That's for sure."

"Training levels?" he asks.

"Long story, I won't bother you with it. So—let's focus on you. Why did you leave the castle?" We begin a slow descent down our first rolling hill. His steps leave an imprint in the flower field. From the air, it might look rather strange or perhaps even more beautiful. Just as the thought escapes, he yanks me off my feet, and we're flying. My anxiety swells again.

"Is this a good idea? I mean, should you turn back into stone—"

"Never fear, princess. I never change when I'm flying. I'll keep you safe."

Princess? Me? I shiver as the wind picks up and pierces my eyes forcing me to close them. Blodd's body is warm, but I've no shelter from the elements riding atop his broad shoulders.

"Where are we going?"

"Back to the fortress. My brothers will want to meet

you."

"I'm so glad you said *meet* and not eat," I joke.

There's a hint of a smile on his face, and I'm thankful for the module creators easing me into this test of my will. Placing me in peril with a *friendly* monster instead of a ruthless one feels like a fairy tale, but it still beats watching Star get her face bashed in and Ozzy's brain turned to goo. I know there's a real challenge ahead, but I'm basking in one of my all-time favorite dreams, flying sans an airplane.

Blodd's skills are precise, soaring high into the sky and back down near the surface with grace. Gliding in between trees and mountains with equal precision taking my safety into consideration with each dip and change of direction, almost as if he'd had years of practice with someone else. I'm lost in my magnificent ride for awhile totally forgetting about aliens and government conspiracies and dismissing the idea that soon I may be in the fight of my life. Chancellor Azuna trying to rip my soul from my dead body, so she can live here.

On the horizon, a stone castle of darkened grey and black juts up from the valley. An angry wall with a heavy wooden bridge and a gate greets us, and a cobblestone path leads directly to the palace steps. There are three empty pedestals along the wall and two above the steps where I figure Blodd's brothers and he perch at night as protectors. But protectors from what or whom, I have no clue.

Our near landing is smooth until out of nowhere Blodd is whisked back into the sky by a monster even larger than him. I jerk backwards from my position and fall. The ground approaches like a runaway train, so I brace for impact. *Thud.*

I never reach the ground. Once again Blodd catches up to me and cradles me in his hands, and we're flying back toward the castle. This time there's a gargoyle escort.

"Your brothers?" I ask.

"Yes. But they haven't seen me in a while."

"I see," I say, trying to get some air back into my lungs.

The path blends back into view through the clouds, and in seconds we're on it, walking this time. Blodd's family stops us just shy of the main gate.

"Why are you here?" His attacker has a strong concern in his voice.

"See for yourself, my brother. I have found her. Our healer."

Healer? A few puzzle pieces take shape as Blodd releases his grip on me, and I stand before them. Blodd has me confused with somebody else.

"You've been banished, Blodd," Another brother says. "The king made that clear, did he not? You must leave before he has you charmed. We don't want to lose you. The Kurd have vowed revenge."

It doesn't take long before I'm swirling in a sea of questions. The last time I checked, I couldn't even heal *myself.* Somehow Blodd senses my confusion and gives me clarity.

"Vincent? Please, see for yourself. She has the marks. I *know* she's the one."

The smallest of the five approaches and examines me. I feel naked in his glare until his eyes light up like Blodd's did when he first saw me. Able to crush me with one blow, there's a compassion and fierceness in all of them. He pushes back the hair from my face as if he's touching a newborn for the first time.

"These marks? Where did you get them?"

I think he's talking about my tattoo, so I explain.

"Well, where I'm from, people like to color their skin with ink. It's called a tattoo." I look over my shoulder and refer to my back surprised by what I find. *My praying mantis is gone?* "But how?"

"The other marks, princess," Blodd says. "On your face? Your arms?"

Suddenly I'm back in my bed screaming with my pillow, my sheets a bloodstained mess and heavy bruises all over my body. And that's when I realize what Blodd means. My disease has returned.

"I have a blood sickness that manifested itself at age 13 in conjunction with my menstrual cycle. I'm afraid you have the wrong—"

Blodd's demeanor changes now. Just when I think he's finally understood that I'm not who he thinks I am, he hovers ten feet off the ground with joy in his eyes. Soon his brothers join him in a merry circle in the air, surround me, and land. Each is bowing before me.

"It's true," Vincent barely breathes out the words. "Just as the prophecy predicted, but you have no place in the kingdom anymore. *We* shall take her inside. The king may see your deed and forgive you."

"No!" Blodd responds. "I brought the sorrow to the kingdom! It is mine to undo!"

"That's suicide!" The largest brother reminds him. "Demas probably already knows you are here. He'll have the charm incantation, the nets waiting, and we'll lose you forever!"

Blodd appears ready to give in to his brothers' request yet hesitant at the same time, and that's when his inability to control his alteration makes his choice *for* him.

12

"Princess Adaline met The Kurd's charge with courage. Our battle was nearly over until she was taken. Dredge the Destroyer took her hostage in the Cave of the Heather quite a distance from here."

I listen to Vincent's explanation as we approach the castle doors. Rand, Krist, and Titus fly back to their platforms blending in perfectly with the stone structure, three monoliths on one mission. Protect and serve. All three are adept at animation as well as conversion. Not experiencing the difficulties of Blodd.

"Who or what is the Kurd?" I ask. Vincent joins me on a flat-rock bench near the front doors.

"They are soul-less demons from the south that've outgrown their own territory, their village, and desire *our* lands;

cursed with dark abilities like affecting the natural elements, manipulations of objects, and inexplicable weaponry."

"Yet, you remain free."

"With a handful of close calls, my princess, but only *one* almost cost us our free will. Alas, the very battle that ended Adaline's waking life."

"Wait! I thought she was just kidnapped? How did she die?"

Vincent's expression mimics Blodd's when I first met him. His voice is raspy now, fighting back his emotions.

"Thanks to Demas, our soothsayer and sage, we found Dredge's encampment in the mountains by the cave I spoke of. Had his army confused, unsure of where the attack would come from next. A spell of bewilderment cast over his position allowed us access to the cave, but Dredge was gone. He tunneled underneath the ground with the princess."

"Then what? How did she perish?"

"Well—Dredge figured out he was vulnerable and wouldn't win. He launched his flyers. As a final sign of defiance, he flew right over the castle pushing Adaline to her death."

"But Blodd? All of you? Why didn't you save her?"

"Four of us were deep in conflict with his men trying to decimate the walls. Explosive crystalline balls shot through handheld launchers met target after target. One blow wiped out large sections it took months to repair. The goal was to take out our first line of defense. The princess had only *one* chance. But Blodd—"

I could have filled in the rest of the story myself, but I wait for Vincent to complete it. My stomach lurches as I recollect my own flight with Blodd and my initial concerns.

"He had no shot at catching her mid-air, so he landed. Untimely, he morphed. His intentions were pure. He broke a portion of her momentum, but she hit her head. Now she lies dormant. No spells or medicines have helped. Blodd was banished. But it wasn't his fault."

I want to comment, sympathize with him, but I am stoic. *That could have been me. No wonder he's drawn to me and calls me princess. But if he thinks I can bring her back, he's mistaken. My mom.*

My memory breaks as the doors open wide and invite us inside. A lovely young girl smiles as we enter. She is slightly older than me with fair skin and a flowing green dress.

"I am Lexi. Demas and the king are expecting you. Vincent? You know the way. I have other chores to attend to."

"Yes, my lady. We understand."

I follow behind mirroring Vincent's steps. A long hallway lined with columns and decorative banners guide us forward. Certainly fancier than anything I've ever experienced, yet not overly ornate. Light blue and off-white color the textured walls, a stained glass window interrupting them every so often to break up the monotony. No open-flamed torches but radiant lights that swell as we pass and dim down once we've gone by. I expect to see a throne laced with gems and red velvet, but I am disappointed. Our stop ends at a secluded room lined with tall bookcases full to the top, an intricately designed fireplace with a dark blue fire, and three people comfortably seated around a round glass table. As soon as they turn around and speak, I'm overjoyed.

"Vincent? Please state your purpose. We've no time to

waste," The king commands.

My jaw drops to the floor as Rico, adorned with stately attire and a golden crown continues to talk, Ozzy and Star to his left and his right.

"Why bring this stranger into the castle? She could be a spy," Rico continues.

A spy? Uh, oh. They don't recognize me.

"The prophecy, sire. She's the one, the *healer*. All has come to pass, just as Demas predicted. Our land and Adaline?"

I cringe at the word each time I hear it. Healer. Not sure of proper protocol in front of royalty, I keep my thoughts to myself for now. I'm searching for something to jar their memories, so we can work together again, but something convinces me a water bottle won't work this time. There's no magic key gonna take us through to the next challenge. I search for wisdom again, only to be thwarted. Maybe I was a bit premature in my Socrates' sister idea.

Ozzy, now known as Demas, stares me up and down finally invading my space. He grabs both hands and spins me around like we're dancing, changing my currently mangled jeans and sweatshirt into a prom dress. Complete with bracelets and pearl necklace. He's quite handsome in his kingly attire. I never really noticed before.

"Let's see," he says. An odd surge of energy explodes through my body like he's giving me a body scan. "You *could* be just a Kurdish manifestation sent to give us false hope and relay secrets back to Dredge."

Vincent is about to come to my rescue, but he's interrupted by commotion outside the room's entrance. The doors burst open, and Blodd enters. Not his usual peaceful self.

"Hear me out!" he cries. "Then I'll go willingly if you wish."

In seconds, Demas waves his hand, and five soldiers with silver glowing cargo nets arrive. They surround Blodd unafraid of his size or his temper.

"So be it," King Rico says. Star nods in agreement noticeably intrigued by my presence. She's either practicing her play acting skills, or she truly believes she's the queen of Saxony, the kingdom of a Niner's imagination. The place carefully designed based upon my DNA, my critical thinking, all the tests Marek and Bale ran. My homemade proving ground. Growing weary, I ask to sit while Blodd defends himself.

"My king, I know I look no different, but since I've found the healer, I've changed. My control is returning, sire. We should try again. *Adaline*. She may awaken," He pleads his case on his knees in front of Rico who contemplates Blodd's request. Demas circles the beast like a scolding father shaking his head and making an annoying *tsk tsk* noise through his teeth. Any signs of the Ozzy I know is gone, as he's immersed in his role as necromancer.

"You've taken great risk returning here," Ozzy explains. "You always *did* have such courage. We could reject all your ramblings, have you charmed, and be done with you, you know?"

"Yes, I know. But you've seen it yourselves. She bears the marks. Otherwise, you would have taken me out when I entered. In the cave, just her presence broke through my stone armor, made me feel like myself again."

"Yet, you have still stumbled. Your curse is not reversed. I know you too well, Blodd. I can see it in your eyes, my friend," Rico says.

I watch the exchange of words like a movie, secretly cheering for the hero to win, but then I feel faint. If Blodd's life rests on my shoulders, with my so-called ability to heal someone who's been gone for over a year, I'm at a loss. Inadequate.

Weeks would slip by as I took care of Mom. Some days were sunny, and she'd play games or watch TV with me. Other days, the rain washed away every ounce of hope as I'd sit and stare for hours wondering if she'd ever open her eyes again. I pleaded for them to unlock one last time, so I could say my goodbyes, but that never happened because she was trapped in another realm. To her, I no longer existed. She'd no longer hear my laugh or my cries. I'd miss her teasing me about boys and her happy birthday dance.

That day arrived, and I drifted down into the earth right with her. Weak. Alone. Worn. Sometimes I'm still there. There's nothing supernatural in me. I'm just Faith—without any.

Demas, I mean Ozzy, pulls a blue gem from his coat pocket and sits by my side. Each time he looks at me, he's measuring my doubt. My lips quiver. I don't know what to say. My eyes beg him to return to the boy I remember, but he's zoned into me now.

"Hold out your hand. If you're a spy, the stone will turn dark. Fulfillment of the prophecy? It will glow bright white." He smiles like he knows the outcome, but I'm not sure if that's a *good* or a bad thing. I reach for the stone and he stops me. I swear a tiny wink catches me by surprise.

"No. I must place it. Hold your hand out like this." He demonstrates.

I do as he says. At first, there's no change in the gem, but it is icy cold, burning a hole through my palm. The blue darkens for a moment, and I wince. I imagine the terrible consequences if they believe I'm a spy.

"Close your eyes until I tell you to open them," Ozzy says.

I agree, but the minutes drag and my arm can barely withstand gravity's push. My shoulder aches at the pressure. Choruses of sighs fill the room as a tablespoon of bile rises up in my throat. I swallow and fight it. I want to look, but I squeeze my eyes even tighter.

A commotion of bodies stirs all around me, whispering things I don't understand. Incantations. Prayers. My curiosity's about to explode when Ozzy's voice finally gives me the signal.

"Open now," he shouts.

When I open my eyes I am blinded. The purest white light erupts from my hand through to the ceiling. I blink, several times clearing the outlying images around me. Everyone in the room gathers around like it's a hospital room visit.

"It is she," Rico yells. "Get her to the vault as soon as possible! Our healer has returned! Adaline will live again!"

His voice brings back my gag reflex because there's no turning back now. Like before, I want to escape. Deny my purpose. What if I fail? They'll know I'm not her. Blodd will die. I'll be, who knows what. Exiled. Killed.

I'm whisked down the long hallway into a much older and darker section of the castle. My new dress kicks up a couple layers of dust as we proceed to an elevator, only more modern. It's all glass, an oval bullet similar to a pneumatic cylinder used at drive-up bank tellers. It's the lone modern invention in the entire area. A sharp jerk sets us in motion down.

A shot of cold air and dank smell meets us as the elevator doors open into a shadowy red chamber. I can tell the module creators went all out in this training level as a futuristic mausoleum engulfs us. At times, the iridescent walls appear to be breathing, almost like we're inside someone's lungs. An altar with a hermetically sealed casket rises up from the floor as we approach, our footsteps triggering the movement. This must be Adaline.

Blodd's head barely fits in the chamber, often ducking to avoid the rocky ceiling. A newfound hope clings to his face as he spreads his wings over the coffin; his way of paying respect again to the fallen. Moments pass, as Rico steers him away from her body to disengage the technology still keeping her alive.

"Wait," I squeak, my heart pounding to the rhythm of the walls. "What now?"

Ozzy winks once again, and maybe I'm nearing insanity and seeing things, or he's dropping bread crumbs, leading us back to our original mission. Adaline's body obscures in the milky white fog under the glass. Ozzy flicks one last switch, and it opens revealing the princess. I'm not certain what everyone else is seeing, but my eyes cross a few times before regaining focus. Marek's words ring over and over again in my mind. *Each training session is geared to each of you individually.* My knees buckle at the sight. It's my mom, a much younger version. Maybe in her twenties, but I'm sure it's her.

"Is this a trick?" I ask.

Ozzy and Rico glance at each other puzzled by my response.

"Trick?" Rico says. "Why do you say such things?"

"This princess, Adaline? It's my mother," I say.

"Your mother?" Blodd asks. "Demas? What's this skullduggery, a spell?"

Ozzy ignores his questions placing a different gem into my palm. Clear. Smooth like a marble. Instead of more winks, his face twitches. Star copies him like they're both working hard to stay in character and incognito at the same time. Pressure builds inside me as I hone in on Ozzy's instructions.

"Now, Princess Faith. Consider your power. The *reason* you're here. What lies *beyond*. When you're ready, slam the gem down on her chest." I wonder if he might be speaking in code, but I'm oblivious, turning my head to the side. My eyes request clarification, but he just presses both hands to his temples, his breathing unsteady.

Rico's soldiers react in defense protecting the casket. Blodd spreads his mighty wings over Adaline's body. I can't get to her now even if I tried. Something's not right. Adaline's face is exposed, and it morphs in and out like a defective hologram. Two faces, then three. Adaline. Mom. And

Azuna. *Azuna?* Mom begs me to use the gem as is Adaline. Azuna's words are aggressive. Demanding I step away from the platform. Her eyes are lasers boring right through me. I receive increasingly stronger jolts of electricity into my soul. An enormous hand pierces right through Blodd's body and tries to grip the essence right from me, but I remain focused and force Azuna's appearance back to my mother's.

"Now's your chance," Mom says. "You couldn't save me, but you can save yourself. The world. Use the gem, Faith! Use the gem!"

13

Mother's words sting my ears. Breathing grows increasingly more difficult with giant fingers squeezing me like a sponge. *Crack!* An explosion under our feet steals our balance. Blodd and the soldiers rock backward as the altar begins to quake. He rises up, his head carving out a section of the ceiling, causing an avalanche of pulsating rock to smother him. Azuna's hand retracts with the commotion. No longer in Azuna's tight grip for the moment, I leap over Blodd's body and nail Adaline's with the gem right over her heart.

The blow sends the rest of us spiraling out of control like gravity has been removed from the room. Bodies, except for Blodd's, are bouncing back and forth off the walls. A small crevice in the floor reveals a black hole. Space. Stars.

131

Incredibly another wormhole emerges. Ozzy, Rico, and Star get sucked in right away, but Blodd pokes his head from the rubble and frees one arm. His pitiful scowl meets my eyes—a way of sharing his disappointment in me. Expecting one last fight from him, I'm shocked by his next reaction.

"Go," he screams. "Now! Before she breaks through to you!"

I shove myself off the ceiling in an awkward arc toward the portal with Azuna's hand in pursuit. I'm about to be free of the crumbling chamber half-way into the swirling void when a strong tug rips me back. Her throbbing hand engulfs both legs. She pulls me back over the now-tilting body of Princess Adaline who's still very much dead to the chaos. Every soldier is buried under the cave-in. Blodd has freed his other arm now, so just his torso immobile. There's little room to spread his wings to attempt flight, but his pure strength and will power gain him a few more feet of freedom. Azuna's nearly absorbed me into the princess's body—a feeble cry whimpers out of me. I am resigned to my fate. Just type *failure* into the report and send me back to Earth.

I close my eyes and wait expecting to wake up to my friends begging me to get up, but that's not what happens. A quick glance to my right brings me hope. Blodd's dug a soldier's pole axe from the debris. One sudden swing later, and I am freed from Azuna's grip and face-first with the comatose princess, her body like a frozen yet thawing lake. Azuna's hand and arm is nowhere in sight. I waste no time being recaptured. Some semblance of gravity returning, I slump off and limp back toward the opening that grows narrower. My legs are barely functional now.

I may be too late. I sense the draw, but it's weak. Little suction left to take me to the next level. Blodd sees my plight and blasts through the rest of his restraint. He staggers over to my escape window. My face pleads for him to do something because I've no words. My voice is gone. My resolve, an engine with no fuel. I gasp a few times, but I'm spent, unable to lift my head or take the *one* step needed to launch me back into the window.

Blodd runs his claw down my back like he's given up too, a sympathetic glint in his eyes. I fall, but he catches me, shielding me from another deluge of rock. Cradling me like a child, he raises my head up, and I catch a glimpse of myself in his shiny black horns and pull back in his hand startled. My eyes glow piercing blue like Marek and Bale's. He panics as well, metamorphosis beginning to take hold of him again. He shakes his head side to side, up and down, and sets me down near the diminishing vortex. Half his body alive, the other entombed in stone. One free arm jams the axe down into the floor, and a *new* doorway forms, much larger. Fully charged. The same arm peels me up off the floor and forces me into the spirals. The last image I see before I'm swimming in gel, is Blodd erupting into a million pieces, and a few remnants fly in with me. His true form's returned. We share a grin and a wave, and I spin head-first through the clear jelly. I am wiser and stronger. *Changed.*

****

I feel the cold compress on my forehead before I even attempt to open my eyes. It hurts just to think about it, but

I need to know where I am. Star sits so close she's almost on top of me. I'm on a grey metal cot wrapped up in a co-coon of blankets. The others surround me but at more of a distance. I stutter a few unintelligible words, and they just smile and nod. Lifting my head off the pillow is a chore, so I don't bother. Star bends down to me.

"Hey there, Princess Faith. Glad you're back," she says.

I feel my brain reengaging now, and I want to respond with something like "where are we or what's next?" But an absence of air in my lungs stops me.

"It's okay," Rico whispers. "We had the same problems. You'll be yourself in no time. Marek's mixing his energy cocktail. You're gonna—"

I tune out the last part of his sentence at the sound of Marek's name. Home. Earth. That's all I can fathom or hope for right now. The training must be over.

"Where are we?" I ask.

I roll my head sideways attempting to get a better look, and Ozzy's sporting a mighty grin. "Ya really wanna know?"

"No. I'm just trying to make some small talk." Sarcasm spills from my mouth; a bit of my attitude is returning. I wish my body would follow suit, but I'm still fighting grav-ity and losing badly. Star sees my frustration and lifts my head for me. Marek and Bale stand over a silver table, more like a contemporary-styled wet bar in a laboratory. Steam floats over the area as Bale stirs a purple concoction in a beaker. My friends look like they've been through a dog-fight, white bandages on their faces and hands. *Who knew souls could be damaged?*

The thought slips out, and I realize the truth. Our bodies take such a beating in life we often forget about the *internal* destruction. Rico and Ozzy move closer as Marek arrives with his energy potion. I still have no idea where I am, but I'm pretty sure I'm not in Kansas or Tennessee anymore. Every so often I hear the deep roar of an engine or loud heater turning on.

"Is the training over? Or is this some *other* level now?" My voice is faint but gaining in strength. Marek's liquid goes down like lemonade on a dry day; it stings and comforts at the same time. I drink slowly.

"All over," Marek smiles. He forces me to drink the entire mixture all at once, when I'd rather pace myself. I do as he says, and there's almost an instant response. Suddenly I'm sitting upright, and I swing my legs over the side of the bed. I catch a much better glimpse of my surroundings. A hospital ward, only the walls don't resemble anything I've ever seen on Earth. Reddish recessed lighting at horizontal intervals in between silver and black tug-a-war rope coils from ceiling to floor. Automatic glowing doors appear and disappear just as fast. Luther's entire family peek in on their way to something more pressing. Cozy cabin in the woods has been replaced by some type of flying vessel, and somehow I'm remembering more and more from our training adventure.

"The camp? Barn? All destroyed?" I ask already knowing the answer.

"Military," Bale says. "They finally got a lock on our position. Some rogue Niners who traveled through the first wave with us must have helped. No way any *human* cracked our stealth code."

"What about the alignment? Has it happened yet? It's not like we know how long we were in limbo, ya know?" My three friends start to shower me with items to make my recovery easier. Ozzy places a blanket over my shoulders like any minute he's expecting me to chill. Incredibly, that's exactly what happens. I'm overwhelmed by a cavernous blast of cold throughout my whole body. I try to lie back down, but Rico and Star impede my progress. Star hands me a box of strange pink crackers, and Rico follows with a mug of water. The crackers taste a little like Cheez-Its and do a nice job of calming my gnawing stomach.

"You gotta stay up," Rico says. "Makes the elixir work faster. You'll be on your feet in no time. We've got more training."

He says it so matter-of-factly now, not an ounce of hesitation in his voice. A confidence and boldness he's never shown, unless you wanna count his battle with Star.

"Alignment's already begun. As you've probably guessed," Marek says.

"Huh?" I mumble. "Whaddya mean?"

Before he can explain, Misty pops her head into my cubicle. A medical center is in the far corner of the ship. Dimmed overhead fluorescent lighting casts a moving shadow on her as she comes toward us carrying her tablet. The one she'd been playing her video game on before we entered our sessions. I can't help feeling like all of this is a part of a remarkable dream, or perhaps I *did* die and I'm on my way to the afterlife. Misty's bright smile makes her pretty blue eyes light up her flawless face. More perfect than any in my old porcelain doll collection.

"How are you feeling?" she asks. "I thought we lost you." She grabs my neck in a death grip. Her strength is way beyond most girls her age.

"Lost me?" I question. "How so?" I pare her away from me, so I can breathe. She sits next to me on the bed while the others find seats on the perimeter. Marek and Bale take turns examining the others, taking temperatures, blood pressure, and redressing some of their wounds.

"Azuna. When the barn exploded, your training session was placed in *pause* mode. She came through the portal right after the fight in the ring. Discovered your location in the system and re-calibrated the module. She almost got your soul."

"Yeah. I was there. But Blodd. He came through. Helped me escape."

"I know. That's how I designed it. Fixed what Azuna unfixed. It took me a few minutes, but I broke through her defenses and altered the ending. I'm so glad you're here." Misty's steady posture shifts to one of defeat, and she closes her eyes, like she's reliving the event in her mind. I flash back as well. Blodd's protecting me from the crumbling rocks. I'm in his arms staring up into his face. Then I see it again, my eyes reflecting in his horns. I scream.

"Ahhhhhh!"

Misty throws her arms around me once again but less aggressively. The others pull in closer sensing my fear. Minute whispers bombard me, so I stand. I run. Right into Marek's arms.

"It's okay. Everything's gonna be okay."

"She took it! Didn't she? Took my soul." I feel my eyes

protrude and start to growl my next words. "We've freakin lost! I couldn't fight it!" I shut down. No amount of comforting on anyone's part seems to help. I clench my teeth, and the pain in my jaw sends excruciating signals to my brain, but I ignore them. I'm lost in my fury until Star places her hand on the back of my head, running her fingers through my mangled hair. I want to hold on to my rage, but her touch overcomes me. I feel her pulse through my veins, a slow metered rhythm flowing down my back through to my feet. My knees buckle as Marek lifts me off my feet and carries me back to the bed. He props me up with a few pillows. *How did she do it? I wanted to escape. Tear the room to pieces. But I lost my will. I've no more soul. I should have stayed dead.*

In the midst of my pity party, Misty dials up a program on her tablet and plays it for me. I'm back in the last level hovering over the princess. The scene switches to Misty working feverishly on her computer. Back and forth between what I experienced and Misty's attempt to save my soul. I look away not wanting to relive any more of it, and that's when I hear it. Not out loud but in my mind. Rico's voice. He's encouraging me to open my eyes. I scream back at him in my head, but he's persistent. *You need to see this, Faith. Open your eyes. Please.*

I pop them open for an instant and see an electronic shield between the princess and me, a white barrier keeping Azuna from extracting my soul. I never noticed it in the heat of the moment, but it's clear Misty programmed it into the module.

"Wait. My eyes! Advance it forward. I swear. I had her

eyes," I yell.

Misty hits fast forward, and we wait to see my reaction when I discover Azuna's eyes reflecting back to me. She replays it over and over, and while my part of the response is still present, there's no sign of Azuna's stare. The shield must have worked.

"But—" I keep up my resistance.

"She's come to Earth, but her time's wasting," Bale says. "In three days, she'll be nearly powerless."

"Nearly, you say? What's the catch?" I wonder.

"She can take any old soul and live a little while longer, but that weakens her powers. You're her only hope, Faith. That's why we must get started. Soon."

"Doing what?"

Rico's voice crowds in once again. His mouth never moves, but I hear his words as clear as can be. *We need some physical training now. Learn how to use our enhancements.*

"Enhancements?" I say out loud.

"Yeah," Star says. "We're not the same people we were when we entered. You've already felt some of what I can do."

"I did? When?"

"Five minutes ago? You were acting like a maniac? I absorbed your anger and stole your strength. Wanna see me do it again?"

"No, no. I believe you. Rico? You stay outta my head, okay? That's just freaky. Ozzy? I don't know what you can do, but I'm tired of being the guinea pig, all right?"

Each of my friends laugh in their unique ways, but I see Ozzy wince and hold his rib cage for some reason. I leap to his aid, almost all of my energy returning now. No aches and pains, headaches, or unbalance. I'm fully ready to continue this wild journey.

"What's up? I saw you cringe." Ozzy takes a deep breath and does a terrible job of faking his *fine* health.

"Bad landing coming in," he says. "Hit the corner of the table. I broke a few ribs. I'll be fine." Instinct compels me to rest my hand on his stomach, and I feel warmth through my normally freezing fingers. My blood condition makes me a walking freeze baby most of the time. Heat rushes up my arm and into my chest, but before I can do anything, a jolt leaves my hand and knocks Ozzy to the floor.

"I'm sorry, so sorry. I didn't mean to—"

Ozzy's unhurt. In fact, he's almost giddy. He clutches his wounded ribs and breathes in and out several times. His face flushes as I help him up.

"Well—we were all wondering what little gift you got from our adventure. Now we know," Ozzy says. The four of us gather like we used to in the module locking arms and leaning forward. We take turns shaking our heads back and forth in awe of everything. Our experiences. Our situation. Our new abilities. Who would believe *any* of this if we told them? No one. This is the stuff of movie magic not real life. George Lucas at his finest.

Our official reunion is cut short by Luther's arrival.

"Better get the move on, folks. Azuna's closing in on us. The rest of her entourage crosses over in two hours, and we've got half a country to cover. The war has begun."

14

It turns out that Marek's spacecraft entered the portal with him years ago. Of course, it doesn't hurt that it's totally radar-proof and so invisible—it's narrowly escaped several collisions with other aircraft unaware of the elephant in the sky. It's a multi-leveled high-rise complete with private bedrooms, a high-tech clinic, and a gym. Well, it's not like any gym here on Earth really because it's designed specifically for sharpening one's *abilities*, some physical and not.

Take mine for instance. Returning from the dead has apparently given me a super charged immune system. So powerful, in fact, that I can give some of it away to others. Broken ribs? No problem. Three-inch cut? I got it covered. *Where was this when I really needed it? Maybe mom...* My past continues to affect me, but I've no time to dwell on it anymore. Ancient history. I keep trying to convince myself that what lies ahead is more important.

Having witnessed Star's talents along with Rico's, I'm curious as to what Ozzy can do. Bale guides us through a series of exercises in the gym to increase our blood flow and purge our systems of, well, being dead for four days in training. Everything Misty described is so true. A simple glass of orange juice this morning exploded in flavor. Every sense heightened beyond belief. We're at least ten feet away from each other, and I can smell Star's body wash, her deodorant, Ozzy's wad of gum. Cinnamon. My own sweat trickling down my back feels unnatural now. This is definitely gonna take some getting used to, for all of us. Too bad we don't have much time left.

We finish our last set of yoga-like stretches, and Bale gathers us together in front of a free weights cubicle. He instructs us to find one barbell we think we can lift off the floor, so I choose a fifty pounder. On his signal, we all lift. Our first three tries go well, and then he whispers something into Star's ear. She closes her eyes for five seconds, and we're told to repeat our lift. Weakness. I brace my legs underneath me like I was taught in phys. ed. and strain to pick up, but the weight never leaves the ground. Rico, Ozzy, and I laugh at our ineptness. Meanwhile, Star's busy showing off by dead lifting at least three hundred pounds over and over again.

"Whoa. Slow down there, Brutus. Gonna rupture something," Rico kids.

Bale pushes a few buttons on his tablet licking his lips with cautious hope, and that's when it happens. Star's strength fades quickly at the top of her dead-lift, but she's saved. Ozzy leads Rico and Bale to her rescue just before she's crushed like a daisy. They are choreography in motion like they knew it would occur. But how?

"Okay. Can somebody tell me what the heck's going on here? That—was a helluva close call there," I speak up since no one else seems to be as concerned.

"Star's having some trouble controlling her talent," Ozzy says.

"Which is?" I ask.

"Not sure of the complexity of it yet, but we think she's able to draw on other people's strength and kind of absorb it. She just can't sustain it so far," Bale explains. "I've never seen this kind of reaction in humans before. Like Luther, some return with great strength, but it's always there. Doesn't come and go like hers. Hopefully, it's just a 'practice makes perfect' kind of scenario, otherwise, it doesn't do her much good."

"But what about Ozzy? I've seen what Rico can do."

Rico pushes a new thought into my head as soon as I say it. *You think so, huh? Believe me, you haven't seen anything yet. Wait until I get you to cluck like a chicken and pretend you're a ballerina.*

"Good luck with that." I giggle out loud.

Ozzy senses my exhaustion from our busy morning and already pulls up a padded chair behind me. He's able to anticipate my actions seconds before I perform them.

"Heyyyy! I get it." My voice gets louder. "You've been doing it all along. You knew she'd have trouble with her last lift before it even happened. You're an event predictor."

What else would you call it? There's no dictionary of superpowers out there. My heart races at the thought of Ozzy's special gift. Foolishness abounds as I grab everyone's hands, and we swing around in a circle like *Ring around the Rosie*. I wonder if this is how *all* superheroes felt when they discovered their powers? Probably not. Most of them weren't teenagers attempting to fight a horde of aliens.

Any lingering doubt melts away for now as we jump around like kids at a toy store. I've never been opposed to fighting as long as the fight was a fair one. Having an increased chance of winning never hurt either. For the first time we've reason to hope, albeit a *small* reason. Somewhat better than *no* reason.

Bale's mildly amused by our antics refusing to join in our dance because he's busy scanning our bodies now. One by one he waves a buzzing wand up and down our frames. Star goes first. A green light. Ozzy? Same thing. Rico. Passes with flying colors. I'm next. Nothing but static. The familiar humming interrupted. Red light. Bale presses a few buttons and turns a few knobs and retries. Red light.

"What's wrong? Am I okay?"

"Yes. Yes, of course," His voice lacks conviction, so I panic some.

"You're sure?" I question.

"Just an anomaly. Probably needs charging. Anyhow, it's just like taking your temperature. A training module can really mess up your organs. Need to make sure yours are all functioning at their peak; rough road ahead. You understand?"

"So, like we're all healthy and everything?" Star asks. "I

mean, even Faith?"

I appreciate her concern, but I have enough worry for all of us right now.

"It might have something to do with her blood illness. We'll need to run a few more tests. Okay? Just to be safe." Bale won't lift his head from his tablet now. He's immersed in the data in front of him. Our immature party grows somber, but I won't let them feel sorry for me.

"What's next? I'm feeling hungry." I change the subject.

"Uh, oh," says Star. "We're not allowed to eat anything until—hey! It's past noon. Okay if we head to the mess hall, captain?"

Bale freaks all of us out when he finally finishes his calculations and casts a darting gaze my way. Not known for his humor, I pray he's just clowning around, but I'm not so sure. He rubs the side of his temple with four fingers eventually making his way to the back of his neck. We brace for terrible news until he smiles.

"Gotcha!" he says. "That food rule was just a precaution. Just ask Luther and Micah about that. When they came out of training they gorged themselves on spaghetti and meatballs. Not a pretty sight. Check with Kandy. I think Loribelle and she whipped something up. I'll see you back here in two hours."

The gang takes off toward the cafeteria ahead of me because before I can take one step, Bale pulls me aside. I'm the runt of the litter. I get it. But I know there's something else going on inside that alien skull. It reminds me of the morning my family doctor pronounced me sick. I smell a *new* diagnosis on the way, blinking my eyes to keep the tears from starting.

"Can you come back a little earlier, Faith? I want to run those tests. It shouldn't take too long."

"Of course. But what's up? I mean, really up? You look suspicious."

He taps a few keys on his laptop and something like a DNA strand pops up with my name in the corner. A few more buttons later, and there's a four window version.

"Notice the top two? This is you *before* you went into training. Adrenaline levels sky high, but the rest of your body normal. Now take a look at the bottom. Your first scan on the left shows signs of damage to your DNA but almost a normal reading given the fact you went through so much. Bottom right?"

My throat tightens, and I can feel my heart through my ears. I stare at the image and cringe, but I've no idea why.

"Why are the two strands overlapping? And what's up with the different colors?"

"No sure yet. Your illness can account for some minor aberrations along with your new ability to heal others, but this is drastic. I need some blood. Then you can leave."

"Sure. No problem. You'll just need two band aids. I'm a bleeder, remember?"

Bale grabs a syringe from the cabinet, ties off my right arm, and *Voila.* He's got a vial full of blood. Before he can attach the cotton and band aid, a stream rushes down my arm then stops. I swear I'm tired or hallucinating because the blood streaming down my arm flows backwards. It's as if I never got stabbed.

"Hmm," Bale and I mouth the word almost at the same

time.

"*That* might explain some things," he says.

"Whaddya mean?"

"Well, do you know when a diver goes deep into the water with gear, when he returns he must decompress?"

"So? What's that gotta do with me?"

"Mixing alien technology, module training, with humans isn't a perfect science. We knew that going in, but we were forced by Azuna to press on, even with the side effects. That's probably all this is."

"Probably?" I say, slipping off the exam table and heading back to my friends. "I guess I just wanna know if I have time to eat before I turn into a vampire or zombie?" Bale's face lightens some. Worrying about something I've no power to change seems foolish right now, especially with my stomach eating away at me. It's hard to fathom the compassion in Marek and him and compare it to the *crazed* version of Azuna; the morphed hand squeezing the snot out of me as I tried to escape. Weren't all aliens supposed to be little green men destined to take over our world? Mate with our women and turn out little alien kids who could sneeze radioactive snot and move toasters with just their minds? These two most definitely crush any stereotypes. Not to mention their *knowledge* of our planet is astonishing.

I find the cafeteria and am pleased to see Luther's entire family again, all tucked in around a long short table like at a Japanese steakhouse. No one's had anything to eat yet because they were waiting for me. I'm praying we aren't having spaghetti and meatballs. I don't recognize the sizzling food on the grill in front of Kandy, but it smells delicious. Some type of stir-fry meal with veggies and rice. Marek sits at the front near the grill. He's donned some new clothes more reminiscent of *his* planet not ours, but he's still quite handsome. He would have made a perfect Marine. If I wasn't 16, I'd definitely be interested in him. There's a constant twinkle in his eyes and a confidence fit for a perfect leader willing to risk everything to do what's right. I can't think of any better place to be at the moment as I crawl in right next to him, the only available spot in the circle. I feel my cheeks burn red at even *thinking* of Marek as more than a brother or uncle. I blame it on my most recent trauma.

"This may be the last time we all meet as a group," Luther begins.

"Yes," Marek continues. "Vortices are cropping up all over the planet now, much like they did years ago when we arrived. Azuna has entered, but her cabinet members got delayed. No close enough matching souls to extract, but please listen. All of them wither and die if they can't link with their *perfect* matches permanently."

"So why can't we just hide or find some cave in the mountains and wait it out?" Ozzy asks. "Why fight them head-on?"

"I wish it was that easy, Ozzy," Marek explains. "All of you without the expiration chip stick out like a Kurd at a peacekeeping summit. Remember, nearly every other youth or child on the planet has the device. You could burrow deep into the earth's core, and they'd still find you."

"What about this ship? It's invisible, right?" says Rico.

"Yeah. We could just stay put," Star adds.

Kandy begins the meal by passing the giant bowl of

steaming brown rice to her left. Next follows the main course. Misty brings two pitchers of drink and sets them down on both ends of the table and joins Junior on her right. One big happy family eating what possibly could be our last supper or lunch in this case. I'm starved, so I take one bite of my meat and savor the flavor. It goes down way too smoothly until I look up and realize I'm the only one who's started.

"I see that *one* of us has already sampled some of my wife's cooking, but let's take some time to also thank our Creator for getting us this far. Before I start, I just wanna say how proud I am of all of you. Unfortunately, your families couldn't be with us, but we know they are safe."

"Safe? Where?" I ask.

"Well, they've been captured by the government, but they've become bargaining chips for all of you," Luther goes on. "There's a small percentage of rebel soldiers still loyal to our side, so we've called them in to assist in their rescue, but they're not our biggest concern right now."

The four of us shrug in confusion. Rico and Star push back from the table but don't rise up. Their mouths open, but they're not sure what to say next, so I change the momentum.

"Uh—Luther? The prayer? Ozzy's looking emaciated over there." We all laugh.

Reluctantly, our two dissenters swing back underneath the table and bow their heads. Luther's prayer is short and sweet. It's not long before we hear a chorus of chewing noises and sighs of relief as the food satisfies our hunger. Four days in training without sustenance has taken its toll on all of us. Misty deflects all our anxiety by passing around her tablet. She's designed a new game, an epic battle between good and evil. I watch as the heroes go down one by one. I don't know why, but instead of being *upset*, I smile.

15

Apparently Marek's ship is a part of a massive fleet on his planet. Once all the elders cross over, in spite of the cloaking capabilities, it won't be hard to find. After we make pigs of ourselves, I mosey back to Bale's lab like he asked. *His* meal lies almost untouched on the counter. It's obvious he's spent most of his time on my blood work and strange readings. Three centrifuges spin clockwise as Bale, complete with x-ray-like goggles, peers through a microscope. I try not to disturb him letting a brief clearing of my throat resonate through the air.

"Oh, Faith. Glad you're back. I'm close to finding some answers." A vote of confidence returns.

I move closer to him then freeze. I am no longer in control of my body. I try to cry out, but I can't. It's no use anyhow because he's frozen too. A myriad of voices flood my brain. My own, panicked and questioning our current condition. Bale's, who's trying to warn me of something. And finally Ozzy's, who's poked his head into the room, behaving very much a statue like the two of us. Even the medical equipment, all the beeps and buzzes suspend in time. Someone's manipulating us, but who? Thankfully my eyes are unfazed, and I scan the room for intruders. Not a soul. I think I see one more arm just behind Ozzy that could be Rico's, but I'm not sure. A warm tingle runs through my body as I try to sort out the confusion of words. I blink twice hoping to change channels, but all that does is land Bale and Ozzy on the floor, still paralyzed. Bale's face reddens like he's battling his attacker. A slow stream of blood flows out of Ozzy's nose—no doubt caused by his sudden impact with the floor. I'm growing angry now. I picture myself clenching my fists and striking out at the force that holds us in place. I continue the daydream recalling Blodd's slicing of Azuna's hand around my body with the pole axe and my face to face with the princess. Then I am free.

I plummet to the floor landing Indian style---still quite a shock to my system. Ozzy, Rico, and Bale reach their knees. In seconds, we gather in front of his workstation to converse only we can't. A mild delay interferes with our communication as if something's wiping the memory from our minds. I'm ready to share what happened. The words right at the tip of my tongue. Body language on guard for the next attempt at subduing us, and then it's all gone.

Bale's right back where I left him talking about finding some answers. I listen intently because I know something's not right. He motions me closer, so I can catch a glimpse of his monitor once again. The DNA strands are back, but they don't appear different than before.

"Here. Take a look," he says. "It's your latest sample. I view a couple of glitches, but almost everything's back to normal now."

I make eye contact with him, tilt my head to the side, and then view the screen. Is he seeing what I'm seeing or what? I examine it again, and he's right. All four slides appear to be equal this time. Maybe my corneas recalled a previous image and filled in the details before.

"Your sickness put you at a disadvantage compared to the others. Your organs had a tough time catching up to the present leaving some blanks. You're almost as good as new."

I hear his voice, but I'm skeptical. Bale's never been one to lie, but none of this seems right. All of a sudden I'm mesmerized by the blood flying around in the machine creating a Van Gogh-like pattern. *Starry Starry Night*. A devilish blue and yellow tint glows from the inside out, but I wonder if he sees it.

"Bale? What's up with this? My blood? Since when is blood blue?"

"Oh, that? No worries, Faith. Deoxygenation. Same reason your veins look blue. It has to do with the iron. And by the way, young lady. Your blood clotting issue? No sign of it. It's gone."

"You're kidding, right?" My voice rises in pitch. I want to jump sky high, but I don't. Not yet. I grow dizzy, so I sit. Bale comes to my side at the same time Ozzy and Rico poke their heads into the lab.

"Guess what?" Bale says as they draw near. Ozzy's holding a rag to his nose.

"Wait! Don't tell me! Faith's been healed. No more disease," he says matter-of-factly.

I want to slug him because his new talent is so annoying. But we hug instead. Bale turns back to his food where he passes it through a plastic white ring, and it heats up. The Niners' version of a microwave, I guess. Rico tries to coax Bale out of his food, but Bale looks relieved now, chowing down on Kandy's oriental dish like a hungry teenager.

"What's up with the rag?" I ask Ozzy.

"Bloody nose. I finished dessert and it started bleeding. Loribelle doctored me up, though. Running over here made it bleed again."

"Here. Let me take a look," I say.

Ozzy's nose was rather large to begin with, but now it's swollen and cocked to one side, like he'd been punched in the face. I pull away the bloody rag and a few drips plop down.

"Have you seen this?" I say, knowing he hasn't.

"Whaddya mean? It's just a bloody nose, right?"

I snatch Rico away from pestering Bale.

"Look!" I yell.

Rico gets a closer view, but I can tell he's puzzled. "Soooo? Looks like a nose to me, or a leaky faucet."

"You don't see it?"

"See what?" Ozzy and Rico question.

"Looks like someone hit you in the face with a hammer."

"Huh?" they say. "You sure? What did you drink for lunch? Hey, Bale? Did you give her medicine or something?"

Rico and Ozzy laugh, but the truth is trying to creep back to me now. A fall, Ozzy doing a face-plant to the floor. I shake my head and shift from foot to foot. Rico borrows a metallic tray from the counter and uses it like a mirror. Ozzy's nose still drips, a crusty dark clot beginning to form in his left nostril. I place my hand over it releasing a soothing warm energy. When I pull away his nose is straight. No blood. No sign of injury.

The tray's large enough to capture all our faces like a picture frame. Only Ozzy and Rico are smiling. I'm lifting my chin, pretending I know exactly what's going on, like I planned the entire charade. A scheme to lighten the mood, only the real part of me, my soul, is rebelling. It's screaming. *You're wrong! Everything's NOT okay, here! I'm not myself. Please! Somebody help me!* None of those words reach their ears. They remain buried inside. Prisoners are banging on the bars demanding justice, demanding to be heard. But their pleas fall on deaf ears. So do mine.

"Luther and Marek want us back to the control room now. I guess some of us are leaving or something," Ozzy explains. "You ready?" he asks me.

I want to continue our nose discussion, but all seems good. Ozzy tosses the rag into the trash and leads the caravan. Bale trails behind, his posture rigid and forced. I feel his hand on my back moving up to my shoulders. Soon two hands steer me forward like we're in a conga line, his voice struggling to enter my subconscious. Tiny pieces of information flash back and forth, but they make no sense. *Contact. Assimilation. Partial. Will. Breakthrough.* Rico begins throwing his ideas into the mix which confound me even more. I'm ready to explode, so I stop halfway there and turn around to face Bale.

"Stop!" I scream.

The whole line jerks to a halt and peers back at me. Guilt mars Rico's face. Bale's speechless. He feels my head with the back of his hand like he's checking for a fever but finds nothing. All the voices have stopped but not their emotions. They still play inside me like an audio malfunction.

"It's okay," Bale says. "You need rest. You had a busy day with heavy news about your illness. The meeting can wait. Take her to her quarters. I'll notify the others."

****

My nap takes on many faces. The face of fear. *What's really going on with me?* No answers arrive, so I float off. The face of doubt. *What chance do we have against beings who can turn themselves into giant hands and suck the life out of you?* No nightmares follow, but I *do* re-live everything so far. The daring transport rescue. Our trip to Waverly. Luther and his family's hospitality. The secret spy barn. Slide after slide changes as I go deeper and deeper into sleep. The face of dread. *When I awake, there's no tomorrow. Four ordinary teens versus an alien queen and her henchmen.* I'm not a 'save the world' type. Look me up in a dictionary, and I'm pretty sure you won't find me anywhere near the hero entry. While school came easily most of the time, my *biggest* challenge in life I failed. Miserably. Now I'm just a living breathing piece of situational irony.

I thumb through all the memories and realize my stairway may have been steep, but at least I'm still climbing. I mean, what's the worst that can happen? I die? Well, technically I've already experienced that. Though I'd like to avoid it in my near future for as long as I can, I'm not too scared. I'll keep my soul until my appointed time, thanks. And that won't be determined by anyone except the one who created me. If that's just Mom and Dad, I'm sure *they* got my back. A higher power? Better Him, than some politician trying to keep his job.

Misty rouses me from my afternoon nap. There's a light that shines through her no matter how dire the situation. Oh, to be that insanely positive all the time.

"How're you feeling?" she asks. "You look better. I mean, all pretty again."

I yawn a smile. "Why? Was I ugly before I went to sleep?"

She's brought a brush, and she starts running it through my hair. Kindness and compassion follow every stroke. I'm sure she's got a dark side, but I've never seen it. I want her innocence again, with her undying faith that things will get better.

"No," she says. "Not ugly. Just didn't look like yourself. White skin, like your hair. Funny eyes."

"Funny eyes? Whaddya mean?" I pause her brushing and take her by the shoulders. She flinches, so I back off.

"Just red, like you were crying." She gulps like she's done something wrong.

I sigh and give her permission to continue her beauty treatment. No sense worrying Misty or anyone else with my psychosis. It's just stress. Surprisingly, her attention calms me, and I feel more like myself again. Stronger. Smarter. Less confused and troubled. With everything that's gone on, I'm compelled to find out more about Misty's abilities.

How was she enhanced by the training?

"Misty, dear? Can you tell me more about your special abilities? I mean, from coming out of the training?"

"Can't you tell?" she says.

"Not really. You said all your senses got stronger, but you didn't mention anything else. Like, you know, I can heal people or share my antibodies or something like that."

"I think daddy calls me his little peacemaker. That's why he sent me in here to wake you. 'Cuz he knew you were upset."

"So you affect people's *emotions*? When they're sad, you make them feel better. Is that it?"

"Yeah. I think it even works on animals. I miss my dogs." She bows her head and whines.

I expect at least one tear to form, but it doesn't. No doubt *her* skill keeps her emotionally balanced too, leaning heavily on the up side. I'd like some of *that* in my life. Maybe it rubs off. Since she's been here, I'm seeing things clearer than they've been in days. Bring on the alien warlords or whatever they call themselves. Ass-kicking 101 is about to begin. I sound foolish.

Oh, who am I kidding? I've only been in one fight, and I lost. Wendy Wigglesworth in the second grade stole my lunch, so I threw her backpack out the two-story window into the street. A truck ran it over. She kicked me in the knee and pulled my hair, and that was that. In a month, we were swinging on the swings together and jumping rope.

Misty and I join the others in the main control room. It is probably the smallest place on the ship, but still the size of a small house. Luther and Marek are behind a couple of monitors mapping out what appears to be our next destination. Otis and Micah are busy reinventing their wardrobes looking more like our Niner friends than a couple of teens from the boondocks. They add lightweight belts with gadgets I've never seen before—no doubt advanced types of weapons, but I'm not sure. Using her tablet, Misty causes all of their suits to light up like they're fully charged. In minutes, Ozzy, Rico, and Star enter without any special suit or gear.

"So when do we get our space suits?" I ask.

"You don't," Marek explains. "The four of you will be under cover. We don't wanna put a target on your backs. You'll blend in nicely with the crowd."

"What crowd?" asks Star.

"We're all going to a concert," Micah says. "One of my favorite bands, *Aquafire*. They're awesome! Intense light show, theatrics, pyrotechnics. We'll look just like security."

"A concert?" says Rico. "What're we gonna do? Shoot them with our laser guitars or something?"

Marek and Luther smile, take deep breaths, and exhale. I want to see trust in their eyes, but they're so difficult to read. After all, they've *more* than fooled us before. I wonder what they *really* think of us? Are we really ready, or are we out of our league? I guess in T-minus one hour and twenty-three minutes, we'll find out one way or another.

"Niners always choose heavily populated areas to enter," Marek says. "Usually where there's a great deal of distraction."

"And *Aquafire's* the perfect band," Junior pipes up. "Last year they made a real tornado on the stage! All the guys swooped down out of the clouds. Just a trick, but everyone loved it!"

I move closer to Luther's screen to inspect our new destination. Berlin, Germany. I think about ancient history. Millions of people slaughtered, all because one man wanted all the toys. A slight twinge in my head joins the squirm in my gut as I consider what we've gotten ourselves into now. There's no slamming screen door and walk in the park to clear our minds. Ready or not, here we come.

Bale enters with a canvas bag full of miniature guns no bigger than the palm of your hand. He gives two to each of us without uniforms along with a disappearing holster. He tells us we may never need to use them, but they're there just in case. The Niner statesmen are non-violent, so once we neutralize their abilities, they'll come quietly. Apparently there's a *third* level of the ship that houses a prison, where in *theory* they'll wither away without their hosts' soul.

The plan sounds simple enough, but I've got so many questions. What about Azuna? What if they don't come quietly or they have guards? Just how do you *really* fight someone who wants your soul? I mean, in training I did such a Wang-bang job of it. Rico must have picked up on my subconscious fear because he starts sending me messages.

You ready for this? I just want it over with, ya know? One way or another, we can't go on like this.

I push a few more signals his way. *You're right. I just---*

He never lets me finish my thought, drawing near and placing his arm around my shoulders. His cartoon-like face is gone now. No more jokes. "Got your back, mamacita. No worries, hey? Only one Holocaust in our lifetime."

"You were listening?" I ask.

"Yeah, sorry. I'm just getting stronger the closer we get to D-day. And you remember what happened, right? News-flash. We won."

"You ever think Hitler was an alien?" I ask.

"Maybe, I mean, he got that terrible moustache from somewhere, huh?"

We laugh, and my head spasms even worse. Rico, Ozzy, and Star pick up on it.

"Bale? You sure she's okay?" Ozzy asks. "She's battling something."

The word *something* flows out of his mouth, but I replace it. *Someone.* I need to tell them, but I can't. I won't. Maybe when we land, or not. Incredibly, the mental train stops. So does the pain. I'm okay. Fine. Azuna. Uh—I mean, Faith. Faith Marie Monroe. *Faith. Faith.* I whisper inside. My ears ring with the sound of the pre-landing countdown. Bring on the Nazis. *Niners.*

16

Some of us arrive at the concert venue, and it's like stepping onto a horror movie set. I say *some* of us because Luther, Otis, Micah, and Marek hitch a shuttle and head off toward England to greet *another* group of Niners crossing into our world. We wouldn't have made it to both places in time without splitting up. Marek assured us they'd be in Berlin before we left, but all of this makes me uneasy. Half an army can't be as good as a whole one.

The air's unusually heavy with several rounds of thunderstorms moving through the city just before we arrived. As we enter, O2 Arena in Berlin resembles the underworld complete with towering water fountains set on fire and uneven rock formations with various appendages sticking up out of the cracks. Aquafire's signature logo, from what I can remember about the band. Not my kind of music really, but I'd seen pictures.

Apparently these wax people musta missed the lake of fire and ended up trapped in hell's core. Molten lava streams down their bloody heads and faces enshrouded in light blue fog. These artistic wonders are fighting over reaching the crystal clear water in the center of the stage, surrounded by vivid red tiki-torches lit and emitting a ripple of black smoke into the ceiling. A crazy exhaust swirls the smoke around before it's sucked through the roof. An excellent effect, if you're into that sorta thing.

Tortured expressions animate the mannequins' faces like maybe they're reconsidering ending up here—along with taking back every time they told someone to 'go to hell.' Crowds of people, some dressed like the band members, others normal by European standards congregate in lines at the various gates. Tattoos and piercings surround us, but everyone's laid-back. No sign of aggression or conflict. Totally unaware that in a matter of hours, aliens will be stepping through a portal to assimilate and call Earth their home.

Unbelievably our fake tickets worked well, and we're just to the right of the main stage about five rows back. Loribelle, Kandy, and Misty all sit side by side, from left to right in front of us. Bale, Junior, and the four of us are one row back. From the time we left the ship, we've been asking about a plan or strategy, but Bale's not offering much. According to Bale, numbers have a tendency to be important to the Niners, so some time just before 9 PM we're to all leave for the bathroom. Keeping us in the dark literally and figuratively is not my idea of a plan, so before the band starts, I push the subject.

"Okayyyyy." I sigh, noticing that I'm the only one not enamored by all the hoopla. The sound-check carries on in spite of us, but we can still hear one another's voices.

"So, like we're here, now what?" I ask. "Is anyone *else* slightly curious about what happens next? I mean, diplomacy might work on humans, but I'm not sure our good looks are gonna get these officials to abandon their mission. Ya know what I mean?"

Bale's staring forward like his eyes are infrared goggles or something. He's calculating the exact entrance point for our Niner *guests*. Just because Marek says they're nonviolent doesn't mean they won't bring a few hostile types with them. Then what? An arena full of fans in the midst of an alien laser battle might not end too well. But then again, given the already graphic scenery, I wonder if anyone would even notice. They'd more than likely think it was all a part of the act. That is, until they witness relatives' heads being severed or arms and legs getting blown off.

Bale finishes his readings and finally realizes we're waiting for something tangible.

"I'm sorry, but pinpointing the precise entrance isn't an exact science. High dosage energy fields show up at least an hour before the window opens, so I'm not getting much yet. I'll try again after the concert starts. So, how can I help?"

Ozzy, Rico, and Star give him a sideways glance while I scratch my head in astonishment. If Niners have a pulse, *his* must be flat lining because there's no sense of fear. No sign of apprehension whatsoever. I tap my hand on the back of his padded chair hoping to coax him into providing us something before hell breaks loose. If I *had* Spidey senses, they'd be through the roof right along with the black smoke.

"So, what's the plan? If they come through on stage, what then? We'll all be in the bathroom," I surmise.

"I know we should think things through, but so much of this depends—"

"On what?" All four of us blurt, trying unsuccessfully to not draw attention to ourselves.

"On your training. Faith, you won't be in immediate danger when they cross, but the three of you will." Bale begins his relentless snacking on his popcorn. He demanded we all pick up a snack to blend into the fan base. It turns out he was right. We're about five minutes from the start, and almost everyone's on their feet in anticipation, half-eaten nachos and pretzels all around us. Thankfully our two rows are still seated, so we look just like everyone else right now. Wait until we whip out our weapons and start firing. There's a good chance *someone's* gonna notice, I think.

Bale continues his explanation in between his crunching. "Counselor Briggs, Rayne, and Ajai are due in this transfer. They are *your* matches." He points to Ozzy, Rico, and Star. "They'll know you're here. Be drawn to you. Nullifying their abilities is paramount."

Ozzy swallows hard. Rico's eyes bulge more than naturally, and Star fades off into yoga-land. I bump her with my elbow because she needs to hear the rest of the plan like the rest of us.

"Hey," she complains. "I'm preparing."

"Why can't we just *block* the gate?" Ozzy asks. "Shut down the vortex? I saw it in a movie once."

"It doesn't work like that, Oz. The Convergence is organic. Natural. Really *any* alien force could enter Earth's atmosphere during this time with the proper technology. From this end, the procedure can't be changed. Like a satellite signal, they're already dialed in, so to speak."

"So you're saying that these leaders will simply hand themselves over to us willingly?" Rico says, with his mouth full of sour gummies.

"Let's just say," Bale says, "we'll use a little *persuasion*. That's *my* job."

Our conversation is interrupted by the host of the evening's festivities. The man's speaking in German, but two giant screens project the English translation along with at least ten other languages. Due to some unfortunate technical accidents in previous concerts, all attendees have to suffer through a paragraph of liability warnings, just in case a rocket lands in your lap or your hair catches on fire. Suddenly I'm not too impressed with our VIP seating.

"I have the neutralizer in my vest pocket. Their first step on earth, and I'll render them powerless. They'll have no choice but to come with us. We'll ensure their safety."

"But won't they recognize you? Know you're against them?" Star asks.

In seconds, she's up on her feet rocking out to the pre-concert jams, head-banging back and forth and side to side. Very uncharacteristic of her controlled personality. Just as quickly, she's back down in her seat trying to hide.

"Did I make my point?" asks Bale.

Misty's the first to burst with laughter, and the rest of us follow. I get the humor, but I stay reserved. If something should happen to Bale, we're screwed. None of us have *that* kind of power. I hesitate to mention it because I don't want to be negative, but I've learned so much over the past few years. One thing's for sure. Almost *nothing* in life goes *exactly* as planned. Let's hope *this* time is the exception.

Two ramps on both ends of the stage light up as the house lights dim. Engine sounds reverberate from both sides. Motorcycles. The blue mist increases, and lasers crisscross through the crowd. The stage fire swells, and while I'm wondering why the fire alarms don't trigger, Junior shouts.

"There they are!" He points to the top platform on the right where four motorcycles are about to descend onto the stage via a twenty-foot jump. The first rider explodes down the ramp, spins horizontally in the air, and lands perfectly onto the waiting platform on the left. The next three all do different tricks before landing, including a complete two and a half upside-down flip, hitting hard but managing to steer out of a possible crash. Soon each rider zooms out of view for a moment and then downstage, removes their helmets, and bows.

Kandy and Loribelle are busy debating whether or not the members actually pulled off the stunts or had real stunt riders. Out of the corner of my eye on both ends of the stage, four men in dark suits appear. For some reason I'm lured by them more than the band. I know live concerts always include security, and there are plenty of those t-shirted bouncers milling about with the signature Security across their chests, but these guys don't fit. Men in black. CIA. I highly doubt they're here for the music. Why are they in Berlin?

Bale's gone into his staring-mode once again, only this time he's getting a signal. It's still weak but growing. He points us toward the middle of the burning water center stage. My knees begin to bounce, only it's got nothing to do with the excruciating beat of the drums. The rest of the gang gets swept up in the music almost forgetting why we're here, and I'm thinking maybe Bale's using his manipulation on them until the real action starts. It's either that, or Misty's keeping everyone calm before the storm.

I scream my questions into his ear. "Since the window is in here, why exactly are we leaving?"

"They'll arrive during intermission. Try to exit without being detected. I'm trying to avoid a public confrontation. I'll seize their minds and march them right into our arms before they even know what hit 'em."

"What about those agents and the suits?" I question.

"Yeah, that's exactly my point. I already *read* their thoughts. Might make things more complicated but—"

"More complicated? How?" I wonder.

"Let's just say, they're not here to worship Aquafire. They're here for *you*. All of us. Someone tipped them off. They knew about the portal, just like us. Only we're gonna snag our royal Niners before they even point a gun."

I admire Bale's confidence. Each word bleeds conviction. While my own faith has grown, I long to experience his fortitude. I get back on the horse, but there's a trace of doubt; a tiny seed that lingers and waits for me to water and feed it again. I thought for sure our training would eliminate it. I guess I couldn't be that lucky,

The concert rumbles on. Our bodies vibrate with the

driving electric guitars and constant bass. I recognize a handful of songs from the radio, and by the time I peek at my watch again, it's already 8:47. Loribelle and Kandy have already taken Misty to the bathroom, but Bale holds the rest of us in check. His phone's equipped with an imaging sensor, and he's confused by what he sees. Like before, he doesn't share his concerns.

We rise and slide past our neighbors on the right out into the aisle. Luckily the band's in the middle of a medley of tunes and everyone's singing. They pay little to no attention to us as we stagger out the exit doors into concession row. A small contingent of fans waits in lines at the stands anticipating the intermission rush, but the walkways are mostly clear. The three girls wait in a pizza line for drinks, still oblivious to the time. 8:55. In five minutes, we'll play *Mouse Trap* and catch us some aliens, but apparently Misty's got everything under control. It's strange, but her skills don't seem to be affecting me like they did before. I'm a mess. Too many 'what ifs' swirl around in my head.

Marek tweets Bale a quick message on his phone that their mission is complete, and they're on their way. But we're on our *own* for the arrival. *Their* ETA around 10 PM. Our rendezvous point is about a hundred miles from the city. Marek expects a full report as soon as our passengers are safely on board.

Bale's face hides his panic, but I sense even more that there may be some trouble in River City. We gather outside the east exit in front of the women's john. Our huddle looks suspicious, but we're not the center of attention. Flat screen monitors reveal the band's current theatrics except that this time, they're not manmade.

An enormous whirlwind emerges in the center of the staged lake, spraying the entire arena with water. Tiki torches extinguish, expensive stage lights burst, and the speakers continue to grind out the instruments and voices. Laser lights fire at random. Even the band members stare in astonishment having never seen *these* special effects before. Rather than stop playing, they continue, thinking the crowd will settle down if they don't panic. Many fans, mostly the wasted ones, start a mosh pit. Security monitors it closely, their perfect Adonis heads of hair wet mops now, but things are progressively getting worse. Punches are thrown. Drinks. Mass chaos.

We watch a few minutes longer, and the stage-side screens project the word intermission. A flood of people shove their ways through the doors as the host implores the roughnecks to stop fighting. Police are involved now gradually restoring order. Incredibly, few people catch the three bodies hurled through the portal into the wax body parts stage right. Those who do, pass it off as just another magic trick. An elaborate illusion, except that's our cue to spring into action. Ready the traps.

17

We *feel* the surge of people before we see it. Hundreds pour out the exits in controlled yet panicked waves. Most react to the concert in the same way, commenting about how awesome the special effects are, and wondering how they got that water tornado to appear. We waste no time trying to adjust their realities because our three detainees have dusted off the effects of their intergalactic trip and are headed toward the south exit. We catch a view in the monitor as we sprint toward them. Misty does her best to clear the way as crazed fans suddenly calm down allowing us to pass by without much resistance.

One doped-up fool in a brown leather jacket and fedora must have escaped Misty's powers because he flies out of the bathroom and blindsides me. I launch sideways, and my head nails a support beam full-force. I'm lucky it's not a wall because it's a direct hit, and I may have knocked myself out cold. A host of bodies including Ozzy and Star help me up. When they speak I swear I see stars again. Free-flowing stars coming out of their mouths.

"You all right?" asks Star.

"Yeah, I think so. But what's with all the bubbles? No. I mean, stars?"

I'm obviously dazed and not making any sense. Standing upright begins to clear the fog away some, and I remember why we were running.

"Just go. Let's go. We can't let them leave without us," I shout, rubbing the side of my head assessing the damage. A smear of blood covers my fingers, but it's just a scratch. No one's spouting crystals out of their mouths anymore, so I think I'm fine.

Our alien diplomats are stuck in people traffic which gives us a chance to cut them off. I have an idea that we should pretend we're on *their* side and escort them to safety, but that's when I see it. *We* see it. Our black suits have already caught up to them and are using their authority to clear them a path. With Bale's abilities, getting by these dudes shouldn't be too difficult.

Kandy takes Junior, Misty, and Loribelle to wait by the outside exits as a last line of defense in case we fail. The rest of us hide behind an abandoned t-shirt kiosk where we have the perfect angle as they approach. They're less than ten yards from us, so we draw our weapons. Their bodyguards exit first. I can tell Bale's already manipulating their minds because instead of moving toward the doors, they push through the chaos to the hotdog line.

Immediately we hear a thunderous rumble from inside the arena. Our heads twist in unison toward the flat screens. The vortex is opened again. Six more bodies sail through the portal landing gracefully on their feet, all dressed more like Marek and Bale with glowing boomerang-like objects in their hands. They hold the same kind of guns we holster; warriors, soldiers. Their leader resembles a Viking, but a much uglier and slightly older version of Thor. Bale greets our council members as they cross the threshold, and they show no aggression, just like he assured. But I'm worried that he's spread too thin. Keeping the black suits out of our way, we are escorting our royal captives, and trying to avoid bloodshed.

Rico and Star move into action, but Ozzy's disappeared. Star fires a few rounds of laser at the lead warrior just to warn him, but he blocks it with his arm brace. It caroms off the floor, hits a folding chair, then it disintegrates. We have no idea who we're fighting or why they're here, but Bale needs us. All six soldiers leap over the clumps of stragglers in the aisles and are nearly on top of us. Bale's almost through the turnstiles when he yells back.

"Hurry! Now!"

His hesitation costs him, as the lead warrior throws his glowing boomerang toward Bale and the three alien leaders. It's a type of stun weapon. Even my ears ring, but I'm far enough away not to go down. We charge ahead hoping to get them back on their feet and onto the ship, but they're already up running. I'm thinking that either the soldiers missed, or maybe their technology doesn't work on earth, and that's when I see him. Ozzy. He's face down with half a cracked full-length mirror on top of him, stunned but still moving.

"Ozzy? What the hell were you thinking?" I scream. "You could have gotten killed!"

It takes him a second to register who I am, and then he's got that big old grin on his stupid face again.

"I saw it coming, all of it. Knew it was gonna happen, so I made arrangements."

"Where on Earth did you find a mirror?" asks Rico.

"The main dressing room. I ripped it off the frame. Anyhow, look!" He points.

The four of us shift our eyes back to our extra aliens, and they're down. With no idea how long they'll stay that way, we turn for the exits and run right into the CIA.

"Enough," The bearded one bellows. "You're coming with us! Their weapons. Don't try anything funny. You kids have no idea what you're doing."

"We can't," Rico says. "All of you are in danger. Those guys back there? They're aliens."

As soon as he says it I laugh inside. I'm ready for my padded room and my straightjacket fitting, but our agents surprise us.

"We know. That's why we were here. Now we need to get back the *rest* of our cargo. Where's the ship?"

The four of us stare at each other as if we've just gotten caught doing something wrong as kids, and no one's talking. With no time to corroborate our stories, we decide silence is the best policy.

Out of the corner of our eyes we watch the alien army

brigade, a bit dazed, peel themselves off the floor and exit the building. I guess *they're* not a part of the CIA's mission because they almost all totally ignore us. I make quick eye contact with the brute who seems to be in charge, and I swear I've seen him somewhere before. He snarls as if that's supposed to frighten me, but I feel pity instead. Soon Rico's sending me happy thoughts interfering with my emotions and memories altogether now. *Not exactly how we planned it, huh? At least Bale got away. Any ideas?*

I want to answer him out loud, but I don't. Keeping our abilities to ourselves could come in handy down the road. Though I'm kinda wishing I got the extreme strength gene right now because something tells me I won't be *healing* my way out of this one. I have no idea why Ozzy failed to see *this* coming and kept us from getting caught. It may have had something to do with his mirror trick. At least, that's the excuse I'm going with until I know better.

"Not gonna talk, huh?" A clean-cut, square-jawed Italian suit speaks as he dips my head into their limo. He taps his chest twice like he's activating something, but we can't tell what it is. Ozzy and Star take seats to the right with Rico and me on the left. Two agents join us on the other side. GI Joe minus the camo gets behind the wheel.

"We're agents DeMarco and Katz. Jordan and Dent are up front," The bearded one addresses us a little more formally now. I'm not exactly getting any goosebumps from their sudden hospitality, but things could be worse. They could have tortured us until we told them where the ship was located. Maybe that comes later, right after the water boarding.

Our evacuation doesn't go as smoothly as they'd hoped due to the plethora of fans leaving early, too much excitement for one night. At least no one got killed. Incessant horn beeping gets us nowhere as we're all in the same traffic jam without a butter knife. Thirty minutes later, and our tires our humming down the expressway to who knows where. I imagine the CIA has a headquarters somewhere in Berlin, but it's clear we're not escaping any time soon.

Ozzy's sporting a few nasty cuts and burns around his eyes and on his hands from the shattered mirror. Agent Katz breaks out the first aid kit and stops most of the bleeding, and I fight back my temptations. I could touch him once, and in seconds he'd be better, but I can't. Star's eyes tell me a story as the orange lights glow through the side window, now cracked open on the agents' side. Escape plan is written on her face. Downtown Berlin almost looks like daylight even at midnight. Even *if* she absorbed all these guys' strength and we got loose, where on would we go? Back to the ship? Bale's long gone by now, reuniting with Marek and the rest. It's best to ride it out and hope for a rescue. Marek won't abandon us. Luther would never let him.

Star's frustration lingers as I see her examining every detail in the car, her relative position to Rico and me and Agents DeMarco and Katz. I'm praying she keeps her ninja skills tucked away at least long enough for us to leave the limo. If she's got a game plan, we're in the dark. We've already seen how well *that* mode of operation has worked tonight, so I'm hoping for a little less excitement.

Exhausted, I tilt my head back against the textured leather seats and breathe in our agents' after shave or deodorant. Probably the most pleasant thing I've encountered all night, which is sad, especially considering they're the *bad* guys.

Rico's wide awake using *his* time to get friendly with our captors. I'm surprised they indulge him.

"Did anybody see Men in Black Seven? Kinda like what we're dealing with right now, huh?"

"Just a stupid movie, kid," Agent Katz finally talks. "We've got better things to do. Country's all F'd up, if you ask me." As a gesture of kindness, he pulls bottled water out of the mini-fridge and hands each of us one. I take a sip, and it burns going down. I appreciate it nonetheless and lean back again. Sleep seems to have overcome Ozzy and Star. They're using each other's heads as pillows. I don't let myself drift off in case Rico's conversation actually goes somewhere. He's not pushed any thoughts into my brain for a while now, so I try working it in reverse. *Rico? You there? Hey, any chance you could pull a Marek or a Bale? Get these guys to let us go?*

Minutes pass with no reaction. He seems tuned into both men, so I close my eyes and pretend I'm asleep.

"What about those *other* alien soldiers who came through the portal? They looked pretty nasty. And they almost killed my friend over there."

I'm interested in their response, so I lift one eyelid to catch their reply. DeMarco puts a finger to his ear and whispers. It's a silly notion because we're so close we can already hear the transmission ourselves. *What's your ETA? We got an unforeseen matter to handle. We need your manpower.*

"Our new alien friends?" Rico questions.

Agent Katz lets out a deep sigh, checks his watch, and begins a temple massage. I keep one eye closed and one open. Things are becoming more interesting by the minute.

"Geez," he says. "Not even finished with *this* gig, and they're already sending us out on another one. We get back to the states, I'm going to look into an early vacation. Get away from this little green men crap."

"Why didn't you go after the diplomats? Won't you get in trouble?" asks Rico.

DeMarco's off the communication device now. "Nah— *they* were the second priority. Rounding up you four was our primary objective. We'll get a freaking medal, right Katz?" His laugh annoys the hell outta me. How can a guy built like a lumberjack laugh like a hyena? Must be steroids or maybe his underwear's too tight. In any case, I can't see this line of questioning going anywhere fast, so I give in to my fatigue.

****

Screeching tires jolt me awake as the car fishtails left and right ending up at an angle in front of a massive warehouse. At first, I'm thinking our daring rescue has begun, but I'm disappointed to see one of the building's garage-like doors going up. Three hooded agents usher us inside. Some official guy with a clipboard and a tablet knocks on our window. The driver engages him.

"Cargo secured, Leo. What's next?" The driver's voice tired, unenthused.

"No worries. You'll get a couple of hours of shut-eye. Chancellor Stevens won't arrive until morning. Her flight got delayed outta DC."

"Thanks. Been a tough night. They're just kids, for chris-sakes. Don't look like no terrorists to me," GI Joe, the driv-er continues. He signs the tablet and pulls the limo into an unloading bay. A small stairway leads up to a burgundy door with no handle, blue sensor at the top. We leave the car, and as we approach the light turns green, and the door opens. We're greeted in the hallway by a few more agents, two women and a man with straight longish red hair and a pen sticking out the back of his ear. Ozzy's sporting an ob-vious limp, so Rico and I practically carry him until one of the lady agents hands him a crutch. Star's using her memo-rization skills again taking in every turn down the corridor, seeking any possible way out.

"I'm Agent Smith. I'll be your host for your stay here. I can assure you that you won't be harmed as long as you cooperate. Oh, and in case you were wondering. Agent De-Marco? Would you please?"

He plucks a lanyard out from under his suit jacket. Al-most looks like one of those emergency contraptions old people use if they've fallen or worse. The center white light pings like a heartbeat.

"*That*, my young friends, is known as a neutralizer. Your powers won't work here, so forget about it. No sense making things worse than they need to be. All right?"

It all makes sense now. Why Rico stopped talking to me inside my head. Star wrestled with absorbing the agents' strength, but she never pulled the trigger. I couldn't have helped Ozzy even if I tried.

I have to really hand it to the Feds this time, they thought of everything. Well, *almost* everything. I say inside as I'm separated from the rest and land in sickbay with a gazillion lights shining in my eyes. Agent Smith handcuffs me to a stationary table, and that's when I know I'm not there for First Aid. Interrogation 101, only they have no idea the effect those intense lights are having on me.

It starts at my ankles and darts up the back of my legs. Something's in my blood. It burns like boiling water. I stare down at the floor hiding my face with my hair just in case they notice the *change*. In minutes, I'm rubbing my fingers over my tattoo over and over again for no apparent reason, and sweat drips off the tips of my hair onto the deadwood floor. They get zero questions out before I finally look up and shatter every light in the place. I lean back and embrace the darkness.

18

"Yikes!" Flies out of Agent Smith's mouth. He's picking glass shards out of his hair and attending to the medics, one man and one woman. Neither is hurt badly. "They told us you had some abilities, but we had no clue. What's up with that neutralizer, Ramsey? See if it needs new batteries or something."

The man leaves the room. I'm still connected to the table. A whisper of light shines through a crack in the door. The woman thinks quickly and lights a Bunsen burner. My creepy crawlies are gone now, but I think I've frightened them. These people must handle the *science* end of the CIA because they don't look brave or capable of fighting their way through any conflicts, which could prove useful later, should my power burst return.

"Tell us about your time with the Niners?" Smith asks, a stutter in his voice. "How much do you know? I mean, really know about them?" He gains strength now he's sure I'm no longer a danger.

"You gotta be kidding, right?" I make my voice harsh. They have no way of knowing what I'm capable of doing, so keeping my mysterious aura is critical. "You'll get nothing from me, from any of us. It's a waste of time bringing us here."

"Well, well—quite the attitude. But you'll be singing a new song when Chancellor Stevens gets here. Don't wanna be cliché, but we *do* have ways of making you talk. We can do it the easy way or the hard way."

I chuckle. "Thought you didn't wanna sound cliché? You're a walking stereotype. Hey, how much do they pay you guys for this? I mean, making those expiration chips, lying to the world. How do you sleep at night?" Both agents smile, but it's just a sardonic gesture.

Another agent drops off two lanterns, and we can all see one another's faces. He relays the message that there was some outside interference on the grid affecting all tech-related gizmos including the neutralizer. I leap at the chance to contact Rico while Smith and his assistant dabble with a laptop and fill a syringe. I need to get Rico a message before they drug me.

Rico? You there? I sigh. I guess I expected an immediate response. *Rico? Put your ears on.*

Faith? Is that you? Really you? Or is it some kind of trick? I push my rolling chair back against the wall and rest my head and eyes. *Rico? I'm in a small lab about 20 paces from where we got split. They're going to drug me.* I wait. He responds again. *Down the hallway to your right. Same kinda room. No sign of Star. Ozzy. Why am I able to talk? I thought they blocked us?*

Agent Smith's walkie-talkie squawks. It sounds like De-Marco, but I can't be sure. It's a report on the techie malfunction. "Three of our dishes on the roof have been fried. Laser fire. We've switched to mobile auxiliary. Back up in ten."

Fried satellites. Probably Marek and Bale. Just hold tight. Don't give them anything, Rico. Nothing.

My last thought slides out under our agents' radar as a needle pierces my shoulder.

"Ouch," I cry.

"Just a sedative," Smith's assistant says. "We want you four to be well rested when the Chancellor gets here. You two have much to discuss."

The drug works quickly. Rico's voice scrambles like I'm in a stadium with poor acoustics, one word overlaps the next. Before I know it I'm out.

****

I awake to a strange metallic taste in my mouth, no doubt a side effect of the sleep serum. I've been moved to a new room with a window. I'm still tethered to a bed. Smith's assistant presses buttons on an IV-caddie, a clear tube now connected to my right arm. I raise my knees to my chest, but it's a chore. My spine's on fire, my calves stiff and sore.

"Your blood disorder? How long have you had it?" she asks.

"What do you care?" I blast back. "You're just keeping

me alive long enough to have my soul stolen anyhow."

"Your disease? It's not what you think it is." She mops my brow with a cool sponge. All of this seems odd considering my fate. But her words grab my interest.

"What do you mean?" I watch her dial up a screen that hangs next to my bed. "Acute promyelocytic leukemia, with some weird anomaly. The cells prove you have it, but something's keeping it from advancing. You needed fluids, blood."

"Gee, thanks, Captain Obvious." Sarcasm fills the room. "There's a cure, ya know?" she continues. A video pops up on the display. It's an operation. Chemo treatments. A young girl around my age alive and well riding a horse. "Angel Stevens."

The name breaks through my cold heart. Suddenly I re-member. Our new Chancellor Stevens' daughter had cancer. I try to extend my conviction and stay angry.

"No, thanks. I think I'll keep my cancer for a while. A certain *alien* leader might catch it and die." I laugh. April, my caregiver frowns. Why? Was she expecting a different answer?

"Suit yourself. Procedure only takes about an hour," she says, pouring me a cup of water. Agent Smith enters carrying a vial of pink liquid. He sets it down on the counter. April hands me the cup, and I drink. My mouth is dry and in need of some mouthwash.

"Steven's is on her way here. She's being briefed in the conference room. She asked to see *you* first," Agent Smith says.

"Hey, just untie me, and I'll bow. I wouldn't want her to feel unwelcomed." I tug at the strap to no avail.

"You *are* a feisty one, aren't you? A damn shame."

"Stop pretending you care. It's not becoming." If I had any saliva, I'd spit on him. April, on the other hand, has earned a slight reprieve. "You care so much, then let us all go. We won't tell anyone." I half-joke.

"Like I was saying," he takes my temperature with a green sticky strip on my forehead, "damn shame you're gonna be assimilated. Hope the alien learns to tame you once she has your soul." He plugs my readings into his tablet and moves toward the door.

"Newsflash, moron, those burnt satellite dishes on the roof are just the beginning. Better get prepared. Cavalry's on its way. It's just a matter of time." I force my tough-girl persona again, but the truth is, I'm not sure anyone even knows where I am.

April follows him out the door. Their standard Fed shoes click in unison as they echo down the hall. There's a small tree or bush outside my window. A grey day, but the sun's trying to burn off the fog. With no clock, I'd say it's around mid-morning. My stomach aches but not in a sick kind of way, just hungry. I'm not on a ground floor but not too high up either. It's like they gave me this view just to torture me.

I try to contact Rico again, but it's no use. My eyes start to water for no reason. I'm crying, but there's no emotion behind it. In fact, I feel almost nothing at all. *Has Azuna already taken my soul?* That's what it feels like. Even my anger wasn't normal. Blah. I'm in no mood to talk to the current leader of the greatest country in the world.

Knock, knock. A voice follows. "Hello? Anybody home?"

Chancellor Stevens enters, her face golden. A smile only

millions could buy. Her sharp white teeth are the perfect accessory to her new blond bob. It's cut long on one side and short on the other. Her thirteen years in office have been kind so far, but why wouldn't they be? With the help of the Niners' gold, our country's back on top where they used to be, almost totally debt-free. Too bad she literally sold all our souls to get there.

"Faith Marie Monroe?" she says in her fake southern accent. "Chancellor Margaret Stevens. So nice to meet you. Please, call me Maggie."

I raise my eyebrows at her entrance but say nothing. The silent treatment worked sometimes with my mother, so I figure I have nothing to lose.

She steps to the window and gazes outside. "Lovely day in Berlin. It was a rough flight. Storms."

I want to tell her I'm sorry her plane didn't crash, but I don't give her the satisfaction of hearing my voice.

She pulls over a chair and sits directly in front of me. I make eye contact thinking it will give her false hope.

"You're in quite a predicament, aren't you? I mean, what were the chances that you'd be the exact match for our parallel universe friend?"

I'm not sure what to say to that, so I look away. She invades my space taking my head in her hands. It's a risk, given how I'm feeling at the moment.

"You want out of here?" she whispers.

I perk up. "Whaddya mean?"

"Shhhh! Can't be too loud. They'll hear."

Stevens grabs hold of both straps holding my arms and begins to untie them, her eyes glossy and unfocused. Someone's manipulating her mind and causing her to help me escape. *Crash.* Just outside my door someone drops something, but I ignore it. My left hand is free. I get to my knees and look out the window toward the ground. It's Marek. I'm nearly loose, when the door swings open. It's Agent DeMarco and Smith.

"What's this?" they question. "What're you doing?"

Chancellor Stevens blinks several times and almost coughs up a lung. My freedom is in jeopardy.

"She's just a kid. Don't tie her up like an animal. She won't try to hurt me. Stand down, agents. I'll be fine."

"You're sure?"

"Yes. Please go. Faith and I have much to discuss."

All along I think Marek has everything under control. I'll be back on the ship soon, with the rest of the crew.

Both agents leave but don't go far. I see the back of their shoes underneath the door.

"So, where were we, then? You know there's nothing personal, right? The procedure is painless, and a part of you will live on in infamy."

The tone of her voice has changed, all her movements her own. I drag my IV caddie back to the window and there's no more Marek. I'm on my own again. Shit.

"Nothing personal? Easy for you to say, ma'am. *You're* not dying."

"No, but I understand *you* are, which is good and makes things a little less messy."

"Thanks for all the compassion. Look, what more can we say to each other? You gave the country's soul to the devil, but that doesn't mean I have to."

"You really don't get it, do you? The Niners will revolutionize the world. Well—to some extent they already have."

"Yeah, well—what about when they don't need *you* anymore, huh? When there *are* no more humans? Everyone a Niner? What then? You know they're never gonna let overpopulation run amuck again. That's for sure."

Stevens ambles back toward the door and pokes her head out.

"We've got squirrels downstairs in the tree line; two, maybe three of them. I'll handle Miss Monroe."

Both agents leave their posts. As soon as the door closes, Stevens' alter-ego resurfaces.

"Hurry. Go out the window. Now!"

"Wait! What about this?" I point to the IV in my hand. "Here. I used to be a nurse."

She tugs at the flexible tubing and withdraws the needle from my hand. Then she's back to the counter locating a bandage. I crank the window open, pop out the screen, and realize I've got about a ten-foot drop. She's found something to dress my bleeding hand, and I'm ready to jump. Midstream, she screams and falls to the floor. I'm not sure why, but I bend down to check her pulse and feel a stab right into my neck. My full weight collapses right on top of her.

****

Not fully awake, I hear the rumble of tires on the road. I can barely lift one eye to discover I'm in an ambulance. I'm not alone. Ozzy, Rico, and Star are flat on their backs dead to the world. No movement. The ride gets bumpy, and my head bounces up and down slamming into the side of the vehicle. There's one EMT in the back with us, but he's reading a book. He looks over top to check on us, so I pretend I'm still asleep. Satisfied, he goes back to his story. I'm strapped to the gurney even tighter than when I was in the hospital bed.

Whatever they put in that injection has given me one whale of a headache. My jaw's so sore I can barely swallow let alone open my mouth. I musta cracked it on the floor when I landed. What was up with the chancellor, though? How many split personalities can a person have? Why encourage my escape then knock me out? None of it makes sense. But then again, tooling around with friendly aliens in a spaceship the size of half a football field does?

There's movement now from Star's gurney. She's a little higher up than me, but I know it's her. A gelled-back Mohawk hangs over the gurney's steel frame. Rico and Ozzy have discovered their location now too. Our EMT stands, pulls a handheld mic from the sidewall, and radios the driver up front. He's a middle-aged guy with a wide flat nose and greying brown hair. There are rings around his eyes where he must have worn goggles for some reason and a silver cross around his neck.

He gets his response from the driver and sits back down. We slow, making a sharp turn to the left. All four beds slide in the opposite direction, but we're anchored. Star lifts her head first and spots me right away. A frozen smile hides her tears. She bites her bottom lip in an attempt to control it, but they stream down her face. Rico and Ozzy stare bug-eyed back and forth at each other and eventually notice me.

"Hey," I break the awkwardness.

"Hey," Rico is the first to reply. "We gotta stop meeting like this. What's up with us and truck rides?"

I can't muster a laugh, so I throw him a crooked smile. Pain. Every inch of me. Now I start to tear up. How stupid ironic is it that I can heal *other* people just not myself? Can I return this ability to the Niner training store for a refund? I don't want it anymore.

Ozzy's having the worst time recovering from the drug. A few words come out, but they're garbled. It takes me back to our training when he was a vegetable. Finally, our EMT escort splashes him with some cold water, and he snaps out of it.

"Where are we? What's going on?" He pleads with the man.

"Airport terminal. Private boarding. You're all headed back to the states. Chancellor's orders."

That answers *some* of our questions, but I pump him for more. "Where in the states?"

"Washington, DC. That's all we have. Sorry. We're just the hired help." He goes back to his novel.

One final turn, and the vehicle stops. The EMT calls to the front again.

"You coming around or should I open it?" Nobody answers. "Jimbo? Clancy? You guys up there?" He lifts the latch on the back doors, and they swing open. *Thud.* A sound like a body bouncing off the jump-step gives us hope. Three dark figures leap into the back and stand over us. Their shadows don't look familiar. It seems our cavalry's gotten a makeover. They're Niners all right, just not the right ones.

19

I think I'm in the middle of a nightmare when something cold touches my cheek. I stir but don't wake up. Blodd, the gargoyle from our training session, clings to my hand as I'm about to plunge into a fiery crevice. He's certainly strong enough to drag me to my feet, but he's frozen. Not back to stone this time. Just in a sort of suspended animation. I catch an occasional blink but no other sign he's with me, truly with me.

The rough edges and spikes on his hand make perfect handles, so I climb my way up his arm to solid ground. My effort is wasted. A couple of rumbles later and a tumultuous crack underneath sends us both down into the abyss.

I jerk myself awake where an icy compress straddles my head. Sandpaper fingers remove it, dip it back into a shallow container of cool water, and replace it. I shiver, but so far, it's much better than the nightmare.

A few minutes pass before my vision clears, and I'm startled by my new surroundings. I've *seen* this type of ship before. It has bulbous breathing walls lined with black tar or maybe even dried blood. It's what an inside of a volcano might look like if one could *live* long enough to get a glimpse. Memories of level three of my training where the princess lay in a coma come to mind, only now *I'm* on the raised platform.

I lift up and see my caregiver attending to the others. I recognize him from the concert, but their leader isn't here. We're no longer tied down to anything.

"Where are we?" I ask.

"Safe," he says, moving through his system of keeping each of us cool. "Our apology for the temperature. Since our ship's entrance, our ventilation units have been damaged. No parts here to fix it."

"At the concert, we saw you come through the portal, but there was no ship. So how?" I sit up, rubbing my temples and pulling my hair out of my eyes. He offers me a yellow liquid, but I decline. I've had enough drugs for one day.

"Ships can't travel through the same vortex as Niners. They have their *own* coordinates. That's how Marek and Bale got their ship through as well."

"You know Marek and Bale?" My voice rises.

"Yes. Enemies. Servants of Azuna." No doubt or suspicion in his words.

Any amount of hope I had dwindles, but at least we're away from the Feds. Ozzy is the next to sit up. His ashen face looks even stranger in the red glowing lights. He's almost highlighter pink. Rico jumps down off his bed and rouses Star. We congregate in the center.

"Everyone cool?" Rico asks. We all nod. I'd like to introduce our doctor, but I don't know his name. Before I even ask, he's by my side leading me to a new section of the ship. Everyone else follows. Dark grey slotted panels filled with an assortment of weapons capture our attention as we stroll down a narrow corridor. We enter an all-glass room with the same wall material on the floor now. It's like walking into an enormous blood vessel. Probably just advanced lighting technology but still eerie, nonetheless. We wait thirty seconds before an elevator rises opposite the entrance. Out steps their Thor-like leader. He's not quite as mean and scary as he was at the concert but every bit as intense.

"I am Dredge the Destroyer, mortal enemy to the Niner government. Now, I want to know why does Azuna want you four? You're merely children." He paces back and forth in front of us, towering over even Ozzy. I'm taken back a bit by his *children* insult, but at his apparent age I guess it makes sense.

"Have you been living under a rock?" My biting tongue returns for an encore performance. I'm getting pretty tired of aliens in general right now. "Azuna and her henchmen need our souls, *if* they wanna keep living on *this* planet that is. I'm surprised they never told you."

"What happens if she doesn't get them?" he asks, a tiny grin lights his weathered face. Some signs indicate he knows the answer to all of these questions, but for *some* reason he's playing coy.

"Bye, bye. Not sure if she melts or just evaporates into the wind, but she dies, along with her council members. She can swap for an inferior soul for a while, but each time she does, she loses power. Hey! How come *you* guys aren't dead yet? No offense."

Dredge pretends he doesn't hear my question. Rico and Ozzy inspect all the weaponry that moves from the room and extends into the hall. Some are mounted on the wall while others are in silver marked containers. The familiar boomerangs are lined up by sizes and colors. Palm-sized laser guns, like an English Billy club with a sensor at the tip. There is an entire arsenal that covers the length of one wall and then some. Our weapons have been removed. The holsters lie there uncloaked.

"You guys are locked and loaded, aren't you?" Ozzy says. "There's enough here to destroy an entire city, maybe even a country."

"We know. We weren't sure of the kind of reception we'd get. But we came through virtually unnoticed. The ship's D-Level has a few more catastrophic *toys*, but we're hoping it doesn't come to that."

Star picks up a boomerang to test the weight, and Dredge is behind her in a flash. For a large man, he's quick. Too quick. Unnatural. "Doesn't come to what? An all-out war?" she says.

He nudges her away from the weapons and back to the rest of us in the room, minus the object of her curiosity. Star obliges without incident. Not even she's dumb enough to test *this* guy's fighting abilities. "That's not why we're here.

We came at a special request."

Dredge walks us back through the corridor into the main deck. His pilots are busy keeping the craft in the air and monitoring the skies. I'm no expert on radar, but there's a large blip to our immediate west. My heart flutters. It must be Marek.

"Special request?" Ozzy says. "From whom?"

"Vice-Chancellor Hunt, the only member of the council willing to listen to reason. I was first in command in the military. Everything you see, I conceived. Created. All designed to ward off all threats. But our people started trusting *me* more than Azuna and her father. Talk of an uprising. Many wanted *me* in charge, and that's when it happened." His warrior face changes. Sadness breaks through his outer shell. We listen intently as he's busy choking back his tears. For a being without a soul, he's a pretty good actor.

"Azuna destroyed my life, my family. I took a few loyal soldiers and fled into the mountains while turning up at calculated intervals to foil *some* of her plans. Her bargain with your planet came from her father, Ajai."

"So you really *were* living under a rock. But you knew of her plans?" I say.

"The convergence was forthcoming, yes. It would occur three times in a decade, and then only once more. Like Marek and Bale, we tried to catch the *first* departure but failed. Azuna unveiled her *own* new technology, a pulse wave to render all her enemies powerless for a limited time, and her portal extenders. We were the test subjects. I lost more men and women that day. Ah, but revenge has many disguises."

"Let me guess? *We're* the disguise?" Rico says, leaning on a nearby stack of empty plastic-like containers. They slide out from under him sending him down to the floor in a heap. His smooth move breaks some of the tension.

"You said Marek and Bale were your enemies, but they've been helping all of us; Luther and my father, even Luther's family. We don't understand."

"Deception, all of it. I'm afraid there is so much you don't understand, much like the Kurd myth."

"But Marek was there under the window at the hospital in Germany, controlling Azuna's mind. I almost got away." I try to refute his logic.

"So sure it was him, are you?" Dredge laughs. What he does next makes me weak. I stagger back into Star's waiting arms. Like watching a police monitor scroll through prime suspects' faces until the right one pops up, Dredge morphs into all kinds of people. First, he's Star. Then he's me. Ozzy. Rico. A few more faces scoot by, and I recognize one in particular. Blodd's. He stops his magic trick and lands on Marek. I swear he's standing right in front of me. Everything was identical including his tight uniform, his broad shoulders. I shake my head.

"*I* stood under the tree at the hospital. I wanted your leader to believe it was Marek. Agents spotted me, so I had to leave in a hurry. Don't worry. I would have caught you when you jumped." He's back to himself now.

Marek and Bale? Working for Azuna? That's crazy. Why even bother to save us during the transport? Take the time to train us? Before I can ask any more questions, Ozzy takes charge.

"What about our training? Strengthening our souls, so Azuna can't assimilate? To what advantage was it?"

Dredge leads us back down a different passageway into a chamber with monitors and a conference table. We sit together as he and his men hit switches and buttons in sequence then join us at the table. All the monitors turn blue like they're waiting for a signal.

"Marek and Bale didn't agree with their mother's plan to kill off your people," he says.

"Wait. Azuna is their *mother?*" Our voices echo through the room.

"She is, only you must understand something about us Niners. We may *look* and *sound* a lot like humans, but that's where it stops. Loyalty has been instilled in us since creation. As much as they hated the idea of activation chips, they wouldn't disobey their own family. They thought they'd find a *better* way for Niners to live on Earth."

"But how?" Ozzy asks. "Last time I checked, no one can create a soul. You either have one or you don't."

Two of his men stand intending to demonstrate something, but out of nowhere Ozzy leaps across the table to stop them.

"No. No need to show us, please," he shouts.

"So—you're a see-er," Dredge says. "Maybe you should tell your friends what you now know."

"*They're* the guinea pigs, Faith. The ones with the artificial souls Bale spoke of. Only, there are terrible side effects. They were about to—" Dredge cuts in.

"True. Let's just say, we can't always *control* our abilities, and our *emotions* get a little out of hand. Sometimes the two don't *mix* very well. That's why the program was scrapped."

"Sounds just like humans to me," Star jokes. "You'll fit right in here."

"But what they have done is not right, playing creator and deciding who lives and dies and when. She would never do that to her own people. In time, we could have *solved* all our problems."

"How?" Rico asks. "We've got our own issues, but your breed pretty much solved *that* one for us, huh? We were killing each other pretty well even *before* they put a chip in us. That's my opinion. Plus all the thousands of diseases still out there."

"Diseases," Ozzy whispers. "The true checks and balances system. No *wonder* your planet is wall to wall people. Why haven't your scientists, your doctors figured it out? They're more advanced than any of us. Just add bacteria or disease back into the environment. It's a simple solution."

One of the smaller Niners clicks a button on a remote, and images appear on the flat screens. A laboratory. Men and women scramble back and forth between something that looks like a monster generator. Out pops a series of round chambers. In one simultaneous movement, at least twelve doctors empty a beaker full of liquid into the individual chambers and they close. The contraption blows off some steam then retreats back into the ground. A steel hexagon marks the spot in the floor. Green lines of light zig-zag back and forth over top of the exit point as two-foot arm-like gizmos rise up and point in all directions. Red lights glow at the tips.

"We call it *Pro-em*, the *beginning* of the end of our race.

Kind of like a worldwide air purification system. As soon as any disease or virus erupts, Pro-em kills it. Nobody dies, at least, not *enough* people. Originally the *expiration* technology was created for *our* planet. A self-monitoring population control device. Earth was the testing ground until Ajai changed Azuna's mind. He convinced her that earth was the *perfect* alternative. We've run out of food and resources. Yet starvation can't kill us, so we suffer instead. Turn on each other," Dredge explains.

"So? Just shut it off or blow it up," Star says.

"Believe me. We've tried. Humans say this is painting ourselves into a corner, or perhaps being too smart for our own good. Hundreds of failsafe devices were built into the unit from massive electromagnetic charges to micro robots all designed for one purpose. Protect Pro-em."

"That sucks," says Rico.

Dredge gives him a puzzled look probably not familiar with that expression. There's a wildness and warmth in Dredge. He's the big brother who will stand up for you against the bullies and sometimes *bully* himself. I feel like I've known him longer, but how is that so?

I flash to the big reveal of his transformation ability and remember a face. Blodd.

"Back to our training," I demand. "Did any of it matter? I mean, how easy is it gonna be for Azuna and her counselors to take us down?"

"I can only assume that Marek needed each of you to obtain Niner qualities *unlike* your future hosts. So when they assimilated, they'd take on those abilities, and it would render them more powerful. They'll all lose some power gathering souls until they receive their perfect match, which they came close to doing already."

Huh? When? My heart races. I can't breathe. It's like Azuna's got her hand wrapped around my waist, my chest again. I work hard to keep my panic attack from the others, but I'm sure they're on to me.

"Faith?" says Star. "You don't look so good."

I choke down my fear, and it is way too easy this time. "In the training module when we met the princess, that was real, wasn't it?" Silence. "Wasn't it?" I scream, not as controlled now. I swing my arm to my side, and Dredge, his two men, and my friends fly off their chairs into the wall. They're dazed but not seriously injured.

"Hold it!" Rico yells. "I *think* you just answered that question. Easy does it, Faith. No enemies here. Right gang?" They rise helping Dredge and his men to their feet then cower in the corner.

"Did she take my soul." Tears form quickly. "Somebody tell me, please?" I raise my hand again as if to strike.

There's no hitch in his step or hesitation in his walk. Dredge transforms into Blodd, my gargoyle friend, and approaches.

"No. Not fully. She tried, but there's something inside you that kept her from gaining access. You destroyed one of her ships. The training moved to real life when she re-calibrated the session. It must have been when Marek's hiding place was compromised."

I simmer down some, but it doesn't last long. A static message squeals from the bridge over the intercom. It's a ship, and we're locked in its radar. Ten seconds to impact.

20

The blow hits us square, but shields hold, a slight turbulence. We're rocked back on our heels a little. Maybe our airline companies should look into this alien spaceship technology. Another round barely rattles us again. The four of us strap ourselves into a padded bench along the far wall just to be safe. Orders from Dredge.

"It's Azuna! She's got military assistance. I believe it's called a helicopter. Faith? You might feel her pull soon. Here. Take this!" Her *pull*?

He hands me a square like a Rubik's cube only electronic.

"What's this?" I ask. "Should I be playing games at a time like this?"

"Yes. You should. *Especially* at a time like this. She won't be able to lock into your energy. It'll confuse her."

"But I hate video games. I don't even know what to do with it!"

"Exactly. Just hit the lit segments, and it'll show you. We've got Marek and his brigade coming up on us too. I'm sorry. I must leave!"

I follow his directions and watch as he steps onto a disc in the middle of the bridge and descends into the floor. Level-D comes to thought and turns my stomach. High-powered weaponry. The *big* stuff. Enough to demolish a whole country let alone a chopper or even Marek's ship. I'm torn. Half my mind focused on the glowing square in my hands, and the other praying Luther and his family aren't shot out of the sky. Marek and Bale? They owe me an explanation for sure, but I couldn't bear to lose Misty or Kandy. Luther's family. *They're* not working for Azuna. I'm sure of it. Just innocent game pieces landing on all the wrong squares.

What a giant mess. Not at all how I imagined it. I wish I could tell the future. The *future*. Ozzy. I stare down the row of us, and he's perched on the end. Sweat beads form on his brow, his shiny head. I beg him for some foreknowledge, but he's too quiet. Rico and Star chime in. We're allies to the end.

"Spill it," Star shouts above the blaring alarm. The pilot at the controls notices our angst, flips a switch, and our ears find relief. "What did you see? How are we getting outta this one?"

"You really don't wanna know," he says, staring smack dab down at the floor. A frog suddenly develops in his throat, and he works to dislodge it.

"Come on," Rico tries. "We're all family here. We gotta know. Do we make it?"

I see the war inside of Ozzy escalating. His nose wrinkles, grimacing as he nods his head up and down in a yes pattern. He's sending mixed signals.

"There's nothing I can do. I've tried. Every scenario comes out the same. I'm sorry. *You're mine so*—" His voice changes.

Three of us slide away from him. This must be the *pull* Dredge was talking about, but I've left the light square on the table. I disconnect my harness and rush to retrieve it, but I'm too late. Glancing over my shoulder at my three friends, their images begin to pixilate. Extreme cold floods my body. I'm light as a balloon. I twist and turn at the square in my hands, punch the lights, follow the designs, but it's no use. I'm disappearing. The artist made a mistake; he's erasing me from their existence. Deep down I laugh and bear down, like it's going to help me resist. All my training is useless now.

Star's the first out of her seat attempting a rescue, but I'm nothing but fine mist now. Her hands, her arms, swipe right through me. They're pleading with the pilot, Dredge's other soldiers to do something, but they don't. They can't. I'm no longer a passenger. I'm the flash shadow on the wall in the fun house, merely an impression. Their faces are strewn with grief, eyes so full of tears they can't see. They can't see my pain. My heartache either. I've failed them, just like I failed my mom.

****

Familiar walls greet me as I awake. My house, exactly how I remembered with all our pictures on my dresser. Ruby, my stuffed elephant propped up in the corner. My closet is open and every stitch of clothing was right where I left it that day. *That day.* Saturday morning. My time to learn how long I had to live with a short trip to the expiration station in Atlanta. An hour's ride, and then I'd have the rest of the day to study.

Dad was already somewhere, but he never left me a note this time. Except things weren't *exactly* the same. Noises. Downstairs in the kitchen. I throw off the covers, jam my slippers on my feet, and practically leap down the stairs. Both feet slide out from under me as I land, but I catch myself last minute on the rail. The TV's on in the kitchen, sound down low. I turn the corner, and I can smell her. Victoria Secrets. Amber Romance. My mom's favorite.

Her back is to me. A fluffy dark blue robe snuggles her modest frame. Her latest haircut looks a bit stringy, unwashed, but still shiny. Slightly shorter style than she was used to, but she'd said it'd framed her face better. Made her look thinner, but she was always thin enough for me. Perfect, in fact.

I approach. I'm caught up in the moment. Mom's alive and busy making blueberry pancakes, our normal Saturday routine.

"Mom?" I whisper. She turns around. It's really her, minus the dreadful circles around her eyes as the cancer took its toll. Glossy white teeth. Penetrating green eyes. A few wrinkles around her mouth, her forehead, but still beautiful.

"Morning, sleepyhead. We had nothing planned, so I let you rest. I hope that was okay."

Not sure how to respond, I sit and begin playing with my fork. The Georgia sun is blazing today; summer heat already radiating through the windows. *Summer.* For some reason just the sound of the season as it leaves my mouth sets my brain to scrambling. Something seems *off.* I rewind my past 24 hours over and over again, but they're not *my* memories. Talking to Jensen until eight when my favorite show came on. Doing a little homework on the computer, helping Dad fix the sink in the bathroom, and finally kissing mom goodnight. It's all there like a ripe fruit ready for me to pick, but it's *too* ripe. Maybe even forbidden. I want to taste and forget. Wallow in the sweet sensations, but with them comes a stabbing. An occasional searing pain right through the heart of my chest back to my shoulder blades. My tattoo burns. It feels bloody and fresh.

The syrup tastes real enough. Ice-cold milk is good. Mom makes light conversation as she joins me and goes on like she hasn't a care in the world. Like she'd never withered away like a raisin and died in my arms. She's fully alive, healthy, and strong even; rising up from the table to carry boxes of old clothing down into the basement. Never out of breath. Never puking until she turned green. Just Mom and exactly how I remembered her.

Her last trip up from the basement's when I witness a first glitch. It's subtle. I probably would have missed it if I hadn't already been feeling slightly off-kilter. Her eyes change from green to brown to highlighter blue and back to her original green. I rush to the half-bath and stare at myself in the mirror. It's me all right; 16-year-old me. Mom died when I was only 13. This can't be real. None of it. Authentic memories linger, but I can't access them. Something is blocking them. A constant pressure forces me back into the moment and won't let me leave it.

Mom brushes by noticing my odd behavior. I turn side to side examining my profile and delve into the mirror with my head trying to hunt for something. *Anything* that could help me remember, but the pain grows. The more I struggle the worse I get.

She reaches into the cabinet and pulls out some ointment, scissors, white tape, and a clean bandage. Before I know it, she's undressing the wound on my back. My praying mantis tattoo appears to be glowing, seeping blood. Her touch comforts and calms me. Most of the pain in my chest, in my head subsides because now she's just Mom taking care of her little angel. Her only child. And I'm not mourning her death or battling anger. I'm letting go, allowing her back into my life. My heart. My soul. *Soul.* A twinge of pain returns, but her strokes on my neck, down my back soothe me. I don't want to hurt anymore or fight. I just want to drink in this twinkle before the stars all go out, before the bright lights from the city make them go away. I forget. Where's my sarcasm and lightheartedness? I'm not me anymore, and it's okay. I'm okay. Faith Monroe. Wanted. Accepted. Genuinely loved.

"Any plans for today?" she asks finishing up her doctor's duties.

I honestly don't know what to say or how to respond. Did I have any plans? What day is it exactly? And where's Dad? Maybe *he'd* help me slay this memory dragon.

"Faith? Are you okay? The doctors said you may have

a few bad days from the chemo and the radiation." Mom escorts me back to the sofa and props me up with her favorite silky pillow. It's obvious I've been spending some time downstairs. Half-empty cups, candy wrappers, and a crusted-over bowl of cereal adorn the coffee table. An abundance of Kleenex lines the floor as well.

"What's wrong with me?" I ask, the words chemo and radiation gnaw at my insides.

"Just rest, Dear. You've had a difficult month going to the doctors with long days at the hospital, splitting time between your bedroom and down here."

I'm confused. When have I ever been this sick? I had a little bitty blood disorder. My growing up and a six-month treatment fixed it all. At least, I thought it did. I keep reaching for the correct multiple choice answer, but I'm not sure which letter to choose. A. nightmare. B. insanity. I haven't ruled B out yet because crazy covers a lot of what I'm experiencing right now. C. Mom is an alien trying to trick me into believing she's my mother. D. *I'm* the alien living in a parallel universe dying of some stupid disease nobody on the planet can even pronounce. While I'm kinda falling in love with choice B, I'm praying it's A. What's the damn rule for choosing multiple choice answers again? If two answers sound almost identical except for a few words, choose one of these. Try to eliminate all distracters. I wonder if that includes the fact that Mom's eyes keep changing colors? Eventually my torture ends when the doorbell rings.

Buzz. Buzz.

Unbelievably Mom sits there in a daze, so I rise to open the door. It's a pizza delivery guy. He looks vaguely familiar.

Dark skin, bushy eyebrows; maybe he is Arabian or possibly Latino. It's not easy to tell with his Mama's Pizza cap on his head turned to the side like a gangbanger.

"Sausage pizza for a Faith Monroe, sorry we're late. Uh—I mean, *it's* late. We had a little trouble with the ship." He's a nervous wreck. Stuttering over his words and rocking back and forth on his feet.

"The ship? Are you high? I can't believe they let you guys deliver pizzas on drugs. Mom? Did you order us a pizza?" I shout. Silence. "Mom?" She finally arrives at the door.

"No. Sorry, young man. You must have the wrong address." Mom's more stern than I've ever seen her before, like the kid's trying to kidnap me or something. She slams the door in his face before he can respond.

"Idiotic teenagers!" she growls. "Always messing things up."

I keep the pizza and carry it to the kitchen counter. No chance Mom's gonna let me return it. It might be a little early for lunch, especially since I just had breakfast, but I open the box. It's a sausage pizza accompanied by a note. Mom keeps her attention out the window at the delivery kid, so I read the letter. *The band is back together now. We want you to join us soon. Be prepared.* The band? What band? I sing a little bit but not loud enough for anyone to hear me. Things keep getting weirder and weirder around here.

I stuff the secret letter in my pajama pocket and take a slice. Not bad if you like cold pizza. Sausage tastes sweet. Just the way I like it. I run the message over in my head a few more times as Mom approaches, her hair a mess and covering half her face. She staggers into a chair placing her head in her hands and rubbing the back of her neck. She looks as bad as I felt a little while ago.

"Hungry?" I ask, acting insensitive. "Tastes pretty good."

"No. Go ahead. You need your strength." I capture an eerie grin as she whips out a hair tie and pulls back her tangled locks. Her eyes dart back and forth to the microwave clock kinda like she's waiting for something or maybe someone. I'm not sure.

"Waiting for someone?" I ask, pure innocence in the question.

"You might say that. A new soul." She snickers.

"Mom? You're scaring me. Who's new soul?"

"Why—yours, my dear."

21

My multiple guess quiz selections slam me in the noggin again, only this time I'm wising up. Letter C, Mom's an alien being pretending to be my mom comes to the forefront along with a lightning bolt of locked up memories. The sausage on the pizza acts like a key to unlock the power over me now. Suddenly I'm me again. The *real* me.

"Azuna!" I take one step toward the front door but get knocked to the floor. My knees feel like they've been whacked with a baseball bat. I fall backwards, whiplashing my head and neck. Azuna stands over me, a horrible sight considering she's my mother. She is a raging version, but still an exact replica of the woman who raised me. How do you mount a counterattack against your own flesh and blood?

She gives me no chance to fight back, twisting her index finger in the air and flipping me over the back of the sofa, a perfect landing flat on my back but cushioned this time.

"Were you going somewhere?" she asks.

The first thing that pops into my mind is *crazy,* but I don't bother wasting any of my good material on her this time.

"Probably not yet," I say, praying the good guys are just outside the door ready to pounce. *Getting the band back together.* That's the best they could do? *How was I supposed to figure that one out?*

Out of nowhere, she turns her robe belt inside out revealing some kind of handheld electronic device. It's much thinner than a remote control, about the size of a credit card. One punch launches a cool green force field around me. The current stands the hair up on my entire body. I'm a prisoner on my very own Lazy-boy sofa. Next she's on a miniature cell phone speaking gibberish, just for my benefit, and circling the doors and windows. She's a pet dog that is begging to go outside. Something's definitely not going according to her plans. A grab and dash for my soul after I die might work on some stiff who couldn't care less about where his soul goes in the afterlife, but I'm still attached to mine. She's gonna have to stay for the full-course meal. No fast food here.

Several calls later, and she's back in my space acting all charming again. She sits in the recliner and puts her feet up on the table.

"Well, now. It looks like we've reached somewhat of a stalemate. I say *somewhat* because you won't be leaving this home without giving up your soul. We will just go about it a little *differently.*"

"Yeah, sure. Good luck with that." Why panic? Obviously she would have already killed me if she could. So there's some reason why she hasn't yet. I'll play her little game to learn a little more before my daring rescue.

"Feisty, aren't you? No wonder you're the perfect match for me. But I assure you, young lady. You're *no* match for me, nor will you ever be. You want to be back with your mother, don't you? I mean, the past hour, didn't it feel so right?"

I want to spit at her, but I'm afraid I'll get electrocuted. How ironic. News headline reads: *Faith kills herself peeing on the fence. Makes it easy for Azuna to swipe her soul.* It's funny, but for a while it *did* seem right. Exactly what I've wanted since she passed. But not now. Not this way. She can't win.

"Can I ask you one question? What's your end game? What do you hope to gain by living here? Our world's almost as screwed up as yours."

"You know nothing about my world. Only what you've been told. My two sons have active imaginations."

So Dredge told the truth. Marek and Bale are related to Mommy Dearest.

"Yeah, about them. They may have a little *trouble* on their horizon. A certain gargoyle? Changes form? High-tech weaponry?"

She looks surprised. A flinch in her confidence, but I give her credit. I don't suppose you get to be the leader of an entire world without some resolve.

"Dredge? He's here? How? We had him imprisoned before we crossed."

"Well, looks like there ain't no prison that can hold *that* big boy. And guess what else? I think he's a little sweet on me. Not too fond of you, though."

I'm shocked by her reactions. I thought she'd be on the phone calling for reinforcements, but she's passive, weak, almost out of breath. My stabbing pain's returned. I'm light-headed. Unable to stay focused. It's a perfect time for some dramatics or a shoot-out, a ride off into the sunset. But I'll need to be carried. No doubt about it.

Azuna gathers herself enough to make her way into the kitchen where she splashes her face with water. Her true form returns. I'm no longer staring at my mother's ghost, which is a good thing. It's funny, but her attempt at reviving herself affects me as well. I no longer feel like someone's trying to rip my heart out of my chest. I'm relieved and afraid at the same time. She's elegant, even when she's ill, all the curves in just the right places for however old she is. Do they even *have* birthdays on her planet?

She's gained back some strength making one more call on her mini-phone. A white earpiece stands out against her wavy dark hair. Once again, the language doesn't register, so I don't bother to eavesdrop. I'm incapacitated anyhow. Too bad I didn't get the laser alien DNA. I consider shooting out my healing energy for a second, but I'm worried about the consequences. She's still in the middle of her chit-chat, so I figure what the heck. It couldn't hurt.

I reflect back to when I helped Ozzy. Zero-in on his wound. I need an object of my compassion, so I stare at the rotten apple in the bowl on the kitchen table. It's not a person, but it'll have to do. Brown. Bruised. Hurting. Out the corner of my eye, Azuna catches on, taps the ear piece off, and steps right in between my blast. She flies through the heavy oak table back-first into the corner, just missing the built-in hutch. I follow the sparks, but the force field holds steady. In seconds, she's back on her feet; a huge grin echoes back at me.

"You're already part of me, you know?" she says, stepping through the green haze and stroking my hair. "But I need the *rest* of you. You have no idea what it's like to feel nothing. Your love for others? It's natural. Inbred. Mine is, well—let's just say, mine's manufactured. Mechanical. We've so much in common."

I push her hand away from my face and plop back down on the couch. I want to drive my fist through her ceramic face, break her perfect nose, but she seems revived, powerful again.

"Leave me alone," I scream. "I'm nothing like you. I never will be. Just get it over with already! Kill me!"

She strolls back toward the side window by the main door as she speaks. "I can't. Not that I don't want or need you to die. I do, if I have any hopes of staying here. But it seems like my son, Bale, has double-crossed me. Your training module. Your *gift*."

At first I'm confused. My logic train has jumped tracks. Maybe Bale really *was* trying to help us? Marek? They're *not* in cahoots with their mom. "Oh, I get it." And I really do this time. "I *can't* die, can I? Not with my healing powers. So you can't take my—"

"True. But—and there is always a but—there is still a way for me to extract your soul. We have the technology, just not here with me now." Her voice is staccato, like she's making things up as she goes, trying to hide something.

I'm getting tired from listening to her mumbo-jumbo about stealing my soul, so I decide to stall a little more. Give my uber talented friends more time to figure out a plan. I change the subject, returning to a question she never answered.

"So you get my soul and live here. Heck, maybe you even get unlucky enough to be American chancellor. So what? How does that help your planet? There's only a few of you here, right?"

"A few hundred, but that's irrelevant." She looks comfortable that there's no one sneaking up on us right now, so she strides back over and sits next to me this time. I wish I had her power to glide in and out of the green screen, but I don't. She goes on with her explanation.

"It's not that we *want* to leave our planet. We *have* to now. All the auric, the raw gold we mined? It weakened the core. I bet Marek and Bale never told you about *that*, did they?"

"Nope. Musta left that out in-between preparing us for a battle we can't win."

"Idealistic, those two boys. Totally against the expiration experiment, especially testing it on Earth. They truly believed they'd find a better way. When my father agreed to the auric exports to your world, he had no idea of the consequences. Once he saw earth's potential, and their tenderness for their people and that overpopulation was a growing problem here as well, he lost it. He grew irrational and shipped way more than we should have. Our world rebelled.

They placed me in charge."

"What if there was another way? Our scientists, doctors? We could work together to solve *all* our problems."

"All due respect, but is there anyone on your planet who's figured out how to beat the time-space continuum? Developed a way to tap into the natural and sometimes unnatural talents inside every person? Manufactured an air filtration system designed to eliminate most disease? Built magnificent high-tech—"

I cut her off in my head before I puke. Niner's advanced technology exceeds ours by a landslide. If anyone could have discovered a way to save their planet, they would have. I hate the fact that she's beginning to make too much sense.

I've missed having these kinds of talks. Mom and I used to do this every day. Watch the nightly news and have all the world's problems figured out before bedtime. While sitting here all cozy with the woman intending to end my existence isn't exactly a favorable substitute, I'm resigned; resigned to the fact that if Dredge or Marek or someone doesn't show up soon, I'm toast. Azuna has every good reason to gain control over Earth. Reestablish her race, new and improved Niners from soulless to soulful. When elementary kids learn the planets in a couple of years, they'll ask, "What happened to Earth? Why'd we change the name?" And of course history will read like this. *Small Town girl, Faith Monroe, sacrificed her very soul to save planet Nine, formally known as Earth.*

Formally known as Earth rings in my ears. We're not talking about a pop singer changing his name, or a gas station changing affiliation, or even a sports legend changing teams. Won't all the online textbook companies have to change their galaxy maps? I make light because the actuality frightens me. I grow queasy. Azuna sees me struggling and does that 'I'm-just-trying-to-do-the-right-thing' pat on my back. Her artificial sympathy beams. It's almost convincing, but I know better. She's not capable of really caring. She's more robot than human. She's programmed to love her people, her planet.

"Remember when I said we have so much in common?" she says.

"Gee—how could I forget." I dazzle her with my humor again.

"We're both dying, you know? You won't perish, but I will. This temporary soul is frail. I can't withstand it much longer."

"Sucks to be you, huh?"

"No, you don't understand." Blood starts to drip from her nose onto the leather cushion. She stands, almost embarrassed by the sight. "I've already stolen some of your essence. Some of your blood now runs through me as does mine through you. Your surge a few minutes ago bought me a little time, but not much. When I die, you'll lose all your abilities."

"You're lying!" I yell. "It's a clever ploy, but I'm not buying it."

Before she can say another word, the front door explodes off its hinges and lands right in front of us. I rise up on my knees in expectation. I've been found. I'll escape. Azuna will die, and I can go back to my boring teenage life.

The dirt and fog from the explosion clears. Azuna taps

her ear once again for an update. I expect fear, dread on her face, but she's thrilled, almost giddy. As giddy as a *robot* can be. An older gentleman enters first, odd clothing, like he plucked a few things off a clothes line. Grey hair, goatee, dark skin. An awfully close resemblance to Azuna. And that's when I remember back to our *first* encounter. Marek took us back in time to his planet for the summit. All the leaders sat around the table, he and Bale arguing against the expiration device. This man right next to Azuna is her father. Oh, shit. And right behind him? Marek and Bale. No Luther. No Kandy. No Dredge. Niners. All of them, one big happy family.

22

Yay! My saviors have arrived. I mock under my breath. Marek and Bale look dirty with dark soot on their clothes and their faces with criss-cross cuts on their hands and neck. Apparently they got the upper hand in a battle, but it wasn't an easy one. Bale walks with a noticeable limp. Marek is his crutch. They move near me like they expect a hug or a handshake, but I pull Mom's pillow up over my face. I don't heal traitors.

"Look who I found roaming the skies," The older man quips. "A slight detour, but everything's under control. Thanks to the American military. They truly appreciated some of our weaponry. Not quite the skill of a Niner soldier, but they learn quickly. Dredge *does* have a weakness, you know."

Azuna nods. Her nose still caked with dried blood. Her eyes are crystal blue but bloodshot, watery. She's hanging on by a thread. A half minute passes when we're greeted by a couple of army soldiers dressed like special ops forces. They drag a homeless woman, about thirty-five, into the house and throw her on the floor. There's no way of knowing if these guys are Niners or Americans, but that's irrelevant as they shoot the woman in the head. I hide behind the pillow, but the smell of gunpowder and the very thought makes me lose it. I empty my stomach down the back of the sofa, trying not to soil my hiding place, my comfy rock.

I peek up for a second and watch as Azuna rips the woman's soul right out of the air and collapses in her father's arms. It's supernatural, eerie. Something I can live the rest of my life without ever seeing again. Azuna's body looks like a lump of clay bulging and bubbling, twisting the woman's soul into her body, at times she looked just like the lady and then back to herself, a sickening special effect from a werewolf horror film. In minutes, her father lays Azuna down on the floor and waits. A black bracelet over his left wrist monitors her vitals. Her eyes open, but rather than a thanks or warm embrace, she slaps him.

"You idiot! I'm losing my abilities as it is! I could have waited until I assimilated Faith!"

"No time, my dear." He rubs his cheek trying to remove the sting of her blow *and* her words. Marek leaves Bale on his own and lifts his mother to her feet, glancing over his shoulder to me like it's some type of apology, but I go back to my blind. I can't stand to look at any of them right now.

I hear a series of boots shuffle around near the executed

woman and pray they've removed her. More unintelligible language occurs, but things are different this time. I understand every word. My brain translates every sentence. More of Azuna's DNA at work, no doubt. *She's scared. I don't blame her. We must find some other way.* Marek's words. *Not an option, son. The summit is near. Every leader on earth desires our auric. Demands our technology. We can't turn back now. They'll let us all die.* Her father's words. Bale's handiwork. *Messed everything up. We'll need the ship's lab.* Azuna. *Uh, that could be a problem. Dredge. Luther. His family.* I expect the worst and figure they all died in the battle. Bale continues. *They've commandeered the vessel. We did what we could. Disabled a few life support systems, but you know how crafty Dredge is. He got them all back online. If grandfather wouldn't have come along, we'd be gone.*

Feeling a bit less nauseous, I end their private meeting. "Yoo-hoo? Just so you know, I just heard everything. So, you can like, use English. I won't mind." I gain some confidence back knowing Luther and Dredge are out there.

"What about my friends? Were they injured?" I ask.

"Not sure. They endured some drastic hits. We're sorry this spiraled so out of control," Bale says.

"Save your apology for someone who cares. You're all a bunch of alien scum to me now. Lying to me. Tricking me into training. Letting you take my blood and screwing with my head and my body. You're a bunch of sickos!"

"But—" Marek tries again, but his grandfather stops him.

"Enough! Chancellor Stevens is expecting us in two hours, and we're not going to disappoint her."

"What about the assimilation?" Azuna asks.

"We have three days," he says. "We'll figure something out by then. It's our best chance at getting *everyone* here! Something we've all dreamed about, remember?"

"Something *you've* dreamed about, Ajai," Bale says. "Not us." That newborn puppy face hits me once again. Bale isn't very good at hiding things. Is there still someone in there I can trust, someone who won't let this happen? Whatever he did to keep Azuna from having her way, must count for something, right? I swear, sometimes I think he does have a soul.

Ajai sends his signal out to the waiting soldiers who enter with ski masks like before and a type of cargo net I remember seeing on the wall in Dredge's ship. Azuna deactivates the force field prison as the men drape the net over top of me. The guy on the left winks as he turns the dial, but it's not intended for me at all; it's meant for Bale. Maybe even Marek, who are both doing their best to distract Azuna and Ajai. The net zings out a current that makes me tingle all over. Both soldiers duck under with me and a bright flash goes off. Soon my home is getting smaller and smaller as I thrust through the roof, the sky, two strong arms keeping me secure. Flaming missiles detonate all around us, but they have little to no effect on our ascent back to Marek's ship. A clear window opens and sucks us back through a tube depositing us into the control room.

"Welcome back," says Ozzy. Star nods in agreement, but I can tell she's been crying. Never one to reveal herself openly very much, she's distraught over something. Luther and one of Dredge's men, my rescuers, disengage the glowing net. Kandy and the rest of the family circle me. One group hug later, and I realize something's missing. Or rather a *couple* of someones aren't there, Rico and Dredge. They step away one step at a time until they're at arm's length, and that's when I press them.

"Okay—so is somebody gonna tell me what's going on? Why all the gloom and doom? The band's back together, *with* our most powerful ally yet. Speaking of Dredge, where is he? And Rico?"

Luther is the first to put his arm around me followed by everyone else. Even Micah gets into the act, normally not one for drama. All of a sudden I'm unsteady. My knees buckle. Ozzy grips me the tightest, but it's only so he can lead me to a stool.

"You need to sit for this. Trust me." He and Star race to get me something to drink, a beaker full of something that looks and tastes a lot like blue Gatorade. "Drink it all. Your little flight up here made you dehydrated. Change in altitude, speed, charged ions from my recalibrations."

"*Your* recalibrations, huh? Are you going all alien on me now too?" I ask, downing the last of my refreshment.

"Nope," Star jumps in. "Genius here tweaked the Niner tech and turned the sucker into a protective jet pack. Knew exactly what to do somehow."

"So? What're you keeping from me? Rico? Dredge? Are they on some other mission? Playing the local comedy club?"

"I think Donte called it stasis," Luther says.

"Stasis? Why stasis? What's wrong with them? Is that a quarantine or something?" I start to panic.

Star spills the truth. Not a word leaves her lips before her eyes water up. She begins then stops to choke back her emotion taking turns looking at the ground and then at me. "Rico took a violent hit from an exploding console on Dredge's ship. He took the brunt of it. Ozzy was already out cold. No way to stop it. Donte figures he absorbed over a thousand volts. He put him in stasis, so he wouldn't lose his soul."

I walk away from all of them to set my emotional bearings. It's always an adventure, a challenge until someone dies. Not just a stranger someone. A friend. Like a brother. Before I completely break down I realize what I have. *I'm the medicine.* I am the cure for his dormant body.

"How long?" I ask, my voice raspy from nasal drip with a throat full of salty tears. "How long has he been dead?"

"Over two hours, Faith. I really don't think—"

Luther tries to talk some sense into me, but I cut him off.

"Don't *think!*" I scream. "None of this makes any sense. Parallel planet, alien powers, superhuman strength; it's all bullshit. I have to try. Ya know? He'd do the same thing for any of us. What about Dredge? I suppose he's a goner too?"

Luther leads the charge into the lower deck as we all pile in the elevator. "Not exactly. We're not too sure *what* happened to him. He turned back into that creature, that gargoyle thing, rock solid. He's down there with Rico."

A waft of gunpowder and stale air hits me as soon as I cross into the lower level. A dozen or so narrow cylinders line one of the walls. I'm no military expert, but they look a little like nuclear missiles, or at least the firing tubes for them. The entire floor is a translucent grid that brightens with the weight of our bodies. Donte, the once nameless warrior and doctor, is busy pulling fried cartridges out of some kind of electrical box. Color coded, only many of the current *crayons* are unrecognizable. This must have been as a result of their recent battle with Ajai and his American traitor army.

Luther and the rest lead me toward a clear sliding door that opens as we approach. Five people-sized pneumatic tubes stand upright. Rico's body is in one. Dredge is in one large enough to accommodate his gargoyle body. A swirling mist comes and goes revealing Rico's face in intervals. Nasty burns are along his nose and neck, but he is still the boy I remember. His nearly flawless English, with a few Mexican hiccups now and then. The same kid willing to take a beating from Star during training, half-way between being scared shitless and in total awe of this sudden alien adventure. Gone, he was stuck in cryogenic limbo just waiting to get his soul swiped and to finally meet his Maker.

"How can I make contact? I need to be close to him," I say, trying to speak through the giant lump in my throat.

"No," Luther explains. "Not now. According to Donte, we can't interrupt the process. You'll have to work through the glass."

Luther's usual confidence has faded. Ozzy and Star look lost just like me. But I'm not buying into this pity party. Who knocked Azuna on her ass back at the house? What's a five-inch thick piece of glass gonna do? I ask everyone, Kandy, Misty, all of them to leave. Any negative energy might sabotage the process. They oblige. The sliding door swooshes shut behind me. I'm certain I can revive Dredge, based upon what I did in the training module, so I focus on Rico.

I place both hands on the cold glass. In seconds most of the mist dissipates, and Rico's face is bathed in reddish-pink. No sign of life yet, but I'm just getting started. I reflect back to the transport vehicle where we first saw each other. Meeting Marek and Bale for the first time. The ride in the back of the truck. Every relatively happy memory I can think of, and that's when it happens. He lifts both of his hands to meet mine. I'm ecstatic. It's working.

More, Faith. Push harder. You're stronger than death.

I continue the pressure, but he's still not with me. His eyes remain closed. No other movement. I'm poised to send one final charge his way, but before I can, I hear him in my head. *Stop! Please don't. I don't wanna come back. Leave me, Faith. Just leave me alone.* His words rip through my soul, but I ignore them. Bad choice. White lightning from his fingers jolt me away from the tube and on to my back. My head cracks against the floor with a thud. Rather than a few stars, I see an entire universe. The whole room is a blur. After my eyesight improves, I glance back to Rico's foggy coffin, and the swirls have returned. A blackened remnant of his two hands are seen on the inside of the glass.

That's the way you want it, huh? Okay. I'll leave. Can't say I didn't try though.

Not sure my message even made it through, I turn to Dredge. Rico wants to run and hide, that's his choice. But I'm tired of running. And—I need *this* guy to lead my brigade.

I have no idea what I'm doing, but I tap a blue failsafe button, and the tube opens. A thick fog pours out. My gargoyle action figure is gone and has turned himself back to stone again. I know just the remedy. No heat-seeking hand warmers or electrical charges. I pull over a chair, step up, and plant a sweet kiss on his cheek. My lips feel almost as dry as his sandpaper skin. His eyes fly open first, and even though I've witnessed this magic trick before, it startles me. The chair kicks out from underneath me and I sail backwards. This time, I miss hitting the ground as Dredge swoops out to catch me. We're sporting matching tears, and here's yet one more example that maybe that scientifically engineered soul really *does* work. Maybe it just needed time to grow. Or perhaps being frozen just activates the tear ducts.

Meanwhile Star and Ozzy have waited long enough as they burst through the door. Disappointment covers their faces as they see Rico still frozen. Misty keeps her cool demeanor helping all of us find the positive.

"Well, one out of two ain't too bad. Besides, he's not dead; he's just sleeping."

I love her innocence. I wish I didn't have his voice in my brain right now, begging me to leave him. I should share it, but why? Dredge is back to his own self, and we've got an appointment with the government. They just don't know we've been invited yet.

I'm ready to lead the group cheer once again, but I pause. Donte's monitoring Dredge's vitals, and there seems to be a problem. He's donned his human body again, but he looks bewildered.

"Where am I?" he asks. "How did I get here? And who

are you people?"

Who knew Niners could suffer from amnesia? I guess we'll need to delay our next move. We have one more day to find all his marbles before we put plan F into action. We better get to hunting. Can't be a secret weapon unless you know you're one. But hey, look at it this way. Nearly a week, and *three* of us are still alive.

Luther chases everyone out of the room, but I remain placing my hands back onto Rico's stasis contraption. And I swear I see his eyes twitch for a moment, and I hear his voice again. *Four.*

23

Apparently being in stasis even for a few hours, can mess with your memory, but that's not all that changed. While Star avoided a significant injury during the battle with Ajai, Ozzy kept his smarts, but his *anticipation* talents have dwindled. Somehow he's gained in other areas like alien engineering and technology. Already having a superhuman intelligence didn't hurt, but now he's almost speaking a different language. We sit on three separate exam tables waiting for Donte and his helpers to give us a clean bill. Ozzy wows us with his *new* skills.

"Converting the neutralizer into an aviation device showed up as a schematic in my head. I merely altered the design. I've made an odd hyperlink with Donte and this ship. All the technical alien DNA reads like a manual in my brain; hydroponic food garden on level two? I can control all the systems in my mind. I don't know. Maybe it had something to do with that little *shock* to my system?"

"Whatever," says Star. "If *you're* smarter now, that helps all of us. I'm still absorbing strength, and Faith—" She stops. I can tell she's about to accuse me of *losing* my powers because I wasn't able to save Rico. She realizes what she's implied and recants it. "Sorry. I just can't believe he's gone. We were a team, and we were all going down together."

"Well, you see, that's where you're wrong," I challenge her. "The coal and the diamond, Star, the coal and the diamond."

"Huh?"

"Remove the pressure and whaddya have? A lump of coal."

"So now we're lumps of coal?" she questions.

Ozzy starts a convoluted explanation of my analogy, but I don't let him finish it.

"Yeah, right *now* we're coal. But the stress? It's melting away every weakness. And we're not just coal anyhow. We're *modified* coal. Thanks to our Niner friends, we've gone from useless to resourceful. I'll be damned if I'm gonna give up now. Everything I do now is for Rico. Mom, my dad—if he's even alive."

"I get it," Star says. "Really, I do. It's just—I mean—why didn't it work? You've healed before. Why not now?"

"Yeah," Ozzy adds. "Are you losing your ability too?"

It's killing me that I can't tell them. Just how do you reveal the real reason Rico didn't pop right out of his milky cave and start cracking jokes again? *He gave up, didn't wan-*

na live anymore.

"Look. We've gotta put a few things together and prepare. It does no one any good to argue right now. As far as my ability, you gotta trust me on this one. Okay? I did all I could. Maybe Rico just didn't want to wake up. Ever think of that?"

I give them a version of the truth to chew on as we leave Donte in the med-wing. The three of us are banged up a bit from our skirmishes but nothing major holding us back from our final mission. Convince every world leader on Earth that Azuna didn't come to give humans a second chance; she came to exterminate. Take over. Wipe planet e Earth off the history books. Diamond cuts glass, even alien versions. Part human? They bleed too. It's time to find their vulnerability. If disease can't kill them, how about a nuke? I can think of at least twelve of them just waiting to be fired.

Luther gathers all of us into the main cargo hold. Donte assigns two of his best soldiers to escort us to the ground via a shuttle. They'll take the lead on this mission. Dredge hasn't recovered enough of his senses to be of much help, so we'll face the fire alone. There's no reason to put any of Luther's family at risk either. Hopefully our gargoyle regains all he's lost and jumps on board. Luther outlines his plan once we touch down.

The summit takes place at the newly renovated Kennedy Center. Obviously security will be high, but that's where our clothing comes in; Niner tech at its finest again. No, not invisible, although that would make things easier. But our outerwear mimics the secret service. Earpieces, dark glasses, and stuffy Armani suits for the guys. Black and white typical slacks and blouses for the women.

I have to admit I make a pretty convincing agent with my chest holster, fitted jacket, and blond hair pulled back in a tight ponytail. Star looks quite boss herself. Her Mohawk is growing out now and fluttering in all directions, looking like she's already foiled a few terrorist attempts. Ozzy's the only one who has the size of a *real* agent, maybe even a little oversized, but his fake afro screams Julius Erving rather than Will Smith. It's a good thing the crowd won't see us as we really are, however. Because deep down I'm sure they'd pick up on the fact that we have no clue what we're doing, even though Luther claims his strategy is brilliant. He and Ozzy joined forces, so I guess we'll have to trust an alien enhanced IQ and a former Special Forces soldier to know what they're doing.

The summit's scheduled for 2 PM, and we arrive on the outskirts of the city around 1:35. A tiny airport runway controller picks up a blip on his radar and gives us permission to land. To him, we're a Cessna just coasting in for a sightseeing tour; businessmen and women out for a quick jaunt through DC.

Luther's set up a Hummer ride through his military connections still loyal to the true American forces. Two Marines are slated to drop off the *rest* of the secret service for security duty. Our lanyard badges are coded to meet the event specs, and we have everything covered as far as breaching the gates. Crashing the party may not be as smooth though. Why would a host of dignitaries listen to a group of spastic teens? The answer to that question is way too easy. They won't. But what if the Vice-Chancellor himself gave a speech? According to Luther, he's already an ally in waiting. He's placed the C-4 but doesn't have the guts to light the wick. Blow all of Azuna and Ajai's plans to smithereens. As soon as they find out the *real* reason for the expiration chips, they'll throw Azuna and her entourage in prison where they'll dry up like the parched Arizona ground.

Other than a slight traffic delay, our jaunt to Kennedy Center goes well. As soon as we step out of the vehicle, two agents approach yelling out orders.

"Where the hell have you been? Chancellor Stevens won't step one foot into that place without a small army. You ask me, she's paranoid, but you gotta get your asses to the parking garage ASAP. You two? Come with us." He points at Star and me. I guess job equality still hasn't made its way into the secret service. They probably need us to get them some coffee or make a lunch run or something.

Luther nods as we split, like we're supposed to know what to do next, but way too much of his plan depends upon him. Ozzy. Who knew Ozzy would suddenly be able to download an entire computer into his brain and Luther could do impersonations too? They're supposed to convince the vice chancellor to spill the beans, but if he's too scared, Luther's going to pretend he's him. Tell the truth. Then I guess the walls of Jericho will come tumbling down, and we'll all be heroes. Only I'm not feeling too much like one right now. It's crazy but the closer I get to my alien soul snatcher, my head pounds. Just the idea I might have some of that woman's blood flowing through me makes me nauseous. From what I can infer, our menial tasks turn out to be completely wrong because we're a part of Azuna's entourage into the center. Five secret service agents, including us, greet her as her electric powered limousine stops right in front of us.

Ajai exits first followed by Azuna, Marek, and Bale. If those two are still on our side, they're doing a great job of pretending. Both order us around like we're a couple of hired servants. Marek is in the front with Bale in the rear. Four of us form a protective circle, which seems rather pointless. *They* all have enough firepower to down a small ship, and we're supposed to protect them? I guess they have to follow their roles for the cameras as paparazzi torture us the second we step off the elevator. Going alien incognito helps keep my identity hidden, so I leap into action.

"Clear the way! No questions! Plenty of time for that later! Come on, people! Back off, or we'll haul your asses into jail. That's it. Now you get it. Ma'am?"

I gesture for Azuna to follow me. Her eyes meet mine, and for a moment I'm worried. The pain behind my eyes intensifies like I'm too close to my Kryptonite. Her reaction surprises me.

"Finally a competent human being. They're not easy to come by." She laughs.

I don't linger too long in her stare continuing to force my way through reporters and cameramen. Star picks up on my deception and surrounds Azuna with her body acting like a battering ram. Regular police officers finally gain some control, and we make it into the auditorium.

The place is decked out with holographic flags from each represented country hanging like pictures in mid-air.

So many have changed their names over the past five years, I don't even recognize some of them. Botswana Prime. Memphisto. Calcitrone.

We tread across the stage like music award finalists. Body motion overhead lights blaze with intricate gobo patterns in every rainbow color on the floor and walls. Security cameras haunt our every move. I gawk at the silver fountains spraying pigmented champagne in oranges and reds. Several ambassadors, presidents, and the like crowd around dipping their glasses under the current for a refill.

Ajai is one of the first to sample the nectar followed by Azuna. Marek and Bale abstain. Star and I aren't sure what our next protocol is, so we stay steady, keeping our eyes peeled for gunman or terrorist bombers. Although right now, I'm thinking either one of those would do the trick. *How do you pretend you'd give your life to save someone else's?* I don't have much time to dwell on the answer before both Marek and Bale corner us.

"Nice work back there," Marek says. "This is not one of mother's favorite things. She hates pictures."

"She does? Why?" asks Star.

"I don't know. I think it has something to do with the camera stealing your soul."

He smiles, and for some reason I get a little nervous. The pounding in my head is steady but not any worse.

I'm dying to say, what soul, but I don't. No sense blowing our cover. The fireworks haven't even started yet. We try to ignore our two traitors by scanning the stage in all directions. It's hard to take in considering each body's clothed in their custom garb and sporting their own unique odor, everything from B.O. and Frankincense to Hugo Hero.

My nose itches especially when our hosts unveil the appetizers. Frog legs, squid, monkey brains, all mixed in nicely with the classics like shrimp cocktail and queso chips. They went all out on impressing these people. Since Star and I are supposed to be on duty, we decline repeated attempts at getting us to sample the delicacies. At one point, Star karate kicks an annoying server down to the floor. She covers herself well by having him arrested for being overly aggressive toward Ajai. He thanks her. We share a congratulatory nod, and he leaves to take his seat around the half-circled table center stage.

I want to communicate with Star, but I can tell her attention has been drawn to a new player in our alien melodrama. Unable to distinguish Niner from human, a rather small man in his early twenties has made his rounds to every ambassador and leader in the place. His off-white tux stands out amongst the colorful foreign threads worn by almost everyone else. She and another assigned agent track him from table to table; their conversation rings in my earpiece.

"Who's the guy in the tux? Looks like a child who never grew up? I think he's personally touched every person in the crowd," Star says.

Not wanting to linger much longer by Azuna and her family, I depart from my station and close in on the friendly fellow too. It's crazy, but he seems to be able to communicate with each person, speaking their languages flawlessly. He ambles past the podium and makes his way toward the Niner placard adjacent to Chancellor Steven's table. So far, she's not arrived, but it's not quite 2 PM. Her reputation for being late to everything and creating a grand entrance precedes her. Star gets to tuxedo man first followed by two burly agents, and then I bring up the rear.

"Sir? May we have a word with you in private?" asks Star. She's really taken this secret service role on to the max.

"A word?" he speaks with a slight British accent. "But of course. I'm happy to be of service."

Before we can whisk him off and interrogate him, Marek intercedes.

"Allow me to introduce to you my mother's head advisor Demas. He's been her right hand man for years now."

Demas triggers an adverse response in both Star and me. He offers us his ring-adorned hand to shake, but a small voice acts as a warning.

"No offense, Mr. Demas, but agency protocol prohibits it, sir." I make up the lamest excuse I can think of to not shake his hand and step in between Star and him. "The event is about to start. Nice to meet you, sir. Enjoy your stay."

We glide back to our stations, and my uneasiness grows. *Demas. Isn't that what they called Ozzy while we were navigating the training module, a magician or mystic or something?*

Ring. All of us jump at the sound of some type of alarm that pierces the air for a few seconds then stops. It's not long before we all know the reason for the noise pollution. Chancellor Stevens. She's arrived in all her glitz and glamour, dressed to the nines in five-inch heels and her favorite little black dress; sexy but all-business, confidence her best friend.

She pays her respects to Azuna and her motley crew and saunters up to the plexi-glass podium. No fancy introduction from her media specialist, she begins her state of the world address. There's been no sign of Luther, Ozzy, or Donte's soldiers. Star and I retreat to our security boxes on opposite sides of the stage while the rest of the agents are seated directly behind the delegation. Steven's alto voice cuts through the auditorium like a fine blade. It's almost impossible to tune her out, but I try.

"My fellow countrymen? Welcome to this year's annual summit. Before I begin, I wanted to thank certain people for making this possible."

She drones on thanking everyone shy of the person who cooked her Eggs Benedict that morning. I'd rather watch a Chia Pet grow than listen to her talk, but I don't have much of a choice in the matter. Thank goodness Vice-Chancellor Burton is next, and we can get this dog and pony show up and running. I can't imagine the pandemonium that will ensue after our distinguished guests get an earful of the truth.

"And in closing, let me just say that the world is stronger than it's ever been. Our alliance with planet Nine has made our world more prosperous, healthy, and advanced. Something we haven't seen for over a decade. Sacrifice on all our parts has led to unity in purpose and secured a bright future for generations to come. Now it's my pleasure to introduce Vice Chancellor Burton to outline the next phase of our journey together. Separate countries and uh—planets. One world."

24

There's no way to tell if Burton is Burton or Luther at this point, so I brace myself. How he's all of a sudden able to pull a Marek and exchange identities is a conundrum, but why question it? Given all we've seen and done these past few days, it's certainly not out of the realm of possibility. I keep wondering when Godzilla will show up. It seems like a giant monster is the only thing missing now.

We've lost total communication with them since we left the limo, having miscalculated the fact that once we arrived, we'd be given *new* earpieces. So the one already tucked inside our eardrums would be useless. Any covert message sent or received would be monitored by the *real* agents, and they'd be on us in minutes. Luther mentioned that even the slightest time lapse of contact with the agency would throw

243

up a red flag, so removing their com device isn't an option either. Waiting is our only course of action, but I hate it. I can't wait to get this Christmas present opened and for these unsuspecting leaders of the free world to hear a dose of reality. They've been duped, fed truckloads of manure by our government and the League of Nations and Planets, formally the United Nations.

Burton begins his speech in standard political fashion, but after a few minutes I see Star's eyes light up. Luther's about to change the mood in this place. That is, as long as his foolproof plan worked. Get to the real Burton and convince him to allow Luther to make his speech *for* him. I wouldn't be surprised if a huge riot breaks out. I wish Ozzy was here. He's got me concerned, but he's also smart enough to handle almost any situation, so I chill. Burton finishes his political gobbledygook then steers his speech down some unpaved roads, finally.

"For the past ten years, our nations have lived in relative peace, but what price have we paid for it? That's the question I want to answer for you this afternoon."

Chancellor Stevens squirms in her chair, but she doesn't interrupt him. Azuna is so caught in the moment, she doesn't even flinch. All of her cabinet members hold their permanent beauty pageant smiles. Burton continues his version of the truth these past ten years.

"Unfortunately, the price we've paid in all this is our freedom. Since when should a *government* decide who lives and dies and when? This *experiment* was never intended to happen to Earth. Planet Nine has had a population control problem for years because they've eliminated all diseases.

But their government didn't have the guts to try it out on their own, so they came here and offered us their auric if we'd test their expiration chips on our own people. And the only reason we agreed was to be honest, we've *all* been struggling. Unemployment sky-high. Not enough food. Countless terrorist operations. I could go on and on."

I raise my eyebrows at Star. Luther's not holding back. A few security agents begin to stir, but they allow him to continue his offensive. I expect to see nation after nation whispering amongst themselves. Reacting and overreacting to his words. But I'm shocked. About every two sentences, several of them stand and applaud him. Almost like they're hearing a different message or something. Like their translation devices have been tampered with, but I don't think that's the case, as I overstep my authority and read Saudi Arabia's teleprompter. Translation is accurate.

"Yes, we've seen our economies soar, have nearly eradicated most terrorism, and food is abundant. But now we are faced with an even tougher decision. Niners have removed so much of their auric; they have eroded their planet's core. Massive earthquakes that make ours looks like a toddler knocking down his Legos have decimated Planet Nine. And what do they want to do? Steal *our* planet. Assimilate soul after soul until their entire planet shows up making earth even *more* crowded. Chancellor Stevens is ready to sign the agreement, but I say we work together with Azuna and her people to help solve their problems instead."

Stevens approaches the podium clapping slowly, making a mockery of Burton's words. He's escorted back to his seat by two agents who stand guard. I expect her to recant his arguments, but she just smiles that annoying smile and acts like we're all about to eat cake and sing "Imagine" together. Every delegate rises giving her an arousing standing ovation. Nearly five minutes of applause later, and I'm attacked, tackled to the ground. A random gunshot fired just above my head before the blitz. Ozzy. He's returned and saved my life again.

"Sorry," he apologizes. "I saw it coming. The premonitions still come and go. There are snipers on the walkway up top. But we've got bigger problems. They've got Luther."

"Luther? Then that wasn't him—"

"Nope, we got to Burton just before he came out to speak, but didn't have any time to chit chat. He already had plans to expose the Niner takeover, but his dressing room got raided, brainwashed American military again. They had orders to take us all in or kill if necessary. Luther tried to *talk* his way out of it, but they had one of those neutralizers."

"So how did you get away?"

We crawl along the floor staying close to the delegates as possible figuring the snipers wouldn't risk hitting any of them. False assumption on our part because the bullets rain down even harder as we reach Star, who's taken cover behind an extra chair rack near the main doors. *Whack. Ping. Clack.* Tufts of renovated carpet fly in the air. Fancy wine glasses and coffee cups shatter and spray in all directions. Playtime's over. Azuna wants us dead.

Nigeria's ambassadors join us on the floor. Stevens is still at the podium demanding everyone remain calm. *Terrorists* (that's us) have infiltrated the auditorium, but they have everything under control. Sudden movement might lead to injuries or death. She drones on, but the three of us army crawl to the back doors. Other agents are preoccupied with the shooters, so we catch a small break and make it into the main lobby. We rise and draw our weapons to make us less conspicuous, but I'm still dying to know how Ozzy escaped.

"What now?" asks Star. "And where's the rest of the posse?"

"Luther and the others got captured."

"How'd you escape?" I ask.

"No time to explain. We gotta head to the tunnels!"

"What tunnels?" I ask, Star mouths the words with me. Something feels wrong. This seems too easy.

He drags both of us to the stairs. We race down, two steps at a time. Gunshots grow more frequent above us. Our secret service issued shoes skate out from under us at every level. The earpieces go stagnant with an occasional squawk, but for a moment I think I hear Luther's voice. He comes through clearer, and with that we stop on a landing to get our bearings. Two-way communication is blocked. All we can do is listen.

"Hundreds of catacombs under this place, the Depot Tunnels. Old subway tunnels they've tried to restore for years. It's our safest and fastest way outta here. Come on!"

He's the genius in the bunch, so we go, but ever since my hospital experience with Stevens, I don't know who I can trust anymore.

The stairs open up to a dimly lit passageway. Light blue lights shine the way. The first scent that hits us is the stench of mildew and death. If I remember right, these same tunnels were used during the Civil War. Lots of people died down here.

Ozzy appears much quicker now. Star and I strain to keep up, but there's no stopping. We have company. A quarter mile back, the scientists have added a few more mice to the maze. Ozzy takes a sharp turn to the left, and we're out of sight for now. My mouth's on fire. It's so dry it's difficult to breathe. Further away from Azuna, I've only remnants of my head pain, so I'm thankful for that. But my lungs may not have much more air in them. I ask for rest, but Ozzy denies it. Star's barely breaking a sweat. I wonder if she's draining *my* strength because I'm moving like a noodle with legs now. I force that thought from my mind as familiar words come back. *You're dying. We're both dying.* Suddenly it all makes sense.

"Stop!" I scream, unable to say much more. "Go—with--out—me. Please. I'm slow—i ng you down."

I don't even get the rest of my sentence out, and Star throws me over her tiny frame firemen style and takes off. I feel awful, but maybe this can buy me some time. I'll be able to join back in soon. I work my way back down from her shoulders piggyback style now, and I stare back; our trackers haven't gained any ground, but we know it's a matter of time. Their walkie-talkies are suddenly loud and clear. Maybe we're near the exit.

The tunnels go on for miles, whitewashed brick walls and abandoned cubicles and kiosks where merchants used to sell their wares. Plenty of cubby holes to hide, but we want out. *I thought this was our fastest way.*

Star carries me at least a mile before I tap her on the shoulder. I know she could go on, but I'm ready to run again.

We position ourselves in a hallway marked restrooms, and that's when we see a red exit sign. Not lit up anymore, but this may be our ticket.

"Exit up ahead," says Star. "We've made it." Some sweat beads up around her eyes. She's a bulldozer. I want *her* workout routine.

"No!" Ozzy shouts. "Not here! We're still too close. They'll be waiting for us."

"Wait! What if we make it *look* like we've taken this exit? Throw them off our trail."

"Right. Sure. Great idea." His words faltering. No convoluted explanation. Very un-Ozzy-like. He launches himself back into the tunnel totally forgetting what I just said. We wave him back.

"Hey! You all right? You're not yourself. The Ozzy I know would have taken my idea and run with it, but you just got back on the trail. What's up? You getting some kind of premonition again?"

He raises his voice a little. "No. Nothing, I'm fine. Just tired of running, that's all."

"Yeah, I mean, we've all been on the run since we left Tennessee, huh?" I say.

"I don't know how much longer I can take this. Just want it to all be over."

"So why run then?" asks Star.

"No choice," he whispers. "Freedom's that way." He points.

Then he pulls the perfect yet simple Ozzy move by flying up the exit stairs and kicking the doors. They don't budge. Star and I add our two shoulders, and they finally

swing open. The air feels wonderful. Just the thought of returning to the catacombs makes me ill, but Ozzy was right.
He's always right. It seems like we've traveled miles from
the center, but we're no more than ten blocks away. Those
tunnels must weave and wind so much it's deceiving.

Just for one added feature to our deception, Star rips off
her jacket and tosses it just outside the doorway. In seconds,
we're back down below, but it's odd. No one's behind us
now. *Did they take a wrong turn?* There's no further communication from Luther or anyone else.

I've gotten some of my second-wind back, so Star's not
burdened with my weight anymore. Though at times, I can
tell I'm just not fast enough for her taste. Why couldn't *I*
get the super strength powers? The tunnels open up into almost a mall-like setting with several storefronts. Barricad-
ed garage doors cover each entrance. There is a half-circle
of stores but no way out. We've run right into a dead end.
Straight above us there's outside light and a glass gazebo
overhead possibly two football fields high. Unless we have
jet packs waiting for us around the corner, we're not leaving
that way.

"Okay, genius." My cynicism returns with a vengeance.
"You've led us to a *mall*. What now? We take a stroll through
Victoria Secrets? Check out the fancy underwear?"

Ozzy's deep in his own little world and puzzled by his
instincts and perceived knowledge.

"Something's not right here," he says like it's some grand
discovery.

"Ya think?" Star chimes. "Let's go back to the exit. We
know it leads out."

"We can't!" he yells, his eyes grow fierce. Mine fill with tears just thinking about how far we've gotten, and now we're trapped. I stare at him demanding some answers, and then I get one. Even in between the blur, I see it, cold blue eyes. They come and go with Ozzy's original brown. Then I do what I should have done a few miles back. I unholster my weapon and point it directly at his head.

"Who are you?" I push the gun closer, keeping my hand sturdy in between steadying my wobbly knees.

Star thinks I'm nuts and tries to talk me down. "Hey! It's Ozzy, Faith. You're tired. Upset. Hell, we all are. We can't start turning on each other. Not now."

"Oh, yeah? Well, then you might as well join him! Over there! Both of you!"

"Faith? What's wrong with you? You've totally lost it. Put down the gun."

"No! Not until you show me who you really are! Tell me stuff. Stuff only I would know about you! Hurry up! Or I swear, I'll shoot you both!"

"Okay—okay—I've got it!" Star's leading the way. Ozzy remains quiet. "Ask me something. *Anything*. I swear. I'll answer it right."

I rack my brain for something to test their allegiances. Something only the *three* of us experienced. It's not as easy as it sounds. We've spent the past week together dodging aliens and trying to fathom their humanness and advanced abilities. No contact ever before that. Then I start to think about Rico. How he acted on the shuttle bus before our journey began, wondering what he was singing and dancing to as soon as he got on. Something from way back when.

Old timers' music.

"Here goes. Rico? Everyone was already on the bus when he got on, but had his iPod in his ears, and he was singing something. What was he humming? Over there! A note pad and pens! Write down your answers!"

Ozzy goes first sharing the pen with Star. I make sure there's no cheating by putting at least six feet between them. Though both are armed as well, neither has given me any reason to shoot, at least, not yet. I collect the pad and read their answers.

Star's: *Staying Alive*. Ozzy's: *I'm Marek*.

25

"Damn! I knew it! Star? Over here! Marek? Your gun? Easy does it. Toss it on the ground." He willingly does.

Star peeks at the note pad and makes a break for it before I flinch. She's got him covered alongside me. I breathe a sigh of relief, so happy she wasn't an imposter too.

"Hey?" I say. "Thanks for being you." She laughs.

"No problem, but what do we do now? *He's* the magician. We're just the beautiful assistants."

He's already started to change back into Marek and forcing thoughts into my mind.

"Stop it!" I roar. "Just talk. I don't want any of your hocus pocus nonsense! Why? Why did you turn on us? You were our friend." I'd like to hold back my emotions, but I can't. My voice trembles. Luckily Star brings me back.

"Hey, mantis-girl? Don't get all weak on me. He's the enemy now. And I'm filling up with his muscle. I think we can take him."

"Wait. Allow me to explain," he pleads.

"Explain what? Why you brought us all the way down here? Why you made fools of us, getting us to believe you were on our side, then pulling the rug? What else is there?"

We force him up against one of the steel garage doors in case he decides to make a run for it. I've never shot anyone before, but I will if I have to. What's moral anymore anyhow? As soon as the Niners showed up, all bets were off.

"You don't understand. I am on your side. Always was. I brought you here to show you."

"Show us what?" Star gets in his face. He flops back into the metal door, and we hear a loud bang inside resonate back. An even louder one follows.

"What's in there?" I ask.

"What I had to show you. Here, let me—" He reaches into his coat pocket, but Star removes the item for him, a round disc about the size of a half-dollar.

"Press the center," he says.

"No!" I shout. "You must think we're stupid or something. A couple of teenage kids. Well, guess what? All this alien DNA shit's rubbed off. Yeah, something you didn't count on, did you?"

He turns his head to the side and almost stares right through me. "Oh, no. We *counted* on it all right. *Expected* it even. Hit the button. I'll show you. Please."

"What? And a whole brigade of alien robots will come flying out? You're zoomed, Marek. We ain't that dumb."

Star and I are on the same page, but she makes a critical error switching gun hands and dropping the coin. *Ding.* It hits the floor, and suddenly the opaque steel door turns see-through. The store's filled with pods like on Dredge's ship. Maybe fifty of them line the perimeter. Most have people inside them, but two are open and empty. A light fog hovers low over the floor but never rises. Star and I keep Marek in our sights, but we advance toward the door.

Wham!

Out of nowhere a deformed being slams into the door, right in front of us. Startled, both of us rock backwards keeping each other from landing on our butts. This guy looks nothing like his pod buddies with straggly long hair and blood-red eyes that seep. Dark stains over his pasty cheeks. Nearly every vein protrudes from his face. Infected gunshot wounds ooze from his naked chest. His lower half is covered in a pair of grey boxer shorts.

Bam! A slight dent in the door forms.

A woman this time, shorter; not quite as rough-looking but no beauty queen either. A new wound on her forehead where she ran into the door accompanies an obvious bullet hole. She looks familiar. It's the homeless woman. Azuna took her soul back at my house.

"Okay, so like you're storing a zombie horde. Why? I know that woman, but who are these people, and why are they in stasis like Rico?"

"First of all, we have no need for the guns. I promise, I'm here to help. I brought you here because I didn't think you'd trust me ever again."

"Well, you're right about that. And why should we?" I

say.

Star follows up my question with her own response. She's slightly more animated, almost pistol-whipping him in the head. He's three times her size, but right now I'd bet on Star.

"Give me time to explain. That's all I ask. Then if you want to kill me, go ahead. I have to get *those* two back into their pods before they really hurt themselves or get out. Then we'd have a real mess on our hands."

"Gee whiz. This isn't bad enough?" I say, as snarky as ever. "Do what you must, but remember? No sleight of hand. Got it?"

"Got it."

It's funny, but he sounds so much more like the Marek I remember now. Like outside of his mother's influence, he's our friend again. But that is exactly what we thought before. This time we're doing things *our* way.

He steps to the left of the door and taps a silver square and a control pad springs out. Three digits later, and several flashes blast through the mist in the room. It must be soundproof because we see both escaped pod people scream in agony, but hear nothing. The same beam of light steers them back to their capsules, but they're not eager to return. Marek assures us it's for the best, and by the looks of how they've torn up the place, I think he's right. The added lights allow us to see a few more of the people in stasis, and I'm shocked. At least five of them are the teenagers from the transport van—the one we escaped from.

"How'd they get out?" asks Star.

"I'm not sure, but quite possibly they never went in to

begin with. They're the latest to be assimilated."

"Huh?" I ask.

"All of these pods? Most are temporary hosts," he adds. "A few are permanent like Valic's match and Radon's. Over ten years of Niners trying to stay alive here on earth."

"But I thought once humans died, you left them for dead? Why put them in stasis? Azuna doesn't seem like the compassionate type to me."

"She isn't, and yet she is. It's so complicated. Besides, she didn't know any of this. This was Bale's idea. Part of his fabricated soul experiments. He thought with enough study, he'd be able to create a *usable* soul, so nobody had to die anymore."

"What about the guys chasing us? What happened to them? They just disappeared. Why?"

"I think humans refer to it as a wild chicken chase." He grins for the first time since we discovered his true identity.

"Uh—that's wild *goose* chase," says Star. "So you're telling us that you sent them where?"

"Up the stairs and outside, following your coat trail; I made them think we all went that way."

Our arms growing weary, Star and I drop our mini-pistols for a minute to get the blood back. Some of the tension eases, but I'm still cautious. He walks to each keypad and checks the controls in each of the stations. Star and I follow closely.

"So how many?" I ask. "How many un-deads are in here?"

"Over five hundred. We ran out of room on the ship and purchased this section of the tunnels. Stevens pulled some strings."

"So *she* knows about what's going on down here?" Star asks.

"Not exactly. Bale told her he was working on a way to please everyone. It just hasn't turned out the way he expected."

"What's wrong with them? I don't understand. If they're soulless, how can they still be alive? I just assumed—"

"I'm not the scientist, so I can't rattle off the specifics. But Bale says when a Niner assimilates a human's soul, they leave a DNA residue behind. In essence, humans turn into Niners."

"Let me see if I'm following you. Assimilation doesn't leave the person dead. He or she comes back to life needing a soul to stay on earth?"

"Holy shit." Star plops down into one of her yoga positions on the floor. Exhaustion sets in. "So all these people would be *dead* if you didn't put them in the pod? That's just cruel. Frigging cruel, Marek. Why not just let them die?"

He moves to her like she's just lost her dog, stoops down to her level, and holds out his hand in a warm gesture. At first, she turns away, and her anger builds. In a little while, she turns back and accepts his kindness. Pain replaces her fury.

"*That*, my new friends, is a question you need to ask Bale. He's so sure he can stop this disaster by creating a substitute soul for these folks. He won't give up on them. Even Faith's been a part of the experiment."

As soon as he says it my heart jumps. "All the blood work? His testing on the ship? He was trying to—"

"Pinpoint your healing genes. He found some strange connection between your ability to heal and your natural soul's will to live. We've never seen a Niner ability manifest itself in this way. Shape-shifting, increased strength, superior cognitive, premonitions, and a few others, but never a healer. Kandy's compassion grew tenfold; Micah's a thought pusher like Rico and me, but you, Faith. The *sickest* of us all, and yet you remain the strongest."

"Hey, thanks for the compliment, I think. So what now? We left a room full of chaos up there, and they have Luther and Ozzy. We're pretty-well screwed as far as our little rebel army goes. Dredge can't even remember his name."

"Not to mention that he hates us, my family and me. I'm surprised he's even still alive. American military pummeled his ship."

"Yeah, we know," Star says. "We lost a great friend. Rico's in la-la land like our pod people here."

"I'm sorry," Marek's apology sounds genuine. Maybe he's telling the truth. We re-holster our guns for now and help him complete his monitoring. Each store checks out. No more lunatics slamming into the doors trying to flee. Boy, how would the world perceive them if they ever got loose? The *real* Zombie Apocalypse, not Hollywood style. *"Excuse me? I don't want to eat you, but can I have your soul?"* The thought twists my gut, and for some reason my headache's returned. I overreact like usual.

"We gotta get outta here. Now," I yell.

Star leaps to her feet. She knows I'm serious. Panic fills her face.

"Why? We've got nowhere to go! Marek? Any ideas?"

He pauses like he's aware of something we're not. His skin flushes red, and in seconds he's on his communicator. We hear the same message he does. *They're in the Depot Mall! The tunnels! Get this ship turned around now!*

"You son-of-a—" Star shares in my reaction.

"Stop! I had nothing to do with this! They've commandeered my ship. It's got infrared tracking. It was only a matter of time."

"Until what?" I ask.

"Until they get what they came for. Mother's not well again. They're going to try manual extraction."

"Manual what? And how do you know this?" I ask.

"Your soul. You can't die, so she has *no* chance at legitimate assimilation. You won't give it up willingly, so she's gonna take it, from *both* of you. *All* of you."

"Wait a minute. How? How can she do that? I thought we had to die?" Star says.

"Bale's lab. He built the technology except—"

"Except these half-deads are the result. Right?"

"Yes. But he's determined to put an end to mother's plans. We wish to save our own planet not take yours. Our ancestors would be ashamed of us. Our little corner of the universe was just fine without all *this*."

"Well, believe me. It doesn't take long for the people in power to grow big heads and forget why they were elected. The *one* plague no one's ever been able to eradicate."

"That's because the virus lies in the heart," Star continues. "Or I guess, the *soul*, if you believe in such a thing. And this *hubris* bug keeps mutating. The best intentioned people catch the fever of corruption and don't wanna get well.

They're happy being sick. 'Cuz sick means they get all the toys and attention."

My head is about to explode. That can only mean one thing; Azuna is close by again. Marek suggests we go back to our previous exit point. He'll cover us if we run into trouble. Three steps back toward the tunnel, and a loud crash makes us look up. It's Dredge in his gargoyle form screaming down through the broken glass. We hit the floor covering our heads from the knife-like shards. Star gets nailed in the back right away, so I leap to cover her with my body. Marek's already moved out of range; his reflexes are much quicker than ours.

Dredge lands in the center of the mall cracking the marble tile like a mirror. He pays no attention to us but swoops over to Marek who he's pinned down. Marek's strength and speed breaks him free for the moment, but having wings is a definite advantage. A growing blood stain soaks Star's white blouse. The splintered glass entered at a crazy angle. I waste no time gripping the piece and pulling it from her body, a blood fountain follows. Using my jacket, I apply pressure and begin to consider happier times with Star. Her carrying me on her back, times when she was healthy and not bleeding like a wounded soldier. A fiery charge shoots through both of my hands, and the alien tourniquet does its job. She passes out from the shock, nonetheless.

I direct my attention back to Marek and Dredge who have just about destroyed the place. No clear winner yet. Fighting through my own pain, I take a huge chance and place myself in the middle of their rage.

"Stop! Enough! We're on the same side."

Dredge completely ignores my pleas and tackles Marek into one of the garage doors. This triggers a domino effect as all ten stores light up. Steel turns to clear glass. I see Star rise to her feet, a little groggy, but she's fine. *If* you wanna believe that looking fine includes looking like she just stepped out of a meat market. She's a perfect character for one of those B horror movies.

Marek's losing his battle, but I've seen enough testosterone now for the past ten minutes, so I try again. Star joins me in my peace talks.

"You two can keep this up and let Azuna fly in here and take us all, or we can work this out."

Marek's more than ready to relent, but I'm not sure Dredge feels the same.

"Listen to them," Marek says, his words barely leave his lips. "Please, Father. Mother needs to be stopped."

Father. Mother. Whoa. I didn't see that one coming. Both warriors fall back, Dredge turning back to his human form. Suddenly I've got a gazillion questions. Meanwhile, Star's made her way back to the keypads trying to reverse the garage door sequence.

"Father?" I look to Marek.

"Dredge was my mother's highest ranked commander. They fell in love, but he had one terrible flaw. Didn't he, Father?"

"I admit it. I was raised in the wild. Settling down was not me, but his mother insisted I could change. *She* could change me. Early on, I strayed often. But by the time I realized what it was doing to Azuna, it was too late."

"Too late for what?" I ask, trying to rub the sharp pain

from my temples. Sooner or later, one way or another, I gotta get this woman out of my head.

"She came to power. Surrounded herself with voices, all kinds of voices, especially Demas, the necromancer. Gifted at an early age with unfathomable abilities, he placed a spell on me and found a way to keep me from straying. This." He splits himself in half. One side Blodd. The other side Dredge.

"But how? Where did he *get* such ideas? I thought gargoyles were an earthly concept."

Marek stands and limps toward Star and me. She's successfully reprogrammed all the doors.

"Azuna may *appear* to have all the power, but it's Demas who drives the machinery. He's studied *every* civilized planets' culture. I guess the notion that something could morph back and forth between civilized and monster intrigued him."

Dredge decides to join into the conversation again. His fury's decreased. "Azuna made a habit of calling me her *rock* during difficult times. And that's exactly what I became. What other woman would possibly want a monster, especially one who couldn't control himself. That's why I offered myself as a guinea pig to Bale. My substitute soul seems to have worked, but it's not without flaws, as you can see. Sorry, son. Sometimes the anger has no motive."

"You'd been away for so long. You had no way of knowing Bale and I did not condone killing humans. I would have made the same graven error."

Having tossed a little dirt on the fire between father and son, we move forward toward our escape. A heavy darkness blots out the only light through the dome. Marek's ship is now overhead. Star's hard work reconfiguring the doors all in vain, as each one not only turns back into glass but also opens this time. Each pod slides open as well. We race to our only exit back through the tunnels keeping an eye on what lies behind. Niner soldiers. American troops. They're scaling down ropes through Dredge's hole down into the mall. Hot on our trails. And who's leading the task force? Demas.

26

It's incredible how fast an exit strategy can materialize when you're running for your life. At least two miles back through the maze, we arrive in no time hauling our butts up the steps and through the doors. Star's jacket still lay in the grass. A blast of moist clean air brings life to my aching dry bones.

Dredge suggests our next move, which is to find out where Donte's hidden the shuttle. He'd parked it alongside the Washington Monument when Dredge left to find us, but it's gone. Military personnel are in mass on every side like they're expecting WWIV. *Three* lasted about a week, until our favorite Russians ended the terrorist threat with their new megaton nuke. They were shot from a Humvee, but had enough punch to take out all of Afghanistan, minus the radioactive fall-out, Hiroshima, *without* the pus, sores, and retroactive cancer. No one's ever challenged anyone since. I guess early Niner tech's done some good after all.

We continue our escape over the lawn blending in nicely with all the rest of the tourists. Some, who've either watched or heard about the insanity at the summit and are just as scared as we are, and others who remain oblivious. Demas and his crew spot us as we approach the Reflecting Pool. Star sees the shuttle before any of us.

"There! At the bottom of the pool! It's Donte!"

"Oh, great! Have I mentioned that I'm an awful swimmer?" I complain.

"Wait," shouts Marek. "I'll signal him. He probably already knows we're here. He's just staying clandestine."

"Hey, Marek? I think you've been having too many conversations with Ozzy. You're beginning to sound just like him." He pulls a weird whistle out of his pocket and blows. His earpiece must have fallen out during the fight. It's the next best thing to wireless, I guess.

No more than a hundred meters separates Demas from our position. Navigating the crowds is much harder with more men, but he'll be on us soon. Gunfire rings out, but there's no place to hide. More and more tourists scatter, and unbeknownst to them, they've become our human shields. Three or four mowed down not ten yards from us. Marek blows the whistle once more, but the transport stays submerged. Dredge makes an annoying face at Marek and dives into the pool. We're about to follow, when I see Star go down first. I'm next, and I watch as Marek raises his hands in surrender. Seeing me struck, he catches me before

I hit the ground. His next words give me strength. Hope. *It's not over. Trust me.*

****

I awake to the sound of my own heartbeat through my ears, amplified. It is louder than a heart should ever sound. I try to take a deep breath, but the best I can do is a series of small ones.

The back of my right shoulder throbs, from there the pain goes down to just behind my knee. *Splat.* The first bullet buckled my legs, and I went down. Marek's arms reached for me, but I never made it into the water. *Whack.* The next one penetrated right above my shoulder blade.

I blink through my nightmare only to realize where I am. Bale's lab. My mind's a little less cloudy. No straps or buckles hold me down, so I rise up. Bad choice. In seconds, I'm lying flat again tossing my cookies off the side of the bed into the trash. Apparently I've been busy doing this for a while, as the sickening smell stares back at me from the bottom. Both a visual and olfactory reminder I'm not well. I should be dead, but I'm not. Why not? That's the question. The only thing I feel like doing is lying down on my side and moaning. After a while I put some prior knowledge to work for me. *Heal thyself.* I focus my last ounce of energy on my wounds, but while my nausea fades some, I still feel like hell. *You can't heal yourself, remember? Only other people.*

Just then I want to strangle my reality. What good is a power if you can't help yourself? Not much else to do for the moment, I dwell on my last thought. Out of all the superheroes out there, did *any* of them think about themselves more than helping others? I back down off my horse and accept my fate, and I wonder what they're waiting for. Azuna's won, and she's got all of us exactly where she wants us now.

Still curious about my wounds, I reach around to my back, but come up empty. It's on fire and quite stiff, but no bullet hole. They must have hit us with tranquilizers. Once again, keeping me alive's still a mystery. Am I *really* invincible? I mutter out loud but don't expect a response.

It's Bale. "Pretty close, except Azuna's made things precarious for you. If she doesn't assimilate soon, you'll *both* be dead. And no amount of *healing* abilities is going to bring you back."

"I don't wanna be a zombie," I screech. He presses a remote and lifts the head of my bed. I anticipate another round of vomit, but I'm okay. My hyper merry-go-round has stopped for now. He encourages me to take the next step by swinging my legs over the bed and sitting up. With his help, I manage, but the garbage can keeps calling my name, so I ask him to get it out of my sight. When he returns he's shoving some water and two brown biscuits into my face.

"Here. These will help the toxins wear off, but there's nothing I can do for the rest."

· "The rest?" I crunch down like he said and swallow. I feel like his pet dog.

"Azuna's trapped herself in between *your* planet and ours. She thought she could handle it, assimilating a full *and* a partial soul."

"Let me guess? *I'm* the partial."

"No guess needed. You knew. Probably felt her struggle

and absorbed her pain. Right?"

"Yeah, wish she would get this whole thing over, so I can think straight. My head is killing me. I don't suppose you have anything in that doctor kit for migraines, do ya? Anti-Azuna meds?"

I watch him fight back a smile. He's so charming even *if* he's the wrong species. How has *he* managed to stay healthy here? Wouldn't Marek and he needed to assimilate too? I mean, with their matching souls?

I down the rest of my doggie treats and glance around the room, no sign of Star or Ozzy.

"How are the rest of them? Have their souls already been taken?"

I can tell by his reaction they have. He backs away in case I strike out, but I've not much strength left. I've had just about enough of these pseudo hospital visits. "I'm sorry, Faith. I tried, but there was nothing I could do."

"Yeah, yeah, yeah—I know. Nothing you could do. So why am I alive?"

"I've already mentioned the complications. She's rid herself of her previous host."

"The woman in the pod at the underground mall?" I whisper.

"Yes. How did you, never mind. In reality, you're the only thing keeping her alive."

"Really?" I mount enough courage to smile as if I'd just won a Grammy. "Get me a gun. A fork or a spoon. Anything. If I die, she will too."

"You know that's not how it works, "he says with a hint of compassion.

"Shit. She'll have the rest of my soul, won't she?" I move the back of my hand to my forehead; it's way too warm.

"I'm afraid so."

"What about Marek and you? Why haven't you two assimilated?"

"We have." He rubs the back of his neck and ruffles his hair. Two deep sighs later, and it's obvious he's attempting to avoid the truth, so I demand it.

"Tell me. Why haven't you two gotten sick?"

"Because we *have* our intended souls."

I stand up. Sour stomach and all, I dash toward him fists out, pounding every inch of his body with weak but incessant blows. He stands silent and unmoving, allowing me to cry and fight my way through my anger. I kick and punch him in every vulnerable place I can think of before I collapse in a heap, my head cracking off the floor. I'm momentarily dazed when I feel him scoop me up and lay me back down in the bed. I drench my pillow and sheets with tears and snot, shrieking until my lungs have no air and my voice is all but gone.

"Ozzy? And Star? *They* were *your* matches, weren't they?" He just sits idle on his stool and stares at me. "Weren't they?"

"No. You've got it all wrong, Faith. Marek and I *found* our matches as soon as we crossed over, relying on temporaries until full assimilation. When I discovered the synthetic souls weren't ready yet, we had to make sure we stayed alive to fight back and convince Azuna she was wrong."

"So where are they? All my friends? Luther and Misty? His whole family?"

"Stasis, until we get these souls to work. I promise. I

promise." He repeats himself, and I may be spent, but it's like I'm inside a stadium. His voice echoes in succession. "We can bring them all back. You'll see. You'll see. You're the key, Faith. You can save them all."

"What's that? Right there? Your words? You don't normally stutter." I limp over and take his wrist. He holds my hand.

"It's mother. You're seeing and hearing through her body at times. The signal doubles. It is time to decide."

"Just what are my choices again?" I stall but unfortunately know what I must do.

"She's in no shape to assimilate, so we'll have to try a manual extraction. You'll be placed with your friends in stasis until I can perfect my experiment. You'll be in no pain. Not even aware until we release you from the pod."

"And if I don't?" One tiny tear distorts my vision in my right eye. The left one follows closely behind.

"You'll both die. No amount of stasis can preserve you. You're half of *us* now."

I can't utter the words, so I just nod my head. Over a week of rebellion against this very thing, and it's come down to this. He puts one of my arms around his shoulder and leads me out through the sliding doors.

Azuna's in the next room over lying flat on her back, just her face visible. She's buried in silver blankets inside something that looks like an old magnetic imager, the open kind. Radiant lights trace her body revealing her internal organs as they shine through her covering. A second platform's prepared for me. As soon as I lie down, the table starts beeping and raising me up to the same level as Azuna. A slow massage-like vibration feels good on my muscles, but I feel so guilty. I never got to say goodbye to my friends. Luther's family? Will I even remember who they were when I return?

Bale drapes me in the same gear as Azuna and injects me with an amnesia drug. He says it will take time to work, but I'll have no recollection of any of this. It burns a little going in, but suddenly I'm distracted by a familiar voice. At first I'm sure it's Marek maybe saying his goodbyes, but I'm wrong. It's Rico. *Listen to me, Faith. Wherever you are, you can't give up your soul to her. You hear me. You just can't.* His voice grows clearer, but it's too late. I've no more options. *Fight back, Faith. They'll do anything to get you to let go. Fight it. She can't win. She just can't.*

The room spins, but I'm not out cold. Bale's hidden himself behind a control panel screen with monitors extending above. I look over at Azuna, but her blankets are in a pile on the table, and she's gone. Where is she? Am I finished? Is she me now? That was fast.

I panic. Rico's voice haunts me. *They'll do anything just to get to you. Fight it!* I kick the blankets off of me and roll off the table. Both wrists take the brunt of the fall, but I'm only momentarily stunned. I crawl about ten feet back to the safety screen where there's a room. Lights are on and the door's ajar. With more strength than I anticipated, I move to a crouch and then stand. Poking my head into the room, I'm astonished. It's Bale, but he's not preparing to hit the extraction activation switch. He's suspended in mid-air by Demas as is Rico.

"Run!" they shout in unison. "They've tricked you. Go,

now!"

I don't wait around to be persuaded and race back into the main room, but I don't get very far. An unseen force slams me back down on the table and holds me there. I strain, but it's useless. More yelling comes from the control room.

"You've ruined everything!" Azuna's yells.

"Give me the new codes, or I swear; they'll all be dead by morning!" Demas screams.

"Never mind!" Azuna cries. "I don't need the idiotic extractor. I'll just do it myself! Get out of my way!"

"You're in no shape to be—"

"Her heart's willing now. She's nearly dead. It won't take much. Keep them here. I'll be back to handle them later."

Her heart's willing. I repeat it over and over again trying hard to refute it, but I can't. Azuna pushes her way through the door, and before I can blink she's hovering over me, her eyes as black as marbles. I'm glued down yet my body's being yanked, split into body and soul. Incredible pressure compels my eyes open, and I feel like I'm inside a drum underwater, floating and smashed back down into the earth at the same time.

Azuna's directly overhead like a spirit now, her hands together in front of her face like she's praying. Soon those same hands fly out to her sides, and my skin's bubbling. Flesh pulling away from bone. I need to close my eyes, but I can't. I drown out her laughter by chanting Rico's blast from the past song. *La, la, la, la, staying alive, staying alive.* Then I hear his voice join in. *La, la, la, la, staying alive, staying alive.* Both of us hold the steady rhythm and get louder and louder. *Her heart's willing.* No, it's not. I'm not ready to die yet. I'm not ready to die. I'm not…

Azuna chokes several times in between her gloating, and I can tell something's wrong. She repeats her prayer motion and flares out her hands, but the effect is wearing off. Some feeling returns to my legs first and then my arms and hands. The amnesia drug has no effect. She stays perched, but I'm off the table in a nanosecond sprinting back to Rico and Bale. They're both gone. A trail of blood takes me out into a corridor I don't recognize. It is a part of the ship I've never seen before. The blood stops at double doors. I hit the key pad, and they open. It's pitch black, but I can't find a switch. I keep the doors cracked to let in some light and realize I've entered a storage room. Pod storage, only they're not empty pods; there are people inside. People I've grown to love. One in particular catches my eye. He's got my ears and my nose. Dad. I slump to the floor at his feet. *Creak.* The doors open wider. Click. Blinding light makes me cringe.

"They *all* have a chance if you comply," Demas' voice breaks me. I say my goodbyes, take his hand, and leave.

27

"I'm ready," I say as we walk back to where I just left Azuna. Probably at least ten more miserable steps back down the hall, into the room, and I'll be gone. The *best* part of me anyhow. Not basing that on any religion or astrological sign or some existential theories, just basing it on experience. The *outer* me is highly flawed. I was never a good enough daughter, a bright student, but one who failed to reach my potential. I run like a marathon runner, but otherwise I'm non-athletic. I finally become something *special,* and *that's* not even reliable. How much easier would it be if I just projected all my healing energy at her, and she miraculously didn't *need* my soul to survive? Alive to do whatever the hell she wanted with this planet, as long as she left my friends and me alone.

We finally reach the extraction room doors, but he stops. "What now?" I ask.

"Hostile life forms inside."

In an instant, those same doors rip open. Marek pegs Demas right in the face with his whole body and lands directly at my feet followed by Dredge. My escort's a squished bug under their weight. Someone's tossing them around like rag dolls inside the room. I duck my head inside, but the room is full of pod people turning on each other. Somebody let them all out. I scan quickly for my father, but he's not there. Neither is Azuna. Dredge and Marek shake loose the butterflies, sweep me off my feet, and tear down the corridor. I protest, but they're determined to get me as far away from the lab as possible.

Pockets of pod people chase us down an alternative hall, but Marek insists we can still make it. To where, I'm not sure. Anywhere but on this damn spaceship sounds good to me. Dredge is forced to fire on our crazy non-deads, and I pray Dad's not one of them, or any of the rest of our family and friends.

We blast our way through to the shuttle bay, and more than half of the crafts are gone. Two remain, but they're already drawing quite the mob. Chancellor Stevens? Brace yourself for the consequences of your own pride. The *pod people* have landed. And you thought a bunch of friendly aliens were so easy to manipulate. Try a crew of hyped-up pissed off pod people who want their souls back.

The non-dead are not exactly the most coordinated since their days or maybe even weeks in stasis. So the three of us bulldoze our way to the last empty shuttle, knocking bodies over the railings rather than shooting them. I feel tons better until I see face after innocent face as they fall to their deaths anyhow. It's not *their* fault they weren't allowed to die peacefully in the first place. We duck our heads through the hydraulic doors and seal them shut behind us. Dredge flicks a few switches and pulls back on the center joy stick. The engine hums for a second then dies. An error message flashes across the dashboard. *Critical battery failure.*

I'm taking it that Niners must not use Duracells or Energizers because we'd be halfway out of here already.

"No, no, no! It can't be!" he screams. "I'll have to override the main cells and use the backups. We might not get far, but at least we'll be safe. *You'll* be safe." He engages the backups, and the humming returns.

"Hey, I know it's not exactly perfect timing, but thanks. Thanks for everything. I really appreciate all you've done for me. For *all* of us."

"Sure thing, princess," says Dredge.

"Yeah, I told you it wasn't over. Remember?" Marek adds.

"How could I forget? You said it at the Reflection Pool, just before everything went black." I pause. "I'm sorry, Marek."

I push two moderate electrical charges from my hands to their bodies, and they're both down for the count. I had to draw on my Azuna mojo just to pull it off, but it worked. It takes a few minutes, but I drag both of them out to the bay landing and head back to the shuttle, shooting a half dozen or so soulless defectors trying to swipe my ride out. This battle with Azuna? It's all mine now. I won't risk losing anyone else. I can't. Chancellor Stevens? Set another place for dinner tonight. I *think* you're gonna have another guest. Trust me. It's gonna be a *blast*.

Only having been in one of these transports once before, I touch the screen, and a series of choices appear. They're not exactly in English, so I pick the *one* icon that resembles a map. Jackpot. Auto-pilot complete with GPS. I know it sounds improbable, but so does alien soul snatching, and I've already partially given mine up. Anyhow, I'm pretty sure it doesn't take a genius to hit a button.

I take a few minutes to research the White House co-ordinates, but they dial in as soon as I find them. I flick the same buttons Dredge did and pull back on the joy stick. *Whir!*

I'm about to strap myself in when I see someone out my side window. It's Misty, the non-dead version. I guess their training didn't do *them* much good either. Her face is riddled with open sores, and she's deadly pale; her gorgeous hair a total rat's nest. She sees me as well and ambles across the steel bridge, her face plastered right up against the window. I want to rush right out, drag her inside, and haul our asses right out of this mess, but I can't. She probably doesn't even know it's me.

"Faith? It's Misty," she squeaks. So much for making this easy on me. "You can't go. Not yet. See?" She holds up her damaged tablet, but there's a leftover image, one of her homemade games. "You're not finished here. Junior and Mom and all the rest? We're counting on you. You gotta let her have your soul."

"Why?" I scream back, nearly damaging my own ears. "If I do, then she wins. Don't you get it."

"No. She doesn't win. 'Cuz Marek told you. It's not over yet. There's a better way. Trust him."

"I did! Look where that got me! I'm not even me anymore! I'm a half-breed! A total freak! Stevens has to pay for this! All of this!"

"She will, just not now. Come back. Please, come back."

I can't believe I'm even considering it as Misty slides down the side of the shuttle and crumbles like a load of laundry. How do I know it's even her? It could be another trick, a hologram or impersonator. Maybe Demas awoke, and he's telling her what to say or manipulating me back to the extraction room.

I tap my fingers on the window praying Misty will hear it, but she's not moving. Every fiber in my being begs me to push the pedals to the floor, lift off, and crash this thing right through Steven's front window, but I hold back. Unexpectedly, there's a rush of cold air at my back. The doors have been opened. It's Bale.

"Don't talk me out of this," I say. "I'd rather *die* than give her what she wants. She can't have the rest of me, Bale. She just can't."

"I know. You're the consummate heroine," he says, shaking his head side to side contradicting his words. "Normally I'd completely agree with you, my dear, especially after all you've put up with. Demas pretending to be me, and Azuna almost assimilating. You gotta be exhausted. But I can't let you kill yourself. Not when I'm so close."

"Demas pretended to be you? How?" My back and shoulders throb. I run my fingers over my tattoo, and it's raised up, swollen. I noticed the pain right after my close call with Azuna.

"A three-dimensional hologram, looks, sounds, and feels like the real thing, but it's not. You know I'd never—"

"Wait! Isn't that exactly what you're doing now? Talking me back into the burning building? No thanks. I just left. It's becoming a little too zombie-like in there for me."

"Thanks to Rico," His voice cracks. He's keeping something from me.

My stomach flips. "He's alive!"

"Yeah, and guess what?" It's the first time he's smiled since he arrived. "He's my first success story. Well, sort of."

"What do you mean sort of?"

"His will to live was even stronger than yours. As soon as I injected him with my serum, including *your* DNA, he woke up. He let everyone else out. But he's the *only* one who shows no aggression and doesn't want to tear the spine out of anyone, at least, not anymore. Not sure how long it'll last."

"But he's soulless now too, isn't he?"

"Yes. I'm afraid I couldn't help Luther or any of your friends. We're out of time."

"Uh—could you do me a big favor? Would you mind if I pinched you or slapped you or something? Just so I know that you're real? I'm a little paranoid, ya know?"

"Be my guest." On first movement from me, he shrinks back. Playing with me like the real Bale would.

I pinch him hard at first, and he winces. I warn him then slap him right in the face.

"Ouch! You've gotten stronger," he jokes. "Satisfied?" I nod. "Good, now let's get Misty and go back inside. Mother's in stasis now. I had no choice. Should you decide—"

"I know. You'll wake her up, and we'll be one. You just gotta give me a little time."

"I understand. But you know, I can't think of a better person. Who knows? Maybe with a real soul, *your* soul, you'll convert her."

"I don't wanna be a zombie. Please don't bring me back until you've perfected it. You gotta promise."

"I promise. You have my word."

"Any chance I can get it back one day? My *true* soul, that is?"

"That's the plan."

Dredge and Marek are on their feet, and they're already tending to Misty. Her open wounds look painful. She's still out, but I wave my hands over her heart, touch her wounds, and she revives. An angry growl knocks me back on my butt as she lunges at my throat. Dredge catches her mid-stream before she can do any damage, and she claws at his eyes. Bale pulls a stun stick from his back pocket, but she's unfazed. He zaps her at least five times before she settles down to a low roar. A quick sedative to the neck puts her back to sleep for now.

"Why are they so violent?" I ask as we make our way back to the lab.

"From what I've discovered, there's at least one hundred fifty percent increase in adrenaline, like a dopamine spike, if you will. Almost as if their bodies fought so hard to keep their souls, and they got stuck in fight mode. They strike out at whatever or whomever is available."

"But Misty spoke to me, knew who I was. She was

pleading with me."

"Her training, remember? She's like you. More equipped to push through, and she did not allow the stasis to completely change her, much like Dredge and *his* alter ego."

"Blodd."

"Exactly. We've tried everything to counter Demas' spell, including the substitute soul infusion but—"

"I'm not any closer to controlling my multiple identities than before. It just doesn't last quite as long, and I'm more aware of my feelings when I'm a monster."

"Great. I'll be an *empathetic* zombie. Yippee."

"Hey, just be thankful you're not doubling as a statue half the time. Are you sure you wanna do this? I mean, we can all still walk away, head for the mountains, live off the land."

Marek agrees. I'm surprised. I thought his loyalties ran deeper. I weigh their suggestion, but I won't leave my friends. Not now. There is too much at stake. Even if Azuna dies, there are enough Niners to take her place, her father, for one and Demas for another. It's not easy to trust, but I have to give it a chance. She's practically me already. If what she said about me dying too is true, I only *have* one option.

"Let's go," I say, a weak flutter starts in my voice. "The sooner we get this over with, the better. Thanks for everything. See you in what, a couple of weeks? A month?"

I'm trying to get Bale to shine a little more light on my darkened forest. Maybe give me a time table for how long I'll be cooped up like Dr. Busby's pet horse's brain he keeps in a jar of formaldehyde. Ain't no way *that* brain's coming back to life, so I'm praying my fate's a little better. I'd hate to wake up in ninety years and find myself on someone else's shelf or locked in their basement with a label on my jar. *Faith Monroe. Experiment number nine thousand. Failed.*

28

An hour later, I suffer through a *rah rah* blurb from Chancellor Stevens that makes me want to vomit in her mouth. If she only knew my original plan to park my shuttle right through her bedroom window, she might be slightly less enthusiastic. I long to share it with her, but I take Marek's advice and play my role to the hilt. It may prove to be quite valuable having her and her cronies actually *believe* I'm doing the noble thing. All along she's unaware that as soon as I get back to the land of the living, I'll make her life miserable. Her chance at re-election will be about the size of an atom after I expose her scheme.

The only window in Marek's ship puts just enough glare on Stevens' face on the monitor she appears to have horns. The cut-out pattern in the segments turns her into a demon—spit flies out of her mouth as she promises to give me a key to the country or some other bullshit commendation. Ironically, I don't say much because if I did, I just may talk myself out of the whole thing. I'd trek it on up to the mountains and let them try to find me. Even if I stayed alive for a year, at least the Niners would have to call an audible. Their holy leader is rotting away in a decomposition pod while they played rock, paper, scissors for her job. I just don't understand why Stevens would let her waltz in and take over. She must be under a spell or trick by Demas. It's a shame Vice-Chancellor Burton's so weak. He would have made the best leader yet. He actually *wants* to make a difference not just talk about it.

The broadcast ends rather abruptly almost like an electrical short in the satellite feed. Soon the ship's leaning to the left as if to avoid sky traffic or something. Then quickly back to the right. An intercom chirps, but no voice can be heard. Bale enters the extraction room more than a bit frazzled.

"It's time. All your vitals checked out. Azuna's prepped and ready."

"Okayyyyy. But what was that? Just now? I almost heaved."

"Not sure. I just came from mother's. She's been wheeled next door. Follow me."

We exit and enter the adjacent room where the first thing that hits me is the smell—a combination of bleach and Dr. Busby's taco breath.

"Ewww! What's with the odor?" I ask.

"Decomposition. Niner bodies decay at a higher rate

than humans. Outside of stasis, what did you expect? A rose garden?"

"Well, no. But you coulda warned me. I thought we were friends?"

Bale's amazing at multi-tasking—carrying on our conversation while systematically sticking me with needles, electrodes, and placing on my head something that looks like a Dr. Frankenstein helmet, only way more high-tech. I'm trapped inside half of a tanning booth contraption—Azuna's body slid into the opposite half. I ask for a clothespin, but Bale's kind enough to outfit me with a mask instead.

Suddenly I'm majorly impulsive glancing up at her rotting body and back to Bale. I go back and forth expecting things to change. A slow churning begins underneath the table. I shiver as it gets louder and louder. Bale grabs my hand—his eyes bluer than I've ever seen them.

"You're sure?" he asks. "It's the point of no return, Faith. I can still stop."

I squeeze his hand. He doesn't let go. My breaths are so shallow he coaches me to breathe deeper, but I'm failing. A familiar stabbing pain in my head starts and matches the deafening thump of my heart. I'm not immobile but feel like I've been wrapped in cellophane. Each muscle in my body spasms, even the one's controlling my eye sockets and cheeks, which are soaked with tears now.

Ahhhhhh! One blood-curdling scream later causes Bale to release his grip and back away, but I must be hallucinating. His eyes tear up. *Niners don't cry. They've no soul. No need for stupid feelings.* Azuna's confidence, her mindset's already taking root, but you'd never know it by my exterior. I'm a weary mess—about to cry out again until a deafening voice rocks my skull. *Brace yourself. We're all going down.*

I can't respond. Bale's almost finished with the extraction and injecting me with a purple substance. All my dreams. All my knowledge and memories grow faint. I fight so hard to hang on, but they leave me. Where did I live? How old am I? What's my name? Question after question with no more answers. One final rush of sweltering pain explodes in my chest, and I might as well be a formless shadow. Thousands of voices ring in my ears. Some are familiar, but I don't know why. Some unfamiliar and panicked. I don't want them there, but I'm not in control. Not anymore.

My arms move remotely. Suddenly I'm up and walking. How can that be? I'm still wearing this contraption. Eyes closed. I still see myself lying there. My head's shaking side to side. I'm squirming. Battling. Lashing out, but it's no use. *La, la, la, la, staying alive, staying alive. La, la, la, la, staying ali—ve.* A horrid hush, and then I meet my own darkened void.

29

"Stop it, Faith. You're not yourself. We're friends, remember?"

I war against my rage, but his words don't register. His face may as well be a giant question mark. All I want to do is hurt him. Wring his neck. Stab him in the heart. He's positioned himself behind a tipped over counter. There's a massive mess of wreckage with sparks still flying through the air and smoldering. Mechanical parts and debris scattered on all sides. I'm hanging sideways strapped into some kind of glass tube. My jaw aches. For some reason I can't stop grinding my teeth. I'm waiting for my fog to lift, but it's taking its good old time.

He tries to capture my attention once again, but he might as well be a cockroach. I want him smashed beneath my foot. Eliminated.

"The ship went down," he says, like that's supposed to mean something to me. "Vice-Chancellor Burton shot us down. We're somewhere in the Blue Ridge Mountains, I think."

Who is this guy? Why do I want to destroy him and protect him at the same time?

"It's the stasis. Please, just stay where you are a little while longer, and you'll remember."

Stasis. I'll remember? What will I remember? So far my brain is engaged, but I utter no words. Animalistic grunts claw their way out of my throat, and I'm tired of not being able to breathe. In one big jerk, I rip away at the harness around my chest and waist and crumble to the ground. Thick dark dirt pushes up through the metallic base. We're most definitely no longer in the air. *No longer in the air.* I repeat this thought over and over again, and soon my ire softens some.

"Stay back!" he screams. "It'll take a little longer than you think."

My murmurs begin to transform as well, allowing me to play parrot with him.

"Take a little longer?" I question, like I'm learning a new language.

"Yeah." He peeks over the counter and approaches. "I had to learn the hard way myself." His head swings down to his right where a body lay. The head smashed in, a coal black blood outline around the skull. I stare but feel nothing. So what? Someone died. It's not me, and that's all I can think about.

"I'm Rico," he says. There's no meaning behind it. "Ozzy and Star. They're gone. Ran off like wolves trying to kill each other. I couldn't stop them. And your dad." He breaks off a three-foot pipe from the rubble to fend me off and mumbles a few more words.

"Bale's dead, Faith. I'm sorry, but I just had to wake you up. I'm all alone out here. You gotta remember. Please."

A reservoir of water in a shattered basin calls to me. A little shaky in my movements still, I crawl to it, plunging my face into my memories. I mull over Rico's thoughts trying to make connections—some are short circuiting with the frigid bath. Others are beginning to register. *Dad. Bale. All these faceless names.*

I submerge myself longer again, finally rising up like I'm drowning, sucking in each breath faster and faster. I'm shocked when Rico's hand cradles around the back of my neck, and I turn slamming down hard on his arm and kicking him to the ground. But in an instant I'm sorry—reaching out my hand to help him up. Continuously shaking out the cobwebs and replacing them with real memories. Faces. Events. Gargoyles. Pod people. A flood of images attacking my mind all at once.

"Faith!" I yell, my voice echoing through the ruins. "I am Faith Monroe, and I am alive!"

Rico tries his best to get technical with me by saying our bodies are *functioning*, but we're basically soulless. I don't care. I know who I am now. Who *he* is. What I want to do and why. I bother him with more questions, as we seek better shelter from an oncoming storm.

He's fashioned a temporary campsite in a cave approximately two hundred yards from the crash site. We're drenched by the time we arrive, but he's already got a fire going in minutes. My limp grew more pronounced through the rugged terrain, so lying down is convenient. I've no pain whatsoever, so the fact that my legs aren't working is more annoying than anything.

"Tell me more," I say. "How did Azuna get away? Why didn't she crash *with* us?"

"As soon as the transfer was complete, Demas showed up in a vortex. He took Marek and Dredge, but Bale got trapped in the pod room with you as the ship went down. He had to make sure your stasis was working, and he gave you the treatment."

"Treatment? What treatment?" I stare through the fire into Rico's eyes. There's something *different* about him. I haven't regained all my senses yet, but half of a thought seeps back in. *My first success story.*

"His artificial soul or something. As you can tell, it takes a little while for it to kick in after the zombie tube, but I think it works. I mean, I haven't wanted to screw anybody's head off for a while now."

"How long have we been here?"

"Days. I'm not sure how many. I heard a few choppers flying overhead yesterday, but around the crash site location, there aren't too many places to land. I guess we better be on the lookout, though. Not sure the government wants *us* alive. Destroy the evidence, ya know?"

Sharp lightning cracks just outside the opening. Wind whips straight through me, and suddenly I remember what it's like to be cold. Dead cold. After a moment of hesitation, Rico slides right next to me placing his arm across my shoulders and back. The flame's intense, but not more severe than the aching in the middle of my chest—an emptiness beyond a physical response. His arm triggers a little more discomfort across my tattoo and adds pressure to my upper body for some reason. He apologizes and pulls away, but I'm enjoying his warmth, and I invite him back.

"I don't get it," I whisper.

"Don't get what?"

"We've no souls, right? So how can we feel? Have emotions? You really think Bale's experiment worked? You gotta take me to him when the rain stops. Maybe I can—"

"Heal him?"

"Yeah, I mean, we're stuck here. Not much food or water. A guy creates a soul? I think *he'd* find a way out of here."

"But what if you can't? Who knows if your abilities transferred over?" He pulls my hair behind my ear, and it's awkward. No boy's ever been this close to me before. I blame it all on the situation. He couldn't possibly be attracted to me. It's his natural kindness shining through.

I divert my thinking. "Well, let's test it. Got any cuts, scrapes?"

"I had a few, but they're better. What about your leg?" he asks.

"Uh—nope. If I recollect, I can't heal myself."

The fire dwindles some. Rico jumps up to add more wood, but I feel a strange charge in my shoulders, a quick twinge in my chest again. *Whoosh.* Sparks leave my hands before I can control it, and the flames shoot up to the rocks overhead sustaining itself for seconds before dying down to an even warmer blaze.

"Wow," Rico says, dropping his sticks on the ground. "Should I even bother?"

I smile for the first time since we left the wreckage. "Guess not. I think I can handle it."

He's draped a silver shock blanket on the ground and over us and grabbed a few towels from the ship to cushion our heads. My mind's reeling with so many thoughts as we huddle together again. *Bale can't be dead. He's the only one who can reverse this thing. Get us our souls back. Where's my father? Will he even know me?*

Rico's abilities must be enhanced too because he's heard all my worries. His improvements are creepy and remarkable at the same time. I never had to watch what I think before.

"Slow down, my friend. You'll find answers soon enough. The band will be back together again." He laughs. "Hah. I just thought of the perfect name." He tosses a few bigger logs onto the fire just to look useful.

"What's that?"

"The Grateful Un-Dead. And now on lead vocals, it's Screaming Faith Monroe!"

It's stupid, but we spend the next few minutes playing air guitar and drums and singing our favorite tune. *La, la, la, la staying alive, staying alive. La, la, la, la staying alive, staying alive.*

We're alive, but for how long? I pause staring at Rico like he's my only hope. He was dead. *Now* look at him. He's jumping around like an idiot but making me realize that maybe we *can* do this. As long as I'm not having one heckuva dream, and we get out of these mountains? Anything's possible. *He's my only success story.* Bale's words resonate again.

Instead of slowing down, the storm gets worse. Even colder air spills in. Neither one of us can explain it, but there's an attraction beyond keeping each other warm. Soon we're back down on the ground in front of the fire. The blanket's not much help, but neither are our bodies. I mean, I sense his presence and feel his touch, but the only true heat comes from my magical flames. Hail mixes with the giant raindrops outside the cave as a puddle develops in front of the opening. I think of it as the moat to our castle because I'm running out of small talk. Not much energy left for any intruders.

"Weeks ago, you ever think we'd be here? I mean, running for our lives? Getting our souls sucked out?" he asks.

"Yeah, right. I'm sure that was right up there with Dr. Busby's *our government's possessed by demonic forces theory.*"

"Dr. Busby?"

"He's a science teacher at my school. He had a lot of odd conspiracy ideas and crap. I think he spent half the week brainwashing us."

"Pretty funny. I guess he wasn't *all* wrong though, was he?"

"Nope. I ever get to see his stubby body again; I'll be the *first* to apologize."

"Not to change the subject, but your lips? They're blue."

"We're soulless, remember? Do you think *yours* are any different?"

We snuggle even closer listening to the violence of the

night. A few really close lightning strikes just overhead. Rico's back to his prayer-mode pantomiming the cross over and over again and spouting his Hail Mary's. I want to make jokes, but I don't. We could all be new cemetery decorations right now, but here we are. We stood up to the big bad aliens. Like Misty's game, we're ready to hit reset.

"Hail Mary? Why her? Why not just talk to God himself?" I ask, really curious about his answer.

"Tradition," he explains, "nothing more. I know who's *really* listening. Besides, it sounds a little better than saying God, God, God. Too whiny." He grins his famous Rico smile again. I never noticed it before, but he's a goofball a majority of the time but also quite handsome. Chocolate eyes with thin stubble over his bottom chin, a light moustache forming after days in the wilderness. I never had the time to notice before. I guess sometimes survival trumps romance.

I wonder what he thinks of me? I probably look like Barbie's maniac cousin. *Oh, no. I forgot. He can hear my—*

"Thoughts," he says. "And you don't look like Barbie's maniac cousin."

"Thanks."

"More like her insane asylum sister."

I nudge him with my arm a little too hard sending him caroming into the side wall. He's laughing, so I know I didn't hurt him.

"Keeping up that image, are you?" he says, crawling back over to me.

"What image?"

"Praying mantis? People wanna get to know you, but

they're scared?"

"Are you? Scared of me?"

"The truth? A *little*. Not enough to give up, though. You're one complicated insect girl." He places a gentle kiss on my ear. I think he missed my cheek, but I don't care. Why did I wait to be dead to start falling in love? I have perfect timing.

We go back to our cuddling to keep warm mode, but then I startle him.

"Shhh. Can you hear it?"

The rain's nearly died down to a drizzle. Thunder growls in the distance. A few leftover flashes brighten up the entrance still, but the storm's passed for now.

Rico's the first to stick his head out of the cave. Our clothes are nearly dry from the fire. Surprisingly, my leg works much better now. I turn back to kick some dirt on our fire as Rico checks for wild animals. No sense leaving any evidence behind should somebody make their way into this part of the mountains. I snag the only source of light we'll have to get back to the ship. A stun stick Rico must have taken his first day in the wild, just in case he'd run into a bear or even worse, the FBI.

A crackle of sticks and shuffle of feet lure me back out of the cave. No sign of Rico.

"Rico? I've got the stun stick. We can use it to—"

"Over here!" he yells. "Back down the trail."

I pull the trigger and illuminate my steps, but when I reach him I let go. Ten yards away, it's Ozzy and Star. They have him cornered on top of a large boulder. A putrid smell wafts my way. They've both got remnants of something dangling from their mouths, but so far they don't see me. I inch my way near them not sure of my next move, but I need to act quickly.

Shock them with the stick. Maybe they'll leave. Rico passes a couple of suggestions to me. I'm within striking distance when they turn on a dime and attack me. I jab back and forth with the stunner, but it has minimal effect. I'm pinned, my back toward a tree, as I dodge angry fingers and teeth. Meanwhile, Rico's created a mild distraction thumping them both in the back with a stick. In seconds, it breaks, and they're right back at me, a black death in their eyes like I saw in the *other* pod people.

Normally outrunning them would be an option, but I'm not sure how far I'd get with my leg. So I think of the next best thing. I toss the stick down in front of them like a grenade, clap both hands together, and they fly back like they just stepped on a mine. Rico ducks as they soar above him and crash into the boulder. He runs to me. We embrace.

"You okay?" I ask.

"Yeah, you?" he counters.

"Fine, they don't even know us. Why haven't they changed back yet? Is there any way we can—" I barely get the words out between breaths. Panic washes over me, and I start stomping my feet like I'm having a tantrum and pounding on the tree till my knuckles bleed. Amazingly, a trickle of pain starts to register, and I've never been more agitated.

"Stop! Stop!"

Thud.

He tackles me away from the tree landing right on top

of me. "Let's find Bale. Stick to the plan. They'll be out for a while. Okay?"

"Right," I say matter-of-factly. "The plan: heal Bale. Get the hell outta here. Stop Azuna. Stevens. Everything gets back to normal.

The hike down the mountain goes faster than the trip up. Dawn crests over the horizon once we reach the valley, but the stun stick comes in handy most of the way. The ship's not as bad as I thought, considering we plummeted at least 10,000 feet. Although weaving through the debris to the pod room is a challenge. Rico drags me over a few more obstacles to where he last saw Bale's body. Immediately, he begins to pace.

"I don't get it. He was right here. I swear. I remember the flashing red lights on this control panel. He lay beneath it."

"You're sure he was dead?"

"As sure as Ozzy and Star are crazed animals sure. I slapped him a half dozen times with no response."

"Maybe he's alive and looking for us?"

We search a couple more adjacent rooms, but he's gone. *Helicopters overhead.* Stevens. She must have taken the body. Azuna would have wanted it. We take the next few minutes scrounging for more useful items to take back to the cave. All this time, not one hunger pang. Not one need for a bathroom. No wonder Marek and Bale could go hours without relieving themselves.

We skip and jump out of the remains with two knapsacks a piece, even some food should our appetites return. A quarter of the way back up, our journey is interrupted.

"They took him," announces a voice neither of us has heard for some time. "We think they took your dad too."

It's Ozzy and Star. Not the hungry wolve's version, but we're cautious, nonetheless.

"You're back?" I question, remembering how long it took for me to regroup. I drop the bags and raise my hands above my head as a threat.

"The explosion. I guess it brought us back to reality. Where are we? How did we get here?" she says, still a bit dazed.

I can tell Star's experiencing the same emptiness I felt by the awkward look on her face. Tufts of fur and flesh hang from both of their mouths. Fresh and dried blood covers their bodies from head to toe. Satisfied they're really back to *somewhat* normal, we detour near a small creek to wash away their stench. All of us decide to bathe, half-naked half-clothed and sharing the two bars of soap.

It was a stream just like this where we were faced with the decision to walk away or move forward. Each of us was at various stages of confidence feeling lonely, broken and unable to fathom our situation. No *real* choice in the matter. Fight for the right to keep our souls or take off.

Why didn't we run? I can't speak for my new family, but I can speak for myself. Dr. Busby's words troubled me. *Dying for your country sounds so noble, until you uncover the real reason they want you dead.* How did *he* know? Was he some kind of alien too? He may have been talking about the military, but I can't help but think he was warning me. Us. The world. Crazy *is* as crazy *does*, but what if crazy isn't crazy at all? Aliens exist, people. They're here. They call themselves

Niners, and they want your souls. Dr. Busby? You were right. But right now? I'm not feeling so *righteous*.

For the first time in days, the sun's rays don't take forever to heat the morning up as we lie spent on the riverbank staring up into the sky. Each of us is refreshed from the clear mountain water but in no hurry to return to the stuffy old cave. Not even the wet underwear and tiny rocks poking holes in our skin's enough to make us get up. An intermittent blow of the wind from the brook reminds us how filthy we were but diminishes nicely with the smell of real soap.

Not too certain of tomorrow, we fight sleep by cracking old knock-knock jokes. Heck. We're not too certain of an *hour* from now, but we know *one* thing. Without Bale and Marek's help and all the training, we'd *really* be dead, and not just soulless.

Buzzards circle us occasionally dipping lower and lower to detect movement, so Rico and Ozzy kick their legs occasionally to shoo them away. We're still the hunted but pose little threat now. The Niners think we're dead. The funny thing is, we *are*.

"You okay over there, praying mantis girl?" Rico asks.

"Fabulous. There's nothing like a cold dip in the wilderness to bring everything into perspective, huh?" I scrub a little more dirt and blood from Star's forehead she must have missed.

"Whaddya mean?" Ozzie says.

"Not sure, but I think I've *finally* found something I'm willing to die for—freedom. Freedom to go out the *organic* way, the method planned for each of us."

"Yeah, Rico," Star interrupts. "Any possibility Hail Mary

can give us another chance at this living stuff? I mean, cats get nine lives, right? Aren't we a little more important?"

I can't wait to add my own wisdom. "Hail Mary, hear our prayer. We promise not to crap in the sandbox, sorry if I offended you. It's who I am." I cross my chest left and right like I've watched Rico do many times. Soon we're all lying on our backs doing it over and over again minus the laughter and joking.

I've seen enough to know in my 16 years that humans make terrible gods, focusing mainly on themselves instead of others, especially lately. In the end, selfish deeds die right along with them, while *unselfish* ones bask in immortality. How sad our enemies are blind to this truth and live without fear of repercussions. Oh, but I *swear* they'll be consequences. They'll rise from the ashes of truth and haunt them.

I'm not sure where all this philosophical mumbo jumbo is coming from, but I suppose my artificial soul's bringing some of it out of me. Bale's special alien formula not only keeps us alive but also infuses us with Aristotle's brains or something. I coax my mind to stop proselytizing, but the data keeps flowing.

Ambitious leaders might sit at the banquet table and pretend they're tiny birds, a morsel here, and a morsel there. Easily ignoring how full they've become. Others are vultures, choking down each swallow and proud of their conquest. Ah—but sooner or later, *everyone* eats—most with no worry whatsoever.

"You think Azuna's still looking for us?" Ozzy asks. "I mean, she has what she wanted, right?

Not sure what to say, I let my muse respond instead.

"Why be scared of what's already deceased? What harm can we do?"

My evil grin starts a chain reaction around our make-shift campfire circle. Because we know when the reckoning comes? The *dead*—got nothing to lose.

Read on for a Sneak Peek of

SOULLESS

BOOK TWO
of the
NINE TRILOGY
By D.M. King

1

"Any chance I can get it back one day? My true soul that is?"

"That's the plan."

Bale's words mean nothing to me now as I spent another sleepless night in the middle of the wilderness as a half-human half-Niner. My *true* soul rattles around in my arch enemy as she's probably busy altering the planet I *used* to know pretty well. The sun's a beauty as it rises over the highest mountain in view, but hope remains hidden. Not even the purples and pinks in the baby-blue sky seem to help much. They bring a tiny smile, but my darkness lingers.

At least I'm not alone in my emptiness. The band's definitely back together for good, but we need something to look forward to. Days drag on with no sign of another human being, just a crap-load of deer and skunks treating us like we're Cousin Vinny or Aunt Millicent invading their homestead. West Virginia deer may be smaller, but they're still annoying. A couple of days ago, they scared the pants off of Rico as he relieved himself. They chased him at least a quarter mile with his underwear wrapped around his ankles, or so he claims. We heard him screaming, but I'm glad I missed *that* spectacle. It might have ruined some of my unexpected feelings for him.

Seemingly not needing as much food or water as we used to when we were alive, the past few days we've been fleshing out a new plan to get back to civilization and start making some rebellious noise. Azuna thinks she's got it so easy now that we're *gone*. She's exterminated the cockroaches. Too bad she's lacking relevant insight. Prehistoric. Before history. Those critters were created to survive a nuclear holocaust. *Be the cockroach*. That's become our new battle cry.

"I think we should go back to the crash site at least once more before we head down stream. There may be something useful we missed, and we're gonna need every resource," I say, packing up my few personal items and loading them into my backpack.

It's a mild morning. A tender breeze blows just enough to dishevel my hair, but it's warm. I'm not sure spring has totally sprung, but it's a heckuva lot more comfortable now than it was when the ship went down. Our cave came in handy at night as we took turns staying up scouting for bears or in our case, Niner soldiers. Thankfully we had no major incidences, unless you want to count Ozzy's reverberating snore. One night Star had had enough and grabbed her stuff to sleep out under the night sky. I just prayed we wouldn't wake up and find her dead carcass strung out all over the ground. Apparently she'd done a lot of camping when she was younger, so she was used to it. I'm not sure even a bear would stand much of a chance against her anyhow. Her artificial soul has magnified her strength tenfold. Maybe we *should* turn her loose? We sure could use a bearskin rug in our humble abode. Not that we'll ever see *that* place ever again.

"Faith's right," Star says. "It's time to go on the offensive. Vacation's over. We gave Azuna enough time to think we're really dead." She finishes up her tai-chi and squats down in a spot of soft moss.

"We *are* dead, remember?" Rico laughs. "Just not buried, right? If we could only find Bale—"

I shoot him an angry glance. I've been more on edge lately. Anxious. Short-fused for some odd reason. I pass it off as righteous anger for the most part because it's all I have left. Besides, Rico's been rambling on almost every day about Bale, but it's time we face the truth.

"Just stop, will ya? He's not coming back. Nobody is. We're on our own now. No Marek, no Dredge, no Luther. Got it! We can't count on anyone but ourselves. Our cavalry went down with the boat or got massacred by the Apaches. Let's head down."

Thanks to me, all of us have healed about the best we can from our dramatic plunge to Earth, so the trip back down the winding slope goes well. We scatter in all directions figuring we won't miss anything that way. I launch myself over what's left of sick bay debris to scour for more meds. With only one stun-stick, I send Rico to collect as many weapons he can carry. We may not know exactly how to use all of them, but I've always been more of a hands-on learner. Hopefully—we won't blow each other up or fire a hole through another barn door in the process. Ozzy and Star search for creature comforts like food, clothing, and anything to make our trek more manageable.

I reach the area where Rico let me out of the pod. And even though I'm adamant about Bale being lost for good, I keep hoping I'll find him buried beneath the rubble still. Work my magic fingers and voila, he's alive again. Some of the pods lie deep into the forest floor while others rest horizontally. They're all opened, at least eighty to a hundred raging lunatics roaming these woods now. Not to mention all the others back in the DC tunnels.

Five-minutes of digging, and I uncover a jackpot of undamaged antibiotics, bandages, and basic first aid equipment, which seems ironic. I'm still not wrapping my head around this current zombie mode *we're* in. I guess technically Bale's artificial soul buys us some more time, but who knows for how long? So we *can* be injured and killed even. We've retained our enhancements from our training too, only Ozzy's has diminished. His hyperlink with the ship's AI ended when the computer blew up on impact. And he hasn't been having his *usual* see-the-future moments as much as before. But I'm even more of an oddity now because while I haven't had to heal anyone lately, my body's like one gigantic electrical current. Sometimes I feel like I exist in a lightning bubble, and all it takes is a wave of the arm or hand to take down a tree or carve a new path through the rocky terrain.

I collect as much as I can fit into a second knapsack and stalk around for Bale's body one final time, using my superpowers to my advantage. I startle at the sight of first a black boot and then a leg poking out from under a half-covered pod. A few more swipes of my hand, and I've uncovered a complete body. It's a pod person who wasn't lucky enough to escape. Middle-aged man with a wide nose and several biker tattoos down his arms and neck.

His skull looks gashed, but the rest of him shows no sign of injury. *Do I bother to check for a pulse? I mean, it's been days. He's gotta be dead by now, right?* I'm insane, but I kneel down and place my tingling hand on his neck. Nothing. Just as I suspected. Before I can stand, I'm distracted by a blood-curdling screech from the other side of the wreckage. It's Rico. I wonder if he's been attacked by another deer. I rise, but in seconds I'm yanked back down to the ground by the pod-man. He's awake and extremely pissed off. I brace myself as best I can as he hauls me face-first down through the dirt back inside the buried part of the tube to retrieve something. He's gathered it before I can even react or loosen myself from his iron grip. *And I thought I was strong.*

We resurface, and I dislodge the caked mud from around my mouth and nose to breathe. My head rings like someone's boxed my ears, and my heart hammers its way up my throat. My abductor drags me by the hair to another upright cylinder next to his, and for some reason I've lost my alien mojo. Arrrrrrg! He lets out a livid scream and let's go for an instant. That's my cue to run.

I make it a few yards before he's back onto me leaping right over my head to stand as a wall. That's when I notice the lanyard around his neck. It's a neutralizer—the reason why I can't zap him and be on my way. *I thought Bale said these pod folks without souls were more like animals? Now they're thinking animals? Oh, boy. Smart zombies. Just what we needed.*

I vault over a plexi-glass cabinet to my left back toward the rest of the gang, but he's much faster. Fury radiates from his pores, his eyes, but I also see confusion and angst. Like the rest of us at first, he has no idea what's happened to him. Why he's a raging lunatic trying to rip out my ribs and feed me to the wolves.

I keep praying Rico will show up with the stun stick, anything to put this guy down for good, but my attacker's gone for the jugular. He leaps—pinning me down, and my head caroms off a steel beam. I'm dazed. I strain to keep his yellow teeth from gouging my neck, but I'm losing my battle. Then out of nowhere, three shots echo through the valley as the man slumps full-weight on top of me. Dead. I'm aware enough to shove him sideways and get to my hands and knees. My vision's blurred, but I catch two strangers out the corner of my eye. I look up at them, but the sky spins counterclockwise, and I'm out cold.

****

"Miss? Miss?" A slow drawl brings me back to the land of the living or whatever I'm supposed to call it now that I'm soulless. "You're fine, ma'am. We killed it."

"You did?" I question, not even aware of what *it* is at this point. My brain aches, and I can't control my gag reflex. Unfortunately—my heroes take the brunt of my vomit projectiles. It's crazy, but they don't even flinch.

"There, there now. Quite the bump you have on your noggin. It could be concussive. Levi did the best he could to patch you up. He stopped the bleeding and all, but alls we had was a butterfly band aide. I think you need stitches, but Levi swears you don't. He's studying to be one of them there paramedics, ya know?"

"My friends? Where are they?" I ask, not even sure what day it is. I should be thanking them, but my anger's rising up again.

"Friends? We really didn't see or hear anybody else, ma'am," Levi, the younger man finally speaks. "Sorry. We haven't even properly introduced ourselves. Levi Jackson. That's my daddy, Ned. We live on down the river a spell in Yancey. Don't suppose you've ever—"

"No. Can't say I have," I interrupt, more concerned about the rest of the *band* than myself right now. "You're sure you didn't see anyone else at the site? A tall African American? Short stocky female with a straggly Mohawk?"

I never get to Rico's description before Ned interjects his backwoods' wisdom. "I suppose if they were being chased by those zombie creatures, they didn't stick around long. If I may ask, what are those things, ma'am? Levi and I saw a gigantic explosion around four days ago, so we took out to explore. Just not too easy to hike these parts on account of there's not many trails. Luckily we followed the skid marks."

"Skid marks?" I question, starting to feel a little relief from my head wound.

"Yup," says Levi. "That there new military spacecraft blazed its *own* trail. So we just followed it on up. That's when we found you and killed that monster."

I'm not even sure where to begin explaining to my rescuers that they're not really monsters or zombies even. How to summarize the last few weeks of my life won't be easy, but I give it the old college try.

"You two get much news in these parts?" I ask.

Ned chuckles. He's a cross between a country western singer and one of those swamp people gator chasers. He twirls his long grey beard around in his fingers as he speaks. Every once and awhile I notice a sparkle in his crystal blue eyes. Kind of like, no matter what I tell him, he wouldn't be a bit surprised by it.

"Well—that's good because all that stuff you've been hearing recently about the new League of Nations and Planets and our signed agreement with the planet Nine? All of it's a sham. It turns out the Niners can't exist on *their* planet any longer, so they convinced our government to install us with expiration chips. Supposed to be a way for them to control their population on *their* planet, but humans were the guinea pigs."

"Are you sure you're feeling okay, ma'am? That's quite a story." Levi shakes his head like I've just told him he's pregnant or something.

"The God's honest truth. And by the way, I'm Faith. Faith Monroe."

"So why are those people acting like a bunch of angry wild boars?" Levi asks, checking the bandage around my head and flashing a pen light back and forth in front of my eyes. He's got his father's kind face and dimples, minus the beard. I'd guess around twenty or so—his hair coal black and longer for this day and age. He keeps testing my reflexes, and in seconds, he jumps back shocked by what he sees.

"You're—uh—you!" He grabs his daddy and draws away toward the path down the hillside then stops.

"One of them? Yes. How did you know? But I can explain—" I stumble forward toward them, my momentum halted by my electrical power surge. It's returned.

Ned jerks Levi by his jacket collar back toward me. "She's different, son. Can't ya tell? I'm not scared of her. But those others? Well—"

"You should be," I encourage. "It's a long story, but those *animals—uh--people* no longer have their souls. In order for the aliens to live here, they need a soul. Otherwise—they shrivel up like raisins and die. I was the perfect genetic match for Azuna, their leader. You may have seen her at the latest world summit. She swiped my soul, and as some of you may say up in these hills, I aim to get it back."

Levi and Ned aren't sure whether to trust me or not, but at least they stay. I'm busy wondering what Levi saw when he checked my eyes. I haven't seen myself in days.

"I swear to you—I'm not dangerous. Levi? Would you mind telling me what you saw? I mean—when you shined the light in my eyes?" I ask, more afraid of the answer than I admit.

"Miss Faith?" He's braver than he looks as he ambles back by my side shedding more pinpointed light in my eyes once again. "Right there, ma'am. You see? They glow. Can't always see it during the day, but at night? That's how we know they're lurking 'round the neighborhood. Pa and I've had to chase them away from our campsite these past two nights. Yancey's quite a hike from here, you understand?

We couldn't do it all at once. Not with Daddy's bad knee."

Deep down I want to hug them and thank them for all their help, but I'm not sure how they'll respond. *I'd never harm them. Would I? Could I?* My mind fights such thoughts, but to be honest, I'm not confident in anything right now. The one thing I could always count on was my conscience—my compassion. Who knows if Bale's fake soul takes that into account or not?

My aggravation grows as Ned appears more and more cautious like at any moment I could turn on them. If I don't do something soon to change their view, I won't have to worry about finding the rest of the gang or out-thinking the pod people. They're liable to just put me out of my misery.

"Please—listen to me," I beg. "You're right. I was one of them, but Azuna's son, Bale, didn't agree with the chip or the assimilation of souls. So he created an *artificial* soul. That's why I'm still alive, and so are my friends. You gotta help me find them." I hate crying in front of strangers, but I can't control it. My incandescent eyes go blurry as I drop to my knees rubbing my aching head.

Both men must be suckers for crying damsels in distress because it doesn't take long for them to lift me back to my feet and ease me on down the most treacherous part of the journey. The river approaches quickly, and all the while I'm forcing back the *power* not wanting to spook them away again. It's a chore, but after a half hour expedition along the riverbank, I have no choice. A medium-sized brown bear and her two cubs block our path across a shallow section of water. Ned fires his shotgun in the air, but it's no use. In fact, momma bear rises up on her haunches like a professional wrestler challenging us to a battle royale.

One flick of my wrist, and we'd all have bear-skinned caps, but I'm torn. *They trust me now. I need them. I have no idea where I'm going.* I decide to go easy for the greater good, but before I can warn them about my ability, four pod creatures tear out of the trees and chase our furry enemies back up the mountain. We attempt to hide behind a few larger shale boulders, but it's too late. They've spotted us. Guttural shrieks echo through the valley, and we're surrounded. Two seem more aggressive than the others—darkened dried blood's caked all over their faces, their hands, and in-between their fingernails. I have no idea, but it looks like they haven't eaten in days, and the three of us must look like a healthier buffet than a few steelhead trout.

Ned used up his fire power trying to chase away the bears, and Levi needs to study harder to be a paramedic—he's no hunter, missing everything in sight until I'm sure he's empty too.

"What now?" Levi asks, his lips quivering as fast as a hummingbird's wings.

Almost as if they're calculating the distance between us and them, the varmints close in.

"Promise me you won't run away and leave me here? I need to know." I test the waters before I awe them with my alien modification. At least they're out of ammo.

Levi and Ned huddle close wrapping their arms around me in a show of support. *Oh, boy. Wait until I unleash my version of violence.*

"Promise," They say in perfect chorus. "We don't wanna die like this."

So I unhinge myself from their iron grip, and like a con-
ductor beginning a symphony of terror, I release a charge.

Acknowledgements:

"Life is like an empty box. Put great stuff in? Get great stuff out."-D.M. King

This novel was written in loving memory of my brother Ernie who conquered his blood disorder but still lost the war, and to my grandsons who will one day accomplish even greater things than their Papa.

Author's notes:

I'm a writer, so I don't want to be cliché, but there are just so many people I need to thank. Distinguished members of the Academy? Cue the music. This might take awhile.

Where to start? I know this is going to sound crazy, but from the age of 14, I was convinced I would be a writer one day, a songwriter. But I remember at least 20 years ago a prophetess came to my church, and I'm not sure what led me up to her, but she kind of freaked me out when she said I would be a writer. Of course I said, "I already write songs, so that makes sense." She stared right through me and countered, "No. Not that kind of writer; a writer of *books*."

Wow! I'm pretty sure that's the first inkling I got to try my luck at novel writing. I'd had moderate success as a songwriter and published my first play, so how hard could it be?

Mighty hard. As an 8th grade English teacher, I've had the pleasure of teaching many YA novels over the years being inspired by writers like James Dashner, Alexander Gordon Smith, Rodman Philbrick, Neal Shusterman, Lauren DeStefano, Rae Carson, Amie Kaufman, and Harlan Coben among many others. So a HUGE thank you to all the writers I've mentioned and the many I didn't. All my Goodreads and Twitter friends have encouraged me to battle through the storms of rejection knowing one day all my hard work would pay off.

Thanks to people like Michelle Hauck and Brenda Drake and others who dedicate so much of their time and talent to set new writers down a healthy path to success with all their contests, advice, etc. I want to grow up to be like you one day. Of course, I owe so much to my incredible editor Leslie D. Stuart from Destiny Rose Editorial. I am indebted to her for many things but mostly for clearing my muddy paths of word debris and showing me how to truly edit my own work better from now on. What a blessing!

To all my students and teacher friends over the years? It was a pleasure to come to work every day knowing all of you had my back and wanted to see me successful. I write because I have a story to tell, but I'd be nowhere without readers willing to tolerate a flaw or two and still enjoy the story. My students have always been my mission field, so please use my experience as evidence that persistence gets rewarded. Never, never, ever give up! Nothing's impossible.

An enormous thanks to Marc Estes and Christian Lee at Snow Leopard Publishing who took a chance on me when numerous agents passed. Their support and expertise made my novel shine, and I'm forever grateful. To J. Ashley Brown who captured my cover vision perfectly and made it stand out on a crowded bookshelf.

My family and friends have put up with my imaginative rantings and claims that one day I'm going to see a return for all my hours of solitude in front of a keyboard and a significant amount of naps just to work out the plot details still giving me trouble. Thanks for believing in me even when you just got tired of hearing me tell you what my latest novel was all about or bounced ideas off of you. Believing in me when the rejections kept piling up in the corner and continued to plague me with insults like "You stink! You're never gonna make it. Nobody likes your writing. You'll never be good enough."

To Logan, Wyatt, and Finn? All I've ever hoped to show you is that dreams can come true when you never give up on yourselves. The legacy I leave behind will be tangible proof that with God all things are possible. He's the reason Papa spends time with you, teaches you new things, and creates adventures for you to read about one day. You inspire me more than you'll ever know.

Finally—my wife Cheryl has been the rock beneath my shaky ground for years. She listens even when she's heard it all before. Endures countless hours of me being away, even though we're sometimes right in the same room. This book could have died an agonizing death, but she wouldn't let me abandon it. Here's to many more days, weeks, months, and years of dazzling her with my wit and my creative chaos at times. I couldn't have done it without her love.

God? You spoke to me through a woman I'd never met over 20 years ago and planted such an amazing seed. Please help me to keep it growing in Your direction wherever it may lead. Thanks to all who bought the book and shared in my ramblings. Stay tuned for the sequel *Soulless*.

D.M. King

35412863R00180

Made in the USA
San Bernardino, CA
24 June 2016